"Rika, this story...you can't do it.

"You could jeopardize national security."

"If anyone's jeopardized national security, Major Huston, it's you."

"You're right. I screwed up, and badly. But you still can't do it."

"I'm a reporter," she reminded him. "I'm dealing with a story. The truth is more important to the well-being of our nation than keeping your secret."

"Noble words," he told her. "Got any idea what they mean?"

She glowered. "Get off your high horse, Major. If this project is supposed to be so damn secret, why were you discussing it over cognac and cigars outside Gramps's study?"

Alex could feel his temper heating.

"Go off half-cocked with misinformation, Rika, and you'll probably sell a lot of newspapers, but it won't do you, the country—or your grandfather—any good. Just remember this isn't about you and me. It's about something bigger."

"You're good, Huston, you know that? But if I've got bad information, why don't you straighten me out?"

"All I can give you is deep background—without attribution," he conceded, "at the strictly unclassified level."

"You're on, Major."

"Shall we seal it with a kiss, Rika?"

"I think a handshake is traditional." She extended her hand. "Alex."

Dear Reader,

Every generation, I think, feels it's created the ultimate weapon, the war-fighting technology that's going to end wars. That's never happened, of course. The history of humankind is a chronicle of battles, large and small, local and international. We may not have a "world war" at the moment, but we most certainly live in a "world of wars."

Then there's love. Talk about a world of war! Remember the slogan Make Love, Not War? Sounds perfect, doesn't it? Except for one detail. Love is a battle, too. A battle of wills, ideals, lifestyles and values. But oh, those peace treaties!

So what happens when a military man intent on keeping secrets meets a beautiful investigative reporter intent on exposing them? Does that sound like a battle of wills?

I had a lot of fun writing *The Major Comes to Texas*. There's a little bit of fact in it and a lot of imagination. I hope you enjoy it.

I love to hear from readers. You can write to me at: P.O. Box 4062, San Angelo, TX 76902.

K.N. Casper

THE MAJOR
COMES TO TEXAS
K.N. Casper

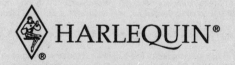

HARLEQUIN®

TORONTO • NEW YORK • LONDON
AMSTERDAM • PARIS • SYDNEY • HAMBURG
STOCKHOLM • ATHENS • TOKYO • MILAN • MADRID
PRAGUE • WARSAW • BUDAPEST • AUCKLAND

ISBN 0-373-70915-3

THE MAJOR COMES TO TEXAS

My thanks to the following people
who generously contributed their time and ideas
to various aspects of this book:
Lori, Connie, Liz, Gaye and Jim, Vera and, of course, Mary.

CHAPTER ONE

"How DID I EVER get elected neighborhood mom?" Rika Philips asked as she wedged a beach ball into the back of the van before bringing the rear window down and clicking it shut.

"Just lucky, dear," her grandmother said. Barbara Tiers was a little woman, not much over five feet tall, with snow-white hair and pink cheeks.

Rika smiled. "I guess you're right." She looked around at the six children gathered in the portico of her grandparents' Italianate-style house. "You kids ready?"

A chorus of "Yeahs" greeted her.

"Climb in," she invited them. "And everybody buckle up. Remember. Safety first. All set? Emily—" she addressed her daughter "—have you put on your sunscreen?"

"Yes, Mommy. Gram helped me."

Rika kissed Barbara lightly on the cheek and slipped behind the wheel of her Voyager. "Say goodbye, kids."

A deafening roar of "byes" ensued. Rika cringed at the high-pitched volume, then smiled happily at her grandmother. "We should be back by five," she announced from her open window.

The four girls and two boys jabbered like magpies among themselves, leaving Rika with her own thoughts. She was still feeling the glow of praise for her last big story, an exposé that had received state-wide attention and boosted newspaper circulation enough for her to wrangle three full weeks of vacation instead of two. But, of course, even that had come with a price. Her editor at the *Michigan Sun* had made her promise to come up with a lead for another investigative report. The question now was how she was going to top bribery and corruption by a state representative.

Maybe surfing the Internet on Gramps's computer later would give her an idea. There certainly wouldn't be anything local to report. Coyote Springs, Texas, was a wonderful place to visit and an even better place to bring up kids, but that was because nothing sensational ever happened here.

Relax, she told herself as the security guard waved her through the main gate at Coyote Air Force Base. This is only your first day of vacation. Enjoy it. Something will turn up.

"WELCOME TO THE WOLF Pack, Major."

Alex looked at the airman standing in front of him. At least six foot four, the two-striper was broad-shouldered but lanky, with a mop of carrot-red hair, enough freckles to qualify as a tan and a youthful face that was probably both a blessing and a curse. He had farm boy written all over him.

"So they still refer to the base as the Wolf Pack." He remembered his father explaining that coyotes, once so prevalent on these vast, open plains, were also called prairie wolves. Alex extended his hand.

"Riley Cavanaugh, sir," the young man said, completing the handshake. "You've been here before?"

"A long time ago." A lifetime ago.

Alex had idly observed the landscape sliding slowly below him in the twin-prop plane he'd connected to at Dallas. As he'd flown west, the terrain had become bleak, desolate and bone-dry in the August heat—until he'd spied a great green splotch at the base of a grayish-brown mesa, an oasis as inviting as the open arms of a lover. "It's still prairie country."

And he was after a wolf, or was it a fox?

They walked around the corner from the two gates that comprised the West Texas town's municipal airport to the dimly lit baggage-claim area.

Riley tossed Alex's luggage in the back of the Air Force van he'd parked curbside. Ten minutes later, as they approached the main gate of the base, Alex suppressed the feeling that he was coming home, but he couldn't keep his pulse from quickening.

A security policewoman stuck her head out of the guard shack, nodded to Riley and waved them through. He gave her a familiar high sign as he drove by.

Alex wasn't in uniform, so it wouldn't have been unreasonable for the sentry to check his ID. Either she'd been told of his impending visit and ordered to let him proceed unchallenged or the missing drone he'd come to investigate hadn't occasioned a heightened state of security.

The main drag was as he remembered it, wide enough for four lanes of traffic, but reduced to two by diagonal parking. The side streets were narrow, laid out, his father used to joke, when heavy traffic was two jeeps passing each other. The wooden buildings gleamed white, most of them double-eaved barracks with dull green roofs. The kind built in the mobilization days of World War II. How many lives had passed through here, and what had happened to them?

Alex ran a hand down his forehead and across his eyes. He'd known he was coming to a familiar place, but he didn't think he'd be entering a time warp. The only thing missing, that would always be missing, was the sight of his father striding purposefully down the middle of the sidewalk in khaki uniform, the stripes of master sergeant proudly worn on his sleeves.

Alex slipped back into the present. His mission here was important, not to his career—it could even be a career killer if he stepped on the wrong toes—but because of its impact on national security. The Top Secret stealth detection system that was still under development may have been compromised. The technology wasn't expendable, and in the wrong hands it could jeopardize the nation's entire defense posture.

He'd ordered continuing photoreconnaissance of the area yesterday before leaving the Aerospace Research Center at Nellis Air Force Base in Nevada, where he was a test pilot for the new generation of "invisible aircraft." He'd also coordinated with Security Command for Master Sergeant Mike Lattimore to head a special mobile intelligence collection team and meet him in Coyote Springs. It would take them another day to get in place.

Riley dropped Alex and his bags off at the billeting office, which would assign him the equivalent of a hotel room in the Visiting Officers Quarters.

"Second floor, Major, overlooking the pool," a

young woman in uniform, a senior airman, said brightly as she handed his key across the counter.

His quarters turned out to be more like a cheap motel in an old movie, with the added disadvantage of sharing a bath with another room. In his father's time, these would have been luxury accommodations, far superior to the open-bay barracks single enlisted men lived in. Nowadays they were substandard for even the lower ranks.

At least his room was located in a corner of the building, so it had two windows, one of which was seriously encumbered by an air conditioner. Someone, intent, no doubt, on conserving electricity, had opened the second, letting in the stifling, dry heat of summer.

He turned on the air conditioner and stepped over to close the other window. Below, a kidney-shaped swimming pool was squeezed in among three adjacent buildings. The enclosure was noisy. The cries and shouts of boys and girls ranging from about five to maybe twelve years of age echoed off the wooden walls.

What caught his eye, however, was the woman stretched out on a chaise lounge in the only spot of sunlight the close quarters permitted. Though modest for a bikini, her swim apparel still exposed more than enough feminine flesh to have an unsettling effect on him.

She had chestnut-brown hair coiled up on the top of her head, long slender legs, a tight belly and trim hips. Even though she was reclining, he could see her breasts were...well, *modest* definitely wasn't the word that came to mind. His curiosity piqued, he wondered what color her eyes were. Sherry-brown to match her hair? Blue? With her tan, violet eyes would be a knockout.

Too bad he hadn't thought to pack a swimsuit. Maybe after he paid his courtesy call on the installation commander, he could stop at the Base Exchange and buy one.

Alex was about to pull down the sash window, when one of the girls went up to the sunbather and said something. The woman sat up, shielded her eyes against the bright sun and answered her. He caught only the shouted, "Thanks, Mommy," as the child ran back to her friends.

Mommy. Hmm. Too bad. Married women were definitely off-limits. What would it be like to come home to a beautiful wife like her and a house full of kids? he wondered, then dismissed the thought. He'd seen enough marriages founder and fail to know family life was incompatible with a military career on the fast track.

He used his cell phone to call General Tiers's residence. Nathan Tiers had been retired for years, but Alex had been ordered to contact him immediately upon his arrival in Coyote Springs. Exactly why, and what part the old man might play in his investigation, he couldn't imagine. But orders were orders. He'd soon find out.

Busy signal. He snapped the receiver shut and unpacked his bags, all the time trying not to think about the woman in the bikini. What was her name? Jeannie with the light-brown hair? Get a grip, Huston.

He removed his uniform from the hanging bag and examined it. Hand-carrying it had been wise. Not a ribbon out of place. No wrinkles. He dressed, made sure his shoes weren't scratched. Not patent leather,

either. These were of the finest leather, spit-shined to
a mirror finish. He adjusted his Scottish wool tie,
wandered back to the window and casually gazed
down. She was gone. Good, he told himself, and tried
not to feel disappointed. He had a mission to accomplish. No time for distractions.

He went back to the phone and was about to poke
in the general's number again, when he heard muffled
shouting through the closed window. He went over
and saw two thrashing figures in the deep end of the
pool below.

Adrenaline rushed through his system, but pilot
training had taught him to keep a cool head. Evaluate
the situation before acting.

He hadn't seen a lifeguard on duty, hadn't even
noticed the usual perch for one. Strange. The Air
Force had very strict policies against unsupervised
swimming. Maybe the rules didn't apply in the Wolf
Pack. Maybe here, patrons were supposed to monitor
themselves—and their children.

Awareness of what was happening took only a split
second. In that time, Alex was flying out of his room
and crashing through the fire door at the end of the
hall. He bounded down the iron staircase that led directly to poolside.

Someone was already in the water, struggling to
save a boy who was flailing frantically. A few feet
away, Alex could see a head with blond hair going
under for what was probably the second time. Kids
lined the side of the pool, excitedly jumping up and
down.

Unsure how deep the churned-up water was, Alex
launched himself into a shallow dive. Two strokes
and he reached the submerged child. He grabbed an

arm and pulled up so quickly half the body shot above the waterline. The girl came down in a panic and clamped onto his head. Sputtering and coughing, she was pressing her belly button against his nose so tightly she threatened to suffocate him. He hit bottom and realized the water was only about six feet deep.

With one arm under her knees, he used his other hand to keep her from gouging his eyes out while he tiptoed to the edge of the pool. The depth diminished as he advanced, and the girl, finally able to breathe, was calming down. Reaching the side of the pool, he set the coughing, still-traumatized child on the tiled edge of the cool deck.

A hand reached out and stroked the girl's arms. "It's okay, sweetheart. You're safe now."

It took a moment for Alex to realize the other person, female type, was in the water beside him, not above. He peeked over. The woman he'd seen from his window. The woman in the bikini. Her eyes were a pale green with golden specks. He hadn't seen or heard her come into the water.

A few feet away, the boy was also sitting on the side of the pool, a strapping young man brushing hair out of the kid's eyes. "You're all right now, Shawn," the guy said, then looked over at the girl. "And Emily's all right, too." He glanced at Alex. "You okay, sir?"

"I'm fine." Except for his heart pounding double time, a half-naked woman next to him with the most beautiful eyes he'd ever seen and his best uniform, from tie to shoelaces, totally ruined. "What happened?"

"Shawn here did a cannonball too close to Emily,"

the man said. "Must have knocked the wind out of her. She's normally a pretty good swimmer."

Alex surveyed the area. In the shade, beyond the view from his window, was a lifeguard's chair on stilts. "You the guard on duty?"

"Yes, sir. Thanks for showing up when you did. Handling one isn't so bad, but two's a bit of a problem, especially when they're both panicked."

Alex observed the green-eyed woman beside him. She was quietly soothing her daughter.

"You, I presume, are Emily's mother," he said.

Even as her hand brushed her daughter's arm, her gaze melted into his. Without thinking, he checked out the woman's left hand. No ring. Divorced? It didn't matter. He had a girlfriend. He didn't need a wife and family.

"I want to thank you, Major—"

A half-forgotten memory flashed across his mind. A boy floating facedown in a stock tank. Sudden, helpless rage surged through him. "Why did you leave her alone? Why didn't you stay and watch her the way you're supposed to? Nothing is more important than a child's welfare," he blurted out before he even realized the words had formed in his mind. "If you had been doing your job as a parent, instead of worrying about your tan and then running off—" out of the corner of his eye he saw a tray of chips and burgers spilled on the ground a few feet away "—to feed your face, this wouldn't have happened."

Her jaw tightened, and her chest rose as she drew in air. "I...I only went...Look..." she stammered.

Alex could see the impulse to lash back warring with what he supposed was the shame and guilt of knowing she hadn't properly protected her child. "Next time watch your kids better."

"They're not..."

He trudged over to the ladder a few feet away and pulled himself out of the water. His dress blues felt like form-fitting leaden shackles and threatened to drag him back into the pool.

"...all mine," she finished in a small voice.

Trying to ignore her, he peeled off his coat and dropped it on the back of a wrought-iron chair, which immediately toppled under the weight. "Damn." He bent down to pick the chair up and almost knocked heads with the woman in the bikini. Still leaning over, he raised his head enough to find himself staring at the water droplets poised in her cleavage.

"Damn," he mumbled again when he realized the indecorous effect her closeness was having on him.

"I'm sorry about this." She straightened and helped him place his sodden coat on the seat. "You should get out of those wet clothes. Better take the tie off right away, too, before the knot tightens and strangles you," she added, motioning toward his neck.

The ghost of a smile on her lips and the hint of uncertainty in her quip drained him of the last ounce of rancor.

He struggled to loosen the soggy knot. Water streamed off it as he pulled the tail up far enough to slip the noose over his head.

When he started to strip off his tailor-made, hundred-percent combed-cotton, light-blue shirt, she looked around nervously.

"I didn't mean for you to take all your clothes off

here," she said in a voice that was stalled between a whisper and a hiss. "The children..."

He searched beyond her. The kids were gathered around, an attentive audience staring at him, some with their mouths hanging open.

"I assure you, there's a limit to how far I'll go," he muttered, and hoped she hadn't noticed how far it had gone already.

She pursed her lips primly, but he also saw a twinkle of amusement in her glorious eyes. They *were* glorious, too, he realized. He couldn't remember ever seeing a color and depth that captivated him so completely.

"Why are you in dress blues in this heat? Major, uh—" she eyeballed the name tag on his jacket "—Huston. If you don't mind my asking."

"I just arrived and was going to pay a courtesy visit on the base commander."

"Colonel Eckert?" She made an "uh-oh" sound. "Today's Wednesday, Major."

He crooked an eyebrow at her.

"Colonel Eckert plays golf every Wednesday afternoon with Colonel Lacy."

Alex stared at her. There was a crisis of potential international proportions, and the base commander and lab director were out nudging little white balls into holes in the ground? The comment he wanted to make wasn't as polite as her delicate "uh-oh." He'd been called in from a critical stealth test flight yesterday afternoon and told to pack his bags. Apparently, the rush to get here had been a waste of time. No one at this boondocks seemed to be letting the current state of affairs interfere with improving his handicap.

He took a step to deposit his shirt with his coat. His V-neck T-shirt was sucked against him like a clammy second skin, and his shoes made a squelching noise every time he shifted his weight.

"Might as well take off the shoes and socks, as well," she said.

He sat down and removed his oxfords—his good handmade Italian oxfords—stood up and bowed formally at the waist to her. "If you don't mind, I think I'll excuse myself now," he announced grandly, only then noticing that several people had come out of the side door of the officers' club and were gathered around to watch the commotion. The lifeguard had a sardonic grin on his face that Alex would have loved to wipe off.

Nuts, he thought to himself, if roles were reversed, I'd probably be laughing, too.

His trousers made a swish-slap sound as he mounted the iron staircase. This ought to teach me to be a Good Samaritan, he told himself as he put his hand on the doorknob to his room—only to realize the latch was self-locking and his key was inside.

"Nice going, Huston," he said out loud. "Welcome to the Wolf Pack."

IT WAS RIDICULOUS to keep looking up at the top of the stairs of the VOQ. The new officer wasn't going to storm down the steps again to rail at her for being a selfish, irresponsible parent. The nerve. The only reason she'd left poolside was to get the kids snacks. Emily had said they were hungry. It wasn't as though she'd abandoned them, for Pete's sake; there was a lifeguard on duty.

Rounding up Emily and her five friends and hustling them into the van took Rika less than fifteen minutes. Her hands shook as she stowed their towels and gear behind the back seat. She'd almost lost Emily today. A cold chill settled in her stomach and a knot burned her throat. The little girl who gave her life meaning, hope and joy had been in trouble, and she hadn't been there for her. Rika had to strain to keep her voice from becoming shrill or breaking as she instructed the children to buckle up.

She glanced once more through the Voyager's tinted window to the black iron steps. He wouldn't come down again. After all, there was absolutely no reason for Major Whatever-His-First-Name-Is Huston to even leave his room—now that he knew the commander wasn't available.

Still, she did feel bad about his uniform. Even dripping wet the chestful of ribbons had been impressive. Of course, with a physique like his, he'd look good in anything—or nothing. She shook her head. *What is the matter with me? Here I am, thinking about this guy's muscles, when I want nothing to do with a military man.*

Okay, he performed an act of heroism, and all he got for it was a ruined uniform and the humiliation of having to strip it off in public. Well, she wasn't going to lose any sleep over injured male pride. Besides, he was probably the type who had more than enough to spare.

But there was something familiar about him. It wasn't the uniform. She'd seen plenty of men in blue and green, black and khaki uniforms. The beautiful bod? She felt a delicate ripple dance through her. Desire? She shivered. If she'd ever laid eyes on that body, she'd remember precisely where and when.

She'd definitely seen him, though, and heard him, too. The deep, strong voice, confident of its authority, was strangely familiar. She searched her memory, trying to pinpoint where it might have been, but drew a blank.

She dredged up a smile and waved at the guard as she drove through the west gate of the base. The youngsters, normally loud and exuberant, were quiet in the back seat, probably because they knew what was coming. Rika took a deep breath. Might as well get it over with.

"Okay, kids. I think it's time we reviewed the rules." She concentrated on her daughter, seat belted into the captain's chair beside her. "Emily, where should you not swim in the pool?"

The girl hung her head, her eyes half closed as she fumbled with her fingers. "Never swim near the diving board when people are using it," she recited in a small, sulky voice.

Rika lifted her chin and peered in her rearview mirror at the boy with the curly brown hair in the back corner. "Shawn, what should you never do when using the diving board?"

"Jump close to other swimmers," he responded humbly.

"So you both knew the rules and you broke them, didn't you?"

"Yes, ma'am," said Shawn softly.

"Emily?" Her daughter was now playing with the wet tendrils of her long blond hair. "I didn't hear you."

"Yes, ma'am," the girl replied in a slightly belligerent tone.

Rika slanted her a warning glance. "Do you all understand now why we have those rules?"

There was an unenthusiastic chorus of "Yes, ma'ams" and "Yes, Mrs. Philips."

"Shawn, you could have hurt yourself very badly and you could have hurt Emily. You were lucky the lifeguard was able to get to you as quickly as he did. Do you realize you might have drowned?"

His expression downcast, the boy whispered, "Yes, ma'am."

"And you, young lady—" Rika's hands tightened on the steering wheel as she turned to her little girl "—if the major hadn't shown up when he did, you could have drowned." She tried to sound stern, rather than let them hear the panic she felt at the thought of what might have happened. "You both could have been killed."

"I just wanted to splash her," Shawn said with that tone of righteousness kids use when they know they've done something wrong but want to justify themselves.

"Splashing is one thing, Shawn. What you did was dangerous and irresponsible. If you can't play by the rules, you won't come with us anymore." In the mirror Rika saw the boy lower his head, a solemn frown of contrition on his face. "That goes for everyone."

She said no more as she drove on. The children stared out the window or whispered behind their hands.

"Mrs. Philips, are we going swimming again tomorrow?" Micki Sanchez asked a minute later, apparently unaffected by her friends' close call and the admonition.

"Not tomorrow—in fact, not for the rest of the

week. You all need a time-out from swimming to think about what happened today.''

"That's not fair," Cindy Roberts whined. "I didn't do anything wrong. Shawn and Emily did. It's all their fault.''

"I didn't say you did anything wrong, Cindy, but you don't have to go swimming every day.'' The mirror reflected five hangdog faces. "Besides," she said, "don't you remember we're supposed to go horseback riding tomorrow morning?''

"Yeah!" came the group reply. Swimming was all but forgotten.

"But only if the bunch of you can keep out of trouble between now and then.'' Rika turned off the main highway onto the ranch road.

The children lived within walking distance of one another on the quiet country lane outside city limits. Rika stopped the van at the foot of the driveways of their respective homes and made sure they grabbed all their belongings. They thanked her for the day and said goodbye to Emily. Calling out promises to come over first thing in the morning, they then scampered off like young Tom Sawyers and Becky Thatchers. If only their lives could always be so idyllic and all the potential tragedies of life could be averted as easily as today's, Rika thought.

She pulled into the driveway of her grandparents' ten-acre miniranch. It had become her home when she was twelve years old, after her parents were killed in a commercial airline accident. When her grandfather, General Tiers, retired from the Air Force after thirty-five years of service, no one could understand how he and Mrs. Tiers, who had enjoyed such an active social life in Washington, could leave it for a little town in West Texas that no one had ever heard of. Rika was very glad they had. The massive cream brick house, with its green tiled roof, appeared very staid and formal on the outside, and some of the treasures within were priceless, but for Rika, it had always been a warm, happy place, full of life and fun and love.

After parking the van in the gravel driveway between the splashing triple-deck fountain and the huge double front door, Rika and her daughter got out and went inside. The first thing that greeted them was the rich warm smell of chocolate cake baking. Then Barbara emerged from behind the central staircase, wiping her hands on an old paisley apron.

"Grandma, I almost drownded today," Emily cried out excitedly, as if it had all been a lark.

"You what?" Barbara Tiers's busy hands stopped and she looked in consternation at Rika. "What happened?"

"I almost drownded," Emily repeated.

"Drowned," Rika corrected. "You almost drowned."

Barbara slipped onto the spindle-back bench opposite the stairs. "What are you two talking about?"

"Shawn cannonballed off the board," Emily prattled on breathlessly, "and he landed right on top of me, and the lifeguard had to jump in after him, and another man came running down the stairs and dived in the pool and saved me. He was real mad at Mommy for not watching us, and Mommy made him take his clothes off—"

"Whoa, young lady. Slow down." Barbara brushed her hand across her great-granddaughter's cheek, then gathered her in her arms. She glanced up curiously at her granddaughter for clarification.

"We had a little incident at the pool today," Rika explained. "Shawn Mullens jumped in and hit Emily, who was swimming too close to the board. They both got the wind knocked out of them and went under. I was inside getting burgers and fries for the kids at the time. The lifeguard grabbed Shawn and a major who's staying at the VOQ leaped in and rescued Emily."

"Yeah, and he had on this big blue uniform and it had a whole bunch of ribbons—" Emily contributed.

And pilot's wings, Rika reminded herself. Out loud she said, "He was on his way to see Colonel Eckert and was wearing his service dress—"

Barbara's eyes widened. "A new major on base?"

"He wasn't very happy when I told him he wouldn't have gotten to see the colonel anyway, since it's Wednesday and Eckert and Lacy golf together every Wednesday."

"Where's he from and what's he doing here? Is he assigned permanently or on temporary duty?" The old woman was almost as breathless now as her great-granddaughter.

"I have no idea, Gram. We didn't stop to talk."

"Well," Barbara asked pointedly, "did you at least get his name?"

"Huston. That's what his name tag said. He didn't give me his first name. All I know is Major Huston."

"What does he look like? Is he married?"

Rika shook her head, half with annoyance, half with amusement. Barbara Tiers was convinced her granddaughter's marriage to Clay Philips had failed because Clay had not been a military man. Gram was determined to match her up with someone in uniform, preferably an Air Force officer's uniform.

Rika wasn't only unenthusiastic about the idea, she had good reason not to get involved with a pilot, especially a fighter pilot. Her first love had been a jet jockey—until she caught him proposing flights of fancy to one of her sorority sisters. She'd given him back his ring and cried for days, never quite sure what was lacking in her that would drive him into another woman's arms. Then a couple of years ago her best friend had divorced her zoom-bag husband for playing around. They were all alike, Cassie had assured her, a breed of their own, irresistibly charming, arrogant, egotistical and totally unfaithful.

"Well?" Barbara asked impatiently.

Rika could picture him with remarkable clarity. Six-two or -three. Broad shoulders. Gray or maybe light-blue eyes…and built…well, like Michelangelo's David, but with hair on his chest. She took a deep breath.

"Now, Gram, don't go getting any ideas. He had gray hair, for heaven's sake."

Barbara's brows knitted in disappointment. "Gray hair? Oh."

Rika fought to keep a straight face and hoped her grandmother didn't get to meet the new officer. "Probably has a wife and six kids at home," she added, although she hadn't noticed a wedding ring on his left hand, and she was sure she would have. After all, she hadn't missed the class ring on his right hand. Air Force Academy. But so what? Just because he wasn't wearing a band didn't mean he wasn't married.

What did she care, anyway? She was perfectly content with her single-mom life. She didn't need a man complicating it. Certainly not a man like Major Whatever-His-First-Name-Is Huston.

CHAPTER TWO

AFTER TRUDGING to the VOQ office and getting a second key to his door, Alex stripped out of his chafing-wet clothes. He'd had the uniform custom-made in Taiwan last year and now it was totally ruined. With a disgruntled sigh, he changed into dry civvies. About the only thing he had time to do now was arrange for temporary transportation. He'd expected to find an auto-rental agency at the airport, and in fact there had been two, but neither of them had been open. Was this a hick town or what?

For dependable transportation, Airman Cavanaugh had recommended Jallop's Jalopies on Travis Street. It wasn't a name to inspire confidence, but Alex found the number in the Yellow Pages, which suggested the place wasn't as fly-by-night as it sounded. He called and made arrangements to have a year-old silver Thunderbird delivered. Fitting, he thought, coming from Nellis, home of the Thunderbirds, the famous Air Force aerobatics team.

He also phoned General Tiers again, but got another busy signal. On the chance he'd been given the wrong number, he called directory assistance. The number was correct.

When the car arrived, it turned out to be a two-year-old Escort that Alex could barely squeeze his tall frame into. The T-bird had apparently developed engine trouble and this was all they had available. He consoled himself with the knowledge that it wouldn't be for long. Justine, his girlfriend back in Las Vegas, was supposed to arrive this weekend with his Jaguar. He could hardly wait—for either.

Justine was the best thing that had happened to him in a long time—beautiful, sexy and not interested in a committed relationship. She had her career in show business. He had his in the Air Force. They enjoyed each other's company, but both of them agreed that neither of their professions was compatible with the institution of marriage.

He took the Ford to the security police building to get a temporary base sticker for the windshield. That way, guards would wave him through the gates of the installation instead of making him stop every time to show his military identification card and sign the visitors' log.

Alex then drove to the clothing sales store on base. After an initial issue of uniforms, enlisted personnel received a monthly clothing allowance to replace and maintain them. Officers, with their higher pay, however, were expected to foot those bills out of their own pockets.

A matronly woman with obviously dyed jet-black hair was stacking blue knitted sweaters when he entered. Never know when you're going to have a cold snap in August, Alex quipped to himself. She turned and greeted him with a broad smile.

"You must be the new officer on base—" her dark eyes brightened "—the one who rescued sweet Emily at the pool."

Alex scratched his head and smiled. *News travels*

fast! The incident had taken place less than two hours earlier.

According to the tag perched on the woman's ample bosom, her name was Henrietta. He introduced himself.

"I need a complete set of blues," he told her. "And new shoes."

She sized him up with a critical eye. "I doubt I have anything in stock that will fit you, Major. I'll have to put in a special order." She looked up at him. Her apologetic expression inquired if that would be acceptable. "It'll take ten days to two weeks."

Alex sighed. He wasn't surprised. Even at large bases he could rarely find anything on the rack that fit him, and in the military supply system, two weeks could take two months.

"I'm here TDY," he said, using Air Force jargon for temporary duty, "but I'm not sure for how long."

She glanced down at his hands, which were splayed on the counter, then smiled at him. "If you have another set at home, it might be faster to have your wife mail them to you."

He'd never given Justine a key to his apartment. Besides, she wouldn't know one uniform combination from another, and in any case, he still needed to replace the one he'd ruined.

"I'm not married," he replied.

"I see." There was a second appraising evaluation before she stepped over to a service counter, dug out an order form and picked up a pen. She pursed her lips in thought. "Let me get your sizes and I'll check with the stores in San Antonio. If they have what you need in stock I should be able to get the items here in a couple of days."

She compiled a list of what he required. "Where can I reach you during duty hours, Major Huston?"

He gave her the lab director's number.

AT 0800 HOURS the next morning Nathan Tiers, General, United States Air Force, Retired, spread strawberry preserves on his English muffin as Serafina Rodriguez poured hot coffee into his oversized mug. He looked up from the comics he'd been perusing.

"Thank you, Sera." He took an appreciative sip of the steaming brew and eyed the empty place across from Rika. "Where's Emily?"

"She went over to Micki Sanchez's house," Rika replied, "to see the pups their collie had last month."

"Hmm, they must be almost ready for weaning." He returned to *Peanuts*. "By the way, Babs," he said casually to his wife, who was sitting at the other end of the long table, reading her horoscope, "there's a new officer on base."

"Yes, dear," Barbara answered without raising her head. "Major Alex Huston. He came in yesterday."

Nathan lowered his paper. After thirty-five years of active service and now another twenty years in retirement, he never failed to be astounded that she seemed to know as much or more about what was going on than he did. But then, fifty-five years was a long time to perfect her "old girl" network.

"Alex? How did you find out his first name's Alex?" Rika inquired.

"He's here on temporary duty to do some work at the food lab," Barbara noted, ignoring her granddaughter's question.

Her husband picked up his paper, refolded to the editorial page and held it in front of his face before he asked, "Babs, how do you know he's TDY to the lab?"

Rika shifted her attention from the sports page. "The food lab?"

She'd met a few people who worked at the Aerospace Food Laboratory. They seemed unusually intense for dietitians doing research to develop space-age meals and supplements. The man she'd met yesterday certainly didn't strike her as a health-food freak. On the other hand, he wasn't likely to have developed that physique pigging out on potato chips and ice cream in front of the boob tube, either. "He didn't look…"

Both her grandparents stopped to stare at her this time, maybe because of the note of incredulity in her reaction.

"You've met him?" her grandfather asked, bushy gray eyebrows peaked.

Rika recounted the incident at the swimming pool the day before.

"My great-granddaughter was in danger, her life saved by a stranger, and you didn't think it worth mentioning to me?"

Rika felt the sting of his quiet rebuke and knew she deserved it. "You had your Air Force Association meeting last night, so I didn't get to tell you about it at dinner."

He'd gone from his eighteen holes of golf to a local restaurant for dinner with some of his cronies, then to an AFA chapter meeting.

"Hrumfp," he grumbled, granting her grudging forgiveness. "This major is brave enough to save Emily's life, but you don't think he's smart enough to work at the food lab. Is that it?"

"I didn't say he wasn't smart, Gramps. I simply meant he didn't strike me as a pills-and-potions type."

The general arched his brows, his blue eyes twinkling. "I see. What type might that be?"

She did it every time. Painted herself into a corner and then had to fight or weasel her way out of it. "I'm sure I don't know," she said, feigning indifference as she turned the page from baseball scores to football predictions. "But I suspect if I introduced you to a guy five foot six with gray hair and a paunch, you wouldn't think him likely to be a fighter pilot, either."

Barbara's lips thinned in a repressed smile while she continued to study her horoscope.

Nathan's eyes hardened, even as his wide mouth simulated a scowl. "There are very demanding physical qualifications required for being a fighter pilot."

"We know, dear," his wife said, still scrutinizing the astrological prognostications, "but I don't think it's appropriate to talk about them at the breakfast table."

Rika struggled to suppress the giggle bubbling inside her. Her grandfather could have been the poster boy for flying aces in his younger days. Tall, lean, strong, square-jawed and steely-eyed. Even now at seventy-seven, with a full head of snowy-white hair, he still projected a daunting presence. It hadn't been his good looks, however, or his flying skills that had gotten him consistently promoted ahead of his contemporaries and well beyond all of them. Nathan Tiers was a man of exceptional intelligence and integrity who had a reputation for being tough and courageous. He had three Purple Hearts to prove it.

As for Major Huston, she hadn't missed the wings above the display of ribbons. It didn't mean he was a fighter pilot, of course. The two thousand flying hours required for the senior pilot designation could have been in bombers or transports or helicopters. Or even little trainers, for that matter. Somehow she didn't think so, though. Major Huston, with his sculptured features, straight carriage and sharp tongue, had egotistical fighter jock written all over him. Which was one of the reasons she couldn't begin to allow herself to be interested in him.

Nathan turned back to his granddaughter. "So you don't think this officer you met yesterday was sent here to work at the food lab?"

"I don't know, Gramps—"

"Your grandfather used to be in food services, you know."

The two other people at the table gaped at Barbara.

"Babs, what are you talking about?" Nathan scowled. "I was never—"

"When he was in charge of an officers' club," she elaborated before taking a sip of her coffee. She smiled at her husband. "Remember, dear?"

He spread preserves on the other half of his buttered muffin. "That was a long time ago, and I wasn't in food services. Besides, it wasn't really an officers' club."

Barbara viewed him over the top of her half glasses, an amused *Gotcha* expression crinkling her eyes. "It wasn't? I'm sure that's what you told me. I know you would never lie."

The general showed annoyance... no, embarrassment. "Well, I may have exaggerated it a little."

"That's one of the qualifications for being a fighter

pilot, dear,'' Barbara said confidentially to Rika. ''You have to be able to exaggerate.''

''Babs, be quiet so I can enjoy my breakfast.'' He stuffed a piece of muffin into his mouth and chewed.

''What kind of a club was it, Gramps, and where?'' Rika wanted to know.

He obviously didn't want to talk about it, which simply spurred her on. Her insatiable curiosity and ability to wheedle information out of people were two of the things that made her such a successful investigative reporter back in Michigan. She glanced over at her grandmother and saw the tiny smirk on her face as she folded the newspaper to *Dear Abby.*

''It was on an atoll in the Pacific. We were flying missions out of there for a year or so. Not long enough to establish a permanent base. Just had a few portable buildings to live in and a bar set up in the day room. We referred to it as our club, but it wasn't officially.''

''Oh, dear,'' Barbara said, raising her head. ''I thought you told me you had a bartender and—''

''Babs, you must have misunderstood. I said each of us took turns playing bartender.''

''As I recall,'' Barbara persisted, the paper turned now to *Hints from Heloise,* ''that nice copilot of yours…what was his name… Frank something… Didn't he tell me you had a few local girls working there…'' She grinned slyly at him. ''Or did he say local working girls there?'' She rearranged her paper to read the *Ann Landers* column. ''You're right, dear,'' she said with a cheery smile over the top of her newspaper. ''It was a long time ago, and memories fade.''

Nathan Tiers's face turned bright red. ''Babs, I never—''

Still holding her paper, Barbara rested her hands on the edge of the table. "I know, dear, but you have to be careful about the stories you tell people. They just might come back to haunt you."

Serafina chose precisely that moment to come through the swinging door from the kitchen. She deposited a plate of sausage and eggs in front of the general and a bowl of hot oatmeal before his wife.

"As for this new officer," Barbara remarked, pouring cream from a Limoges pitcher onto her cereal and mixing it gently with her spoon, "Henrietta tells me he's polite and quite charming. Of course, what he did yesterday shows he's a person of action, courage and high moral convictions. I like that in a man, don't you, dear?" she asked Rika.

"Well...yes...I guess so." Clay, Rika's ex-husband, had been a wimp at times, especially when it came to his grandmother-in-law.

"Of course you do, dear. A man is supposed to know his own mind. He's got to get things done. Can't be wishy-washy. Take Major Huston, for instance. He clearly felt a sense of duty in a crisis and rose to the challenge."

Rika rolled her eyes. "Gram, I bet you've got every woman on base checking this guy out, haven't you? You probably know his entire life history by now."

"Leave exaggeration to your grandfather, dear. He's the fighter pilot."

"Babs, will you please be quiet and let me enjoy my breakfast—in peace for once," the general said. It was an old plaintive tune, but the harshness failed to mask the deep devotion he had for his wife of over half a century. Rika couldn't help grinning. Life wouldn't be the same without them.

"Yes, dear," Barbara agreed, apparently deciding she'd teased her husband enough for one morning.

"By the way, Gramps—" Rika tried to be casual as she scanned a local sportswriter's overblown expectations of the coming high-school football season "—how did *you* know about the new officer on base?"

He continued to read the editorial section. "The major telephoned this morning." Nathan stabbed a generous piece of sausage and shot a glance at his wife. "Seems he tried to call several times yesterday afternoon, but the line was always busy."

Apparently oblivious to his implied criticism, Barbara turned to her husband. "You did invite him to visit, didn't you?"

Might as well give up trying to fathom the female species, he decided, especially this particular member of it. "Ten o'clock," Nathan mumbled between forkfuls of scrambled egg.

Barbara ate a spoonful of cereal and commented to Rika, "You'll have a good opportunity to see how he is around children if you take him out riding with you and Emily's friends this morning."

"Riding?" Rika gasped. "I'm not taking him out riding with us."

"Maybe your grandfather's boots will fit him," her grandmother rambled. "I don't imagine he'll have any of his own with him."

"May I remind you, Babs, that Major Huston is here on official business?" the general said with some asperity.

Serafina reappeared with Rika's half grapefruit and honey-wheatberry toast, already lightly buttered.

"You didn't mention yesterday that he was an Air

Force Academy man, dear,'' Barbara commented to her granddaughter.

Nathan lowered his paper. "Academy man?"

"The ring," Rika muttered. She'd seen it on his finger, and apparently Henrietta—whoever she was—had, too.

"You were right about the gray hair, though."

Nathan poised the last bite of sausage on the tines of his fork and glanced at his wife. "An Academy man, five-six, overweight and with gray hair." His voice dripped with playful irony. "Is that who you're trying to set up our granddaughter with, Babs?"

Barbara took a mouthful of cereal and swallowed it before answering. "I think you misunderstood Rika, dear. She never said Major Huston was short and fat. She only said you wouldn't consider someone of that stature to be a very likely fighter pilot. Actually, Major Huston is… what would you estimate, dear," she asked Rika, "about six-three? And quite handsome, I'm told. Not an ounce of fat on him, either. As for the hair…" She took another spoonful of oatmeal. "I wonder if it turned gray as a result of some terrible trauma or if it runs in the family." She considered her white-maned husband at the other end of the table. "Do you remember the Svensen boys? Their hair started turning when they were still in their teens. Was completely gray by the time they were twenty-five."

"When did you say he would be here?" Rika asked, not at all sure the acidic grapefruit was what her jittery stomach needed at the moment.

"Ten o'clock," her grandfather answered.

She checked her watch. An hour and a half from now. Maybe she could make herself scarce, move up the trail ride with the kids to nine-thirty. That way she wouldn't be around when the major arrived.

"I know the children are excited about horseback riding with you," her grandmother remarked, "but I think it would be a good idea to postpone it until later in the day. You'll want to join us for lunch with Major Huston and thank him again for saving Emily's life."

So much for Rika's change in plans.

ALEX HAD CONSIDERED visiting Lieutenant Colonel Lacy at home Wednesday evening, but decided against it. What they had to confer about involved highly classified information, and Lacy's private residence, with family around, wasn't the place for such a discussion—or a confrontation. He also didn't want his visit to be construed as social. Instead he'd spent the evening reviewing the attaché case of unclassified files he'd brought with him and doing searches on the Internet from his laptop computer.

After a restless night in which he kept imagining himself wiping drops of moisture from a certain brown-haired, bikini-clad female with green eyes, he presented himself to the base commander at 0730 hours on Thursday morning.

Colonel Eckert's secretary—Tilly Silvers, according to the shiny brass name plaque on her desk—was a six-foot, reed-thin woman with mousy-brown hair pulled back at the nape of her scrawny neck and tortoiseshell half-moon glasses. She might have been old enough to be Alex's grandmother, but she moved with the brisk confidence and efficiency of someone who knew she was in charge.

She surveyed his uniform—dark-blue pants and tie,

light-blue short-sleeved shirt and shoulder epaulets with his gold leaves of rank.

"Excuse me, Major, but shouldn't you be in service dress?" She flipped open her lapel watch. "If you're staying at the VOQ, you have time to change. I'll explain to Colonel Eckert that you were unavoidably detained."

"Thank you, ma'am," he said politely, "but I'm afraid my dress uniform was ruined yesterday afternoon in an accident, and I haven't had time to replace it."

She rolled her muddy-brown eyes cynically—a woman who had apparently heard excuses before. "Very well. If you'll just have a seat, the colonel will be ready for you in a few minutes."

He sat on a hard wooden bench across from her desk and picked up a two-month-old copy of *Airman* magazine. But his mind wasn't on the glossy pictures of paramedics or rescue operations.

He let his eyes roam. The knotty-pine waiting area probably hadn't changed much since his father was stationed here twenty-five years ago, a master sergeant bucking for promotion.

When Alex's commanding officer at Nellis had given him this assignment two days earlier, he hadn't mentioned that Coyote Air Force Base had bad associations. The Wolf Pack was the last place he'd lived with both his parents.

He was nine years old when his mother, tired of her Air Force wife's role of grass widow, had divorced Amos Huston and taken Alex with her to Florida. Alex had seen his father cry only once—the day they'd said goodbye.

"The colonel will see you now," Tilly Silvers announced, and held the door open for him.

"Thank you." Alex rose, adjusted his belt buckle and made sure his gig-line, the line formed by the seam of his shirt and the edge of his fly, was in perfect alignment, before stepping across the asphalt-tiled floor.

He knocked once on the door frame, waited for instruction to enter, then strode, stiff shouldered, across the thick carpet, to stop two paces in front of the commander's desk. He clicked his heels as he came to rigid attention, brought his right hand up sharply and held the salute while he recited the formal words: "Major Alex Huston reporting as directed, sir."

Colonel Eckert wore the same uniform-of-the-day combination Alex had on, except his dark-blue epaulets were embroidered with the silver eagles of a full colonel. Eckert returned Alex's salute with the laconic carelessness that only senior officers could get away with. Alex lowered his arm and heard the door close behind him.

"At ease, Major. Take a seat." Eckert waved to the brown leather armchair on his left.

Alex sat, his shoulders not quite touching the back of the chair, and quietly studied the man. Bull-necked, baldheaded, with a jowly, florid face, Eckert was in his midfifties and probably close to retirement.

The colonel referred to a piece of paper. "This message, informing me of your immediate assignment to my base, came in two days ago. I expected to see you yesterday."

Alex hadn't missed the reference to "my" base.

"I'm sorry I missed you. I understood you were playing golf yesterday when I arrived."

Eckert braced his arms on the edge of the desk and leaned slightly forward. "I play golf on Wednesdays only when my duties permit. Yesterday I was here all afternoon with Colonel Lacy and the lab's chief scientist, Mr. Brassard, discussing the possible cause and impact of this missing drone."

"Obviously, I was misinformed, sir."

"Coyote Air Force Base is one of the best-kept secrets in the Air Force, Major. It's quiet and not very exciting, and we like it that way. But don't let the laid-back atmosphere fool you. We're still serious and professional about our work."

Eckert's hostility was understandable. Alex was worse than an inspector; he was an investigator. As the commanding officer, Eckert was responsible for everything that happened on "his" base, whether he directly supervised it or not. He undoubtedly wished fervently this entire episode would go away and his neat little world could resume its unhurried pace, at least until he retired.

Eckert eased back into his leather chair. "The message says you're to probe into this business." He pushed the paper to the side. "I hope you resolve it quickly, Major. I'm sure there's a simple explanation for this thing's disappearance—malfunctioning controls, something like that. I am fully aware of the need to assess the damage such a loss might have. But if you think one of my personnel compromised this project, either through incompetence or by intention, I must tell you you're barking up the wrong tree. The people here are honest and trustworthy."

"I hope you're right, Colonel," Alex said sympathetically, and meant it. An innocent mechanical breakdown would be a lot easier to handle than malfeasance or treason.

But Alex had read enough classified reports to know spies didn't wear signs saying *Villain,* didn't don black cloaks or speak with funny accents. Most of them were the proverbial man next door, a neighbor, the guy you borrowed tools from and invited over for a Sunday afternoon barbecue in the backyard. When a traitor was caught, his friends and associates were invariably stunned by the news. Many of them would never entirely believe the pal they went bowling with could possibly have done the dishonorable things he—or she—was accused of, or that they themselves had been so completely duped.

Eckert toyed with a pen on his blotter. "I believe you already know Lieutenant Colonel Lacy. Goodie tells me you're old friends."

Alex had thought they were—once. But if a person would break faith with a colleague and buddy, who else might he betray?

"We worked together at the Aerospace Research Center at Nellis Air Force Base," Alex responded without emotion.

"Yes. He spoke very highly of you when I told him you were coming."

I bet he did, Alex thought. "He must have been unhappy," he ventured, "when his name didn't appear on the promotion list for full colonel this last go-round."

Eckert glared and his voice assumed a strident tone. "The man's a brilliant scientist, an excellent manager, a born leader, and he has an impeccable service record.'' He shrugged. ''Unfortunately, the system doesn't always work the way it's supposed to.''

Sometimes it does in spite of itself. ''How'd he handle it?'' Alex asked, echoing the concern of a friend.

''Like a gentleman, of course. He'll probably retire next year. I know he's been offered several high-paying positions with industry.''

As unhappy as Alex was with his onetime buddy, he didn't want to think of him as corrupt, willing to sell out. But it was a possibility he had to consider. Could Lacy have compromised his work as a bargaining chip to wrangle a job on the outside?

''I'm sure he'll do well at whatever he pursues,'' Alex commented diplomatically.

Eckert entwined his fingers in front of a belly that was a bit paunchy by Air Force standards. He cracked a smile for the first time. ''Are you married, Huston?''

''No, sir.''

''Divorced?''

''No, sir. Never been married.''

Eckert nodded slightly, and Alex could see the wheels turning. Don't ask, don't tell, don't pursue. Alex put on a bland face to hide his amusement. Let the old guy think whatever he wanted. As soon as Justine showed up with his Jaguar, Eckert would realize the new major on his base was definitely heterosexual.

''By the way,'' the colonel added, as if it were an afterthought, ''I understand your uniform was ruined in an accident yesterday.''

So Tilly had passed on his ''excuse.''

''Yes, sir. A young girl fell into the Officers' Club

pool, and I jumped in after her. Unfortunately, I was wearing service dress at the time.''

''She all right?''

Interesting, Alex thought. The woman at the clothing sales store knew all about what happened at the pool, but the word apparently hadn't yet reached the base commander or his secretary.

''Yes, sir. A little shook up, but otherwise she was fine.''

''Good.'' Eckert stood, and Alex jumped to his feet. ''Keep me posted on your investigation, Huston. I like to know what's going on. I don't appreciate surprises. Is that clear?''

''Yes, sir.''

''A little piece of advice, Major. It's a good idea when you're traveling on official business to carry two sets of dress uniforms for just such an emergency. You don't get a second chance to make a good first impression.''

CHAPTER THREE

"HELLO, JOHN."

"Rika! How is my star investigative reporter doing deep in the heart of Texas?"

"It's hot as Hades down here." She shifted the phone to her other ear. "Temperature hit 102 yesterday."

"Yeah, but what was the humidity?"

"Oh, about ten percent."

"Well, darlin', we've got the other ninety percent up here."

His attempt at a Texas drawl always made her smile.

"But you didn't call a couple of days into your vacation to talk about the weather. What's up? Have you come across an interesting story down there?"

An interesting man. "Does the name Alex Huston mean anything to you?"

"Hmm." The line was quiet for a moment. "No, not off the top of my head. Should it?"

"I don't know." That was the most frustrating part of it. "I met this guy yesterday—"

"Ah."

"John, don't you start, too."

"Too?"

"Between you and Gram…" Matchmakers, she thought derisively. Why couldn't people believe her when she told them she was perfectly content as a single mother? She'd had her taste of marriage, and didn't need another man complicating her life. If sometimes the nights were lonely, well, that was the price she had to pay for her independence.

"This guy Huston," she continued, "he's an Air Force major, and I have the feeling I've seen him or met him somewhere before, but I can't remember where."

"He's apparently made quite an impression on you."

"Actually, he saved Emily's life yesterday when there was an accident at the pool."

"A hero."

"He's also a pilot."

John snickered. He knew her aversion to flyboys. "Nobody's perfect, darlin'. Maybe you ought to give him a chance."

"To what?"

She heard John's soft chuckle on the line. "Is there a story in his rescuing a sweet little girl from Davy Jones's locker?"

"Not really, but there's something about him…"

"Have you asked him where you've met?"

"No, I was hoping you might recognize the name. Huston, without the *o*." She spelled it for clarification. "First name Alex. I don't know if that's a nickname or if he has a middle initial."

"It's enough for a search. I suppose you want me to authorize remote access so you can check our files to see if we have anything on him?"

"Would you? You're a dear."

"Don't you try buttering me up, young lady. It won't work."

Rika chuckled. As gruff as her boss tried to be at times, he was really a teddy bear. "I wouldn't think of taking advantage of your sweet disposition, John."

"Hey, watch it. Word gets out that I'm a nice guy, and I'm finished, wrapped up, kaput."

This time she laughed at his self-mockery. There wasn't a single employee at the *Michigan Sun* who didn't love Uncle John. "I promise to protect your reputation to my dying breath."

"So what is it about this major that's giving you strange vibes?"

Besides his body, his voice, the way he insists that children are the most important thing in the world? "I don't know…exactly. He's here on temporary duty and somehow he doesn't fit."

"Okay, darlin', see what you can dig up in the morgue on him."

The morbid expression for delving into back files always made her shudder. "Thanks, John. I'll talk to you in a couple of days, if you don't call me first. You have the number here at my grandparents' place?"

"Yes. How are they, by the way?"

"Absolutely great." When they're not matchmaking.

"Say hello to them for me."

After she hung up, Rika wondered if she wasn't overreacting. There was no reason an Air Force officer shouldn't pay an official visit to the Wolf Pack. Just because the sight of him made her pulse do a pitter-patter didn't mean he didn't belong there. It's simply my instinct for a story that has my curiosity piqued, she told herself.

ALEX CHECKED HIS WATCH as he left Eckert's office. Just after eight. Almost two hours before his meeting with Tiers. Alex still didn't have a clue about the retired flag officer's role in this investigation.

What he did know was that Tiers had served with distinction in World War II, Korea and Vietnam. He'd also written two books and any number of scholarly articles on the use of air power and advanced technology as tools of war. His public renown had only been established, however, when he penned a more reader-friendly volume entitled *Blood, Sweat and Tiers,* a memoir that had been both profound and whimsical. It had also earned a rare place—for a military book—on the national bestseller list. Alex had read and reread the general's works and gotten more out of them each time, but he'd never met the legend. The old fighter ace was a polished writer, an insightful historian and a bit of a moral philosopher, but what did any of those things have to do with a missing stealth drone?

Patience, Alex told himself. In less than two hours he would know. In the meantime, there were other players to face—at the Aerospace Food Lab.

The name still made him chuckle. Who said bureaucrats didn't have a sense of humor? Food stood for *Find Object On Demand,* the cover term for the stealth technology detection system they were working on here at Coyote AFB. To anyone inquiring, the lab was engaged in research into space-age nutritional needs and food supplements for a weightless environment.

A telephone call confirmed Lieutenant Colonel Lacy was at the lab, that he was expecting Major

Huston and that there would be someone to sign him in when he arrived.

The one building separate from the others on base was a hangar at the far end of the flight line that could be accessed by only one narrow, shoulderless two-lane road. Chain-link fence topped with barbed wire surrounded the massive structure, while security forces manned a checkpoint and roamed the perimeter. Alex wondered how many people honestly believed the cover story.

Two NCOs were on duty at the guard shack. One of them scrutinized Alex's ID card and confirmed his service number against a roster of authorized visitors. The other telephoned to someone inside, announced Major Huston's arrival and requested an escort. A minute later Riley Cavanaugh popped his red-haired head into the tiny building, a broad grin animating his freckled face.

"Welcome to the AFL, Major."

Alex snorted. Was the airman's sole mission to welcome him to places with strange-sounding names?

The two-striper signed on the clipboard beside Alex's signature, waited until his charge had clipped on a visitor's badge, then led him to the building's main entrance.

"I didn't realize you worked here," Alex said as the tall, gangly young man flashed his access card across the electronic scanner that controlled the reinforced steel door. Alex did the same. A computer system logged the times individuals entered and left. "How long have you been assigned?"

The mechanism clicked and Cavanaugh pulled the door open. "Six months. Basic training, tech school, then here."

"Interesting job?"

They waited to make sure the door latch engaged behind them.

"My uncle worked on Star Wars," the airman boasted. "I wish I could tell him about this project—it's better."

Alex nodded. He would give anything to be able to talk to his father about the duties he was performing, about the career he'd built for himself in the Air Force. Would his father be pleased, proud? He liked to think so. It made Amos Huston's absence all the more painful.

"Maybe someday you can," he said to the young man. "If not him, then at least your kids."

Cavanaugh left Alex at the director's door, which was only a few paces down the wide, carpeted corridor. A secretary, who looked like one of Charlie's Angels, sat behind an uncluttered desk, stapling a sheaf of papers.

She eyed him but didn't greet him before picking up the phone. "Major Huston is here, sir."

So much for friendly West Texas, he thought. The word was obviously out that he was the enemy.

"Go right in, Major," the woman said, nodding to the door on her right.

Lacy didn't come out to greet him but was waiting in the middle of the room, his hand extended, a smile pasted on his face. "Alex. It's been a long time."

"Yes, it has." He accepted the outstretched hand, then realized they weren't alone.

The office was large. At the end opposite the executive desk, two men stood at a conference table.

"Major Huston," Lacy said formally, "this is

Keith Nelson, my deputy and strong right arm. He handles day-to-day operations here at the AFL.''

Alex shook hands with a short, round, middle-aged civilian in a bland gray suit, white shirt and dark-blue-and-red striped tie.

"And this is Pascal Brassard, my chief scientist."

"Mr. Brassard."

"Everybody calls me Brassy," the man said as he clasped Alex's hand.

He was taller, younger and thinner than Nelson. A bachelor, Alex surmised from the rumpled, slightly off-white knitted shirt and fuzzy white socks showing under high-water, baggy chinos.

Nelson passed Alex a mug and poured hot coffee from an insulated carafe, then refilled his associates' cups. They sat, Lacy at one end of the polished conference table, Alex at the other, the two civilians in the middle.

"How has the project been going?" Alex inquired.

"Very well," Lacy replied flatly.

"I've compiled a series of folders, documenting every aspect of our program and its progress to date," Brassard informed him. "I think you'll be impressed. Less than two years and we've—"

"The report is classified, of course," Lacy cut him off, "so you'll have to read it here. I've set up a small office across the hall for you to use. It's available whenever you're ready."

The scientist appeared unfazed by the interruption. Alex crossed his hands in front of him and addressed the other man. "Tell me the sequence of events that led to the drone's disappearance."

Brassard was about to say something, then seemed

to think better of it. With a slight bow of the head and thinning of his lips, he deferred to his boss.

"There's really not much to tell," Lacy began. "Last Sunday we flew the drone—the XS—on the old flight line, as we've done on many occasions. This time, however, when it passed over the tree line to the east, it veered off course and kept going. Naturally, we initiated an immediate search—but found nothing."

"Who was present?"

"Three members of my staff were on the flight line. Three more were monitoring the equipment in the old tower. There were also half a dozen RCers— uh, the radio controllers—of the model flying club."

Alex stopped in midmotion as he lifted his cup to his lips. "RCers from what model flying club? Is this a base organization?"

"No, civilian, from downtown." Lacy seemed determined to meet his visitor's penetrating gaze, but Alex sensed more bluster and defiance than confidence in his hazel-brown eyes.

"Our runway was shut down years ago," Lacy continued. "It's only four thousand feet, too small for modern aircraft. The base has been letting the RCers of the High Flyers Model Club fly their planes there since then. Good public relations."

"Are you telling me the drone was flown with a bunch of model airplanes under the control of un-cleared civilians?"

"Why not?" Lacy countered. He might sound calm, but Alex detected the defensive challenge in the question. "The best place to hide something is in plain sight." He mimicked a grin as he waved his hand. "No pun intended. So that's what we did. It was also as good a test of our equipment as we're likely to get.''

"Look, if the model club didn't already exist,'' Nelson said, coming to his boss's defense, ''we'd have had to invent it. What better cover than the real thing?''

The theory was sound, Alex realized. The execution was questionable. A fictitious club would be under complete government direction. Lacy was likely to be in for serious criticism for exposing highly classified technology to outside scrutiny.

"How soon after the drone went off course did you start looking for it?'' he asked.

"I told you. Immediately,'' Lacy snapped, then backed off. ''We never fly without having a team of observers standing by.''

"Yet these observers couldn't see where it went.'' The words framed a question and an accusation at the same time.

Lacy raised his coffee to his lips, but to Alex his jaws seemed too locked for him to sip the brew.

"It veered off in a sector that's heavily overgrown with mesquite and not easily accessible,'' Nelson answered as his boss lowered the cup carefully to the tabletop. ''We checked every square inch of the area, but didn't find anything.''

Anything that you've reported, Alex thought. ''What about the ELT?''

The emergency location transponder was a beeper that could be honed in on.

"It stopped transmitting about the same time the craft disappeared,'' Brassard replied.

Alex slowly panned the three faces, which were

focused on him, waiting for his reaction. "So you were sabotaged," he concluded.

"Not necessarily," Lacy shot back, then immediately softened his tone. "Maybe the same malfunction that made the XS deviate from its programmed flight path also caused the ELT to terminate operations."

"They should have been two separate systems," Alex noted.

"They were," Brassard confirmed. "I personally supervised the installation of them myself."

"How, then, do you explain their both failing at the same time?"

The gangly, sallow-complected man's response was despondent. "Coincidence?"

Alex smiled at him, intentionally making him uncomfortable enough to squirm in his seat. Scientists didn't believe in coincidence. "That strains credibility."

"If you're suggesting," Nelson said tightly, "that someone in this lab intentionally—"

"Until you give me solid evidence instead of nonsensical conjecture," Alex countered, "that's exactly what I'm saying."

He'd considered playing the nice guy, lulling them into trusting him in the hope they might let something slip, but he wasn't comfortable playing the fool. He doubted his old pal, who had suckered him once, would buy it, either.

"In any case," he went on, "we have to assume the technology's been compromised. Are you still looking for the drone?"

Lacy inhaled deeply. "Of course. I have a team of four exploring every field and gully within a twenty-mile radius."

Alex rested back in his chair, his hands outstretched to the cup on the table in front of him. "Four people trying to find a needle in a 125-square-mile haystack. We're talking lottery odds here."

"What do you suggest?" The lab director flared, then reassumed a calm, professional tone. "Alex, I've been directed not to call in military or civilian police forces—"

"Including the OSI," Nelson interjected. The Office of Special Investigation was the official Air Force detective force.

"—because," Lacy continued, "it might disclose that this isn't just another model airplane. Which means all I have are my own people and the RCers from downtown who are willing to help."

"Frankly, I'm not sure who we're supposed to be keeping this secret from," Nelson added with a hint of disgust. "Whoever took it—if someone did—certainly knows it's missing!"

"This could have happened anywhere," Brassard offered defensively.

"You may be right. In any event, I need to study your report," Alex told the man at the opposite end of the table, "so I can assess the extent of the damage."

RIKA HAD JUST HUNG UP the phone when her grandmother came into the office.

"Oh, there you are, dear." She dried her hands on the old-fashioned bib apron she wore whenever she interfered in the kitchen. "Could you do me a favor? Sera is fixing taco salads for lunch and needs fresh tomatoes and avocados. Could you run into town and get them? It would save her time."

"Of course, Gram. I've been meaning to stop off at the newspaper and say hello, anyway."

Ten minutes later Rika was on the road. She wouldn't have time to get much done at the *Coyote Sentinel*. Checking their morgue to see what they had about the base and the Aerospace Food Laboratory would take a couple of hours at least, and she wanted to talk to the reporter who routinely did articles on the Wolf Pack.

She'd already compiled a mental list of questions she wanted to ask. When had the lab been opened and how had the base Public Affairs office handled it? Was all the information "canned" or were Air Force people willing to answer questions about the place and its mission? What subjects, if any, did they stonewall? Had PA given a tour of the facility? If so, how carefully had it been choreographed?

Rika double-tapped the horn as she came out of a blind curve and approached a T-intersection—a combination of Texas-friendly driving and self-defense. The road junction was a menace and the scene of more than one fender bender. Sure enough, she'd had to veer around a little car pulling out of the side road. She was already over the crest of the hill and cruising down into the draw by the time she looked in her rearview mirror, so she didn't get a second glimpse of the driver.

Not that she needed to. One instant had been enough to recognize the gray hair and angry eyes of Major Huston. She smiled to herself. The car must be a rental—it definitely didn't fit the fighter-pilot image. She glanced at the dashboard clock. Ten to ten. He'd be right on time, which ought to please her grandfather.

Ascending the other side of the dry gulch, she checked the mirror again. He was out of sight. Now, if she could just get him out of mind. She didn't want, and she certainly didn't need, a flyboy messing up her life. Gram, of course, had other ideas. Avoiding this particular fighter pilot was going to be difficult, considering he was—temporarily, at least—the focus of her journalistic curiosity.

If only the man weren't so damn good-looking. She'd lain awake half the night visualizing the wide set of his shoulders, the thick muscles of his broad chest and how it narrowed down to a slender waist. The washboard belly. She'd also wondered what a smile instead of a scowl might do to his chiseled features. He had full lips. She'd tried to imagine the ends curling up in a grin, and what they might feel like touching hers.

Why was she obsessing about this guy? Okay, so it had been some time since she'd had a "relationship" with a man. That was no reason to be as giggly as a teenager over her first crush. Besides, his body wasn't his only impressive feature. There had been something about his eyes when he scolded her. Not anger really. It was more like sadness.

A red traffic signal came into view. She applied the brake and ordered her imagination to do the same. Her interest in Major Huston was strictly professional, and she was damned well going to keep it that way.

Rika turned left at the second light and forced herself to concentrate, not on the man but on her research.

Probably the most important question she would have to ask at the newspaper was what the reporter's impressions were of the attitudes and atmosphere of base officials.

She felt a familiar lightness in her chest, and her pulse thrummed with the excitement of adventure. It was because of her work, of course. She loved it. Pawing through dusty old files could be tedious, and sorting through scraps and snippets of information frustrating—like trying to assemble a jigsaw puzzle when you didn't know what the picture was supposed to be—until pieces started to slip into place and an image began to manifest itself. Then the exhilaration of exploration took over, a thrill more stimulating than anything she'd ever experienced.

She parked across the street from the downtown supermarket Sera always used. August heat smothered her when she opened the van door and climbed out, only to be followed by an arctic blast of refrigerated air redolent with the tangy spices of cumin and oregano inside the food store.

There were other things to research, too, she mused as she selected three ripe avocados from the produce department, a cool head of romaine lettuce and a plastic container of bright-red cherry tomatoes. Some of the additional information she could check on her grandfather's computer, like the biographies of the senior officers on base.

On an impulse, she picked up a package of chocolate-covered mint cookies. High adventure called for extreme measures, she told herself. Nothing like chocolate mints to stimulate brain cells.

ALEX WAITED until he'd driven off base before pulling out his digital cell phone. The number he dialed was answered on the second ring.

"Sam's Sewer Service. You got a problem?"

"How deep do you dig?" Alex asked, using a pre-arranged procedure.

"It depends. One, two, three—"

Alex hit the button that would encrypt the call. Anyone trying to intercept it would get nothing but static.

"How do you read, Mike? Where are you?"

"Read you loud and clear. Just cruising through the scrub cedar and live oaks north of San Antone. Should be in your neck of the woods sometime this afternoon."

"You're not going to find many wild oaks here, my friend."

He and Master Sergeant Mike Lattimore had met at a national-level intelligence course on surveillance techniques five years before. Mike had joined the Air Force right out of high school, expecting one hitch to give him the time he needed to find out what he really wanted to do with his life. Assigned to low-level intelligence gathering, he'd found the work fascinating, and his superiors had discovered he was exceptionally skilled at it. Eventually, he'd earned degrees in electrical engineering and communications science, but too late for him to get an officer's commission. He had no regrets, saying he preferred the enlisted ranks, where the "real" work was done. Alex was sure his father would have liked Mike.

"This is mesquite-and-cactus country," Alex told him.

He stopped at an intersection, waited for a car coming in the opposite direction to pass, then turned left onto a two-lane road that went through an industrial area. If he correctly remembered the map in the telephone book, it led to Prairie Dog Lane, where the general lived.

"I haven't had a chance yet to figure out a place for us to meet when you get here. I'll do it later and let you know this afternoon."

"How about a steak house? Mesquite does a fantastic job scorching a T-bone."

Alex snorted. "I knew I could count on you to think of your stomach. Okay, I'll see what I can find." He unfolded the sheet of paper he'd gotten from the AFL before he left. "I have a list of the lab's employees. We need to run a national agency check on them since their last security updates and—"

"NACs have already been initiated," his friend interrupted. "I accessed them from the master list at HQ before we left."

Alex chuckled. "I should have known you'd be ahead of me."

"Just trying to keep up."

Alex clicked off his cell phone. His watch said twenty minutes until his appointment with the general. He turned down another secondary road and saw a sign that read Prairie Dog Lane. He took it and looked for 6918, but the house numbers here were still in the three digits.

Would the general be royally ticked because Alex hadn't contacted him immediately upon arriving in town? Officers didn't rise to star rank by being nice guys, and the attitude of command didn't always change when they retired from active duty.

I'll just have to take my chances, Alex told himself. *At worst, I'll get a good dressing-down. Oh, well, it won't be the first one, and at the rate things were going, it won't be the last.*

Dressing-down. He chuckled at the thought. That's exactly what he'd been in the process of doing at the pool yesterday after he jumped in to save the girl. He still remembered the look in…what was her name? Mrs. Philips…in Mrs. Philips's gorgeous green eyes as he was taking off his shirt, and the way she stared in panic at the notion that he might go further. In different circumstances—

What the hell is the matter with me? Just because she isn't wearing a ring doesn't mean she isn't married. Off-limits. Although, come to think of it, he hadn't seen any tan line where she might have removed one to go swimming, either.

Didn't make any difference, he convinced himself. She had a daughter. He wasn't interested in getting mixed up with a ready-made brood. How did he know there weren't other kids at home? When he decided it was time to settle down—if ever—he'd create his own family.

Just because it had been a while since he'd been with Justine, and just because this particular woman happened to fill out a bikini in a way that reminded him how long it had been, didn't mean he was interested in her. Attracted, maybe. But definitely not interested.

Locating the general's house turned out to be more of a trick than Alex had bargained for. Prairie Dog Lane meandered around the golf course that bordered Little Coyote Lake, then looped back to the same country road he'd entered by. He could have bypassed the residential area altogether if he'd just stayed on the main drag, but he didn't realize it until he'd wasted ten minutes in a fruitless search for an address that was probably another three miles farther along.

He was at a T-intersection and was just completing a left turn onto the main thoroughfare, when a Voyager coming from the same direction forced him to pull sharply onto the shoulder. The driver offered a quick and cheery double tap of the horn and sped by. Alex glanced over and found himself staring at Mrs. Philips. Their eye contact lasted hardly longer than a nanosecond, but the slightly nervous smile she gave him immediately conjured up the image of wet skin and soft brown hair tumbling down onto very feminine shoulders.

Alex's heart gave a momentary thump as the car came to a rocking halt in a clump of mesquite sapling just off the shoulder of the road. With arms outstretched on the steering wheel, he expelled a lungful of air in a whoosh. Of course she hadn't been wearing a bikini, but for the life of him that was all his mind's eye could see. A bewitchingly slender, golden-tanned body. Deep cleavage haltered in a thin band of white cotton. Tantalizing flat belly flaring out from navel to...

Shaking his head to dispel the erotic image, he slipped his foot off the brake, checked the rearview mirror and backed onto the hardtop. He'd barely started to accelerate, when he felt a sluggish pull to the right. Clamping his jaw, he guided the vehicle once more onto the unpaved shoulder of the two-lane road. He left the engine running, opened his door and got out to examine the front end of the car. Just as he'd suspected. A flat. One of those spindly mesquite branches had imbedded its long, sharp thorns in the sidewall of the tire.

With anger approaching the boiling point, he yanked out the offending twig and marked the time on his watch. Ten minutes before his appointment with the general. He'd hoped to get there a few minutes early. Not a chance now.

Unfamiliar with this particular make and model of American car, he wasted five precious minutes finding the jack and lug wrench tucked into the fender well of the trunk and another six minutes locating the handy-dandy hiding spot in the glove compartment where the special tool to unlock the hubcap was stored.

He checked his watch again. He was already late. Maybe if he called ahead and explained…He picked up his cell phone from the front passenger seat, hit the general's number. Busy. Nuts.

Alex went back to the trunk and scowled at the donut spare. He was going to look like something out of the Beverly Hillbillies, tooling up to the general's house. Well, at least there'd be no doubt why he was late. He removed the undersized tire and carried it to the front of the car. It took only a few minutes to replace the flat. He'd dumped it in the trunk and was about to slam down the lid, when he saw the stain on his uniform pants, right above the knee. Great. What next?

CHAPTER FOUR

RIKA DIDN'T have time for more than a quick stop at the *Coyote Sentinel,* but it would be enough to develop rapport for future visits.

The paper had been established after World War I to cover local news but over the years its mandate had grown to include the national scene. It hadn't lost its small-town flavor, however, even after it was bought out by one of the major news syndicates—obituaries remained on page two and high-school football still monopolized the sports section.

Rika knew exactly who she wanted to see. Stella Brown. The Wolf Pack was her beat. Rika had met her at various social events during previous visits, exchanged views on the current state of journalism and traded stories about the joys of single motherhood.

"I'm sorry," the woman at the cluttered reception desk told her, "but Stella is off this week. Is there someone else who can help you?"

Rika identified herself as a journalist with the *Michigan Sun.* "I was hoping to talk to her and get some background on the Aerospace Food Lab out at the base."

"She's definitely the person you want to talk to, then," the woman replied. "She does all the stories about the air base and knows just about everything that goes on out there—and everyone."

Stella's absence was disappointing. Rika glanced at the big-faced clock on the wall behind the desk. There wasn't enough time to begin her research in earnest, but maybe she could get some idea of the scope of her job. Computers made locating and extracting information from stored files easier than it used to be. Key-word searches could save countless hours of fruitless reading, and uncover references in places one would never think of looking.

"You won't find anything about the AFL, though," the woman said when Rika mentioned the morgue.

Rika's jaw dropped. "How come?"

"Politics. It's not just the AFL. We rarely identify units by their official designations anymore."

"Don't you think that's strange?"

The woman shrugged. "Eccentric, maybe. The relationship between the town and the base has always been very good. When the commanding officer makes an occasional suggestion that seems a tad out of the ordinary, we're inclined to go along."

Rika shouldn't be surprised. The phenomenon of going along to get along wasn't restricted to small-town newspapers. She wondered if anyone had challenged the CO's request.

"When will Stella be back?"

"Monday. She and her boy went camping down at Big Bend. I can leave a message for her that you called."

Rika dug into her purse, removed a business card and handed it over. "Does she use one particular photographer?"

"She likes to work with Wes, but he's out on assignment right now for the sports department. They're covering college football training, though how anyone could even think about football in this heat is beyond me. He should be back tomorrow.''

I'm batting zero for two, Rika told herself. It was a long shot that the photographer would be able to tell her anything useful, anyway.

''I'll give Stella a call next week sometime.''

THERE WERE NO RAGS in the trunk of the rented car, much less stain remover, two items Alex always carried in the ''boot'' of his Jag. With filthy hands he gingerly extracted the handkerchief from his hip pocket and tried gently to remove the thick gob of dirty brown grease from his pants. He succeeded only in spreading it. He felt his blood pressure rising. How could one place wreak so much havoc on uniforms? He'd have to check to see if this was a common experience in the Wolf Pack, or if fate had singled him out for special treatment. Maybe the woman was the jinx!

He poked in the general's number on the cell phone again. Buzz, buzz, buzz. Another busy signal.

''It's all a conspiracy,'' he muttered. ''They ruin my clothes and then won't let me communicate with anyone.''

Should he go back to base, change clothes and reschedule the appointment? He was already late. What would the general's reaction be? Alex hung his head but couldn't keep from laughing. He'd missed another chance to make a ''good first impression.'' Plod on!

Rumpled, sweaty and far from chipper, Alex crawled back behind the wheel of the Escort and proceeded down the road. The mismatched front tires reinforced his feeling of being off balance and definitely out of control.

He drove past cotton fields on one side, corn and milo on the other. Had he gone too far? Missed a turn? Then he saw trees canopying the road ahead and stately homes set back from behind massive gates.

Impressive house, Alex thought as he pulled up the circular driveway at 6918 Prairie Dog Lane. He left the car in the portico and walked to the oversized front doors. A dignified chime sounded deep inside when he pressed the shiny brass button. He was admiring the covered entranceway, when the door opened. A small round woman with salt-and-pepper hair and dark eyes peered up at him.

He took a step forward. "I'm Major—"

"The general is expecting you, sir," she said with a discernible Spanish accent.

Alex caught her discreet glance at the smudge on his trousers. He entered a large, formal foyer. The floor was black-and-white checkerboard marble tiles, the walls wainscoted and papered. A crystal chandelier was suspended from the high molded ceiling.

The woman closed the door quietly behind him.

"I had a flat tire," he explained, as she turned to face him. "I was wondering if there was some place I could wash my hands first."

"Of course." She extended her arm to a door at one side of the entranceway.

He went into a small half bath. The pristine cleanliness and sparkling fixtures made him feel all the more disreputable. It took him several minutes to get the worst of the grease out from under his fingernails. He'd torn a nail, too, down to the quick. Unfortunately, he didn't find any clippers or files. A tiny dot of blood appeared when he bit off the jagged piece.

I should have gone back to base, he told himself. *Better still, I should never have gotten up this morning.* He carefully wiped out the white enamel sink. *Ideally, I'd never have come to Coyote Air Force Base to begin with.* He ran a comb through his gray hair. *It'll probably be white by the time I leave here,* he mused, *if I haven't pulled it all out by then.*

The Hispanic woman was waiting patiently for him when he finally emerged.

"This way, sir."

Down the hall, she tapped on a pair of double doors opposite the broad staircase, entered and beckoned him in. He crossed the threshold. She shut the door behind him.

The general stood behind his desk in front of a pair of French doors. The backdrop of sunlight streaming in cast him in semisilhouette, so that his features were shaded and unreadable. He veered around the desk as Alex stepped closer, and extended his hand.

"Major Huston, Nathan Tiers."

He was taller than Alex had expected, well over six feet, with broad, rangy shoulders and a loose-limbed carriage that belied his years, which Alex calculated must be approaching eighty.

"I'm sorry to be late, General," Alex said. Their big hands were well matched, their grips equally hardy.

"You look like you went through combat to get here," the general observed, stone-faced except for the twinkle in his sharp blue eyes.

"Had to fight a flat tire." With a careless gesture

toward his ruined trousers, Alex acknowledged the ugly stain. "I'm a little battle-scarred, but I won."

"Victory is all that matters." Tiers turned and walked to a side table in front of floor-to-ceiling bookcases that filled one entire wall. "Coffee?" he asked over his shoulder as he poured the dark beverage from a silver pot into a heavy porcelain mug.

"Thank you, sir. Black."

Tiers handed the drink to him and poured one for himself, then moved confidently toward his desk. "Please take a seat, Major."

Alex sat in one of a pair of matching leather straight-backed chairs across from his host. The sheer curtains on the glass-paneled doors muted the brilliant colors of the garden beyond into hazy pastels, reminding Alex of a subtle Japanese painting.

Tiers settled into his seat. "I presume my tickets have been passed to you," he said, referring to his authorization for access to classified information.

"Yes, sir." Before leaving Nellis, Alex had been informed that the retired general still held a Top Secret clearance and was authorized access to a variety of highly sensitive weapons programs.

"Do you need to see some identification?" the general asked.

Personal recognition was the surest means of confirming identity, but since Alex had never met the man before, standard practice called for examining his military ID, checking that the number on it matched other records and verifying that the color photo on it was that of the bearer.

"I don't think that'll be necessary, sir. I've seen your picture on the back of your books often enough to be pretty sure you're you. Besides," he added with a grin, "if you are an impostor, I have a feeling your ID card would pass muster with flying colors. On the other hand, you might want to check mine."

Tiers chuckled. "Ah, but I have seen you before, too, Major. Last year at the Senate hearings."

"You were there?" Alex was surprised he hadn't noticed so distinguished an attendee and was sorry he'd missed him.

"In the background," the old gentleman responded. "By the way, Major, this room is not bugged. I personally performed an electronic sweep before you arrived, so we can talk freely."

Alex nodded. It was unusual for an individual to maintain that level of security, but Alex also realized he wasn't dealing with an ordinary man.

"Before we get started," Tiers said, "I must offer you my deep gratitude. Rika told me only this morning about what you did at the pool yesterday."

Rika? Who was Rika? The girl he'd pulled out of the water had been called Emily. He tried to remember the other children who'd been there. The name of the boy involved in the accident was Shawn, and there'd been several other girls and boys, but he didn't remember hearing their names.

"I really didn't do anything anyone else wouldn't have done," he insisted.

"Perhaps," the general replied, his tone not so certain. "Nonetheless, I'm deeply indebted to you. Now, let me explain why you've been asked to visit me."

Alex nodded again. At last he was going to get some answers.

The old man took a hearty swallow of his coffee, then set the mug aside. "I'm under contract to the Department of Defense," Tiers went on, "to track technology transfers and evaluate their possible repercussions on our military posture.''

Alex expelled an inner sigh. The situation was beginning to make sense. ''Not an easy job.''

'' 'Eternal vigilance is the price of freedom,' '' the old man said. ''For some time now stealth technology has been our ace in the hole. It gives us the freedom to fly undetected into unfriendly territory and remain invisible to weapons control systems while operating there. But we can't be complacent. We won't monopolize this technology forever. Someday someone else will have it to use against us.''

''Which means we'll have to be able to detect the undetectable,'' Alex supplied, recognizing now where the old man was headed.

''Your MADAM concept is both timely and brilliant, Major, which is why I'm pleased you've been sent here.''

Alex's pulse skipped a beat. Few people were privy to MADAM. Even fewer knew it had been his idea. He'd proposed the concept for detecting stealth fighters two years earlier, only to have it snatched out from under him by a certain senior colleague.

''I'm not aware of anyone better qualified,'' the general went on, ''to investigate and evaluate this possible compromise of the program.''

Alex felt a surge of pride. To be credited with the concept by a person of General Tiers's distinction was significant. ''How did you know—''

''That it was originally your idea?'' Tiers's mouth curled in a reversed frown. ''I have my sources, Major. But that's not germane at the moment. What is important is the serious blow this incident might have on our strategic national defense capability. The question is—with the disappearance of this drone, have we truly lost the technology?''

Alex lifted his shoulders and dropped them heavily. ''I haven't had time yet to determine how far the lab has progressed in developing or perfecting MADAM, or what particular technical problems they may have encountered. Until I find out if the plane was stolen, and for what reason, I can't give you an answer. I wish I could.''

''But you will find out.''

A vote of confidence, Alex realized, but it was also a command.

''When you do, I need to know,'' the old man continued. ''What have you learned so far?''

Alex told him about the lab flying the drone on base with the model club from town. At the general's scowl, he added in trying to be fair, ''It wasn't a bad idea. As Lacy's deputy pointed out, if the club didn't already exist, they would have had to create it. But they should have formally documented the relationship and obtained headquarters' approval. That way they could at least have done checks on the club's members to see if any of them had criminal records or foreign connections. As it stands now, they have no official sanctioning for the procedure and have technically compromised security by allowing uncleared people access to the restricted test equipment.''

''Lax security,'' the general noted. ''Do you think it was a matter of intent or incompetence?''

''It could have been simple expediency. You said yourself in your book, sir, that it's often easier to ask forgiveness than permission.''

The old general smiled at the reminder and nodded.

''Security is inconvenient,'' Alex continued, ''and

time-consuming. It's not uncommon in the excitement of the moment to temporarily forget it or gamble that it isn't necessary *this time*. Of course, after it's been neglected successfully once—"

"Complacency sets in." The old man frowned.

"I did some scouting around last evening, sir. I'm driving a rented car with a temporary sticker on the windshield, but I had no trouble going anywhere on base, including the old flight line. No one stopped me or asked who I was, where I was going or why. I did pass a security patrol on the perimeter road. We waved to each other."

The general's brows buckled. "Given the high level of protection required for the research being conducted on base, every vehicle, official or otherwise, should be scrutinized. Especially outside normal duty hours."

"Yes, sir."

"These security problems you've identified will be addressed, Major," the general said sternly. "Now, what else have you found?"

"Poor contingency planning. Lacy says he had a team standing by to pick up the drone if it went off course, yet he waited until Monday morning to report this mishap. The delay has cost us. Had he reported immediately and asked for aerial surveillance, we might have been able to locate it. I've ordered photoreconnaissance of the entire area and expect a report in tomorrow. As you know, infrared can capture the residual heat patterns of things that are no longer present. In this case, time and high temperatures are working against us."

"Dereliction of duty," the general snapped, as if he were marking off another item on a checklist.

From the scowl on the general's face, Alex was positive he didn't want to be the subject of the old warhorse's report back to the bigwigs in Washington. Terms like *lax security* and *dereliction of duty* were career-killers, and if someone was out for blood, those words could lead to a court-martial. In Lacy's shoes right now, Alex would be damned worried.

The general shifted impatiently in his chair. "If there's anything I can do to help you, Major, you have only to ask. Should you need any assistance, additional assets, let me know and I'll arrange for them."

"I've been given the best, sir. A van with the latest in high-tech equipment will arrive this afternoon. It can intercept virtually any kind of communications from primitive Morse code to the most advanced microwave links."

"How soon will it be ready?"

"My team will be tapping phones and computers ten minutes after they set up. I found a spot for them close to the microwave tower and telephone relay station."

"What's your plan of attack?"

"First, we'll find out who's talking to whom and what's being said. Then we'll see if any unusual patterns jump out at us."

"It sounds like you have everything under control, Major."

"Thank you, sir. I do have one question. Are Colonel Eckert and Colonel Lacy aware of your involvement in this investigation?"

"No," Tiers replied. "I think it best they not be informed." He took a thoughtful sip of his coffee. "I understand from Rika you're staying in the old VOQ overlooking the pool. Is that correct?"

"Yes, sir," Alex said with a smile. "Simple but adequate." *That's the second time he's mentioned Rika,* Alex mused. *He seems to think I know her. Who the devil is she?*

"But not suitable," Tiers declared. "Eckert is basically a good man, but he gets in a snit sometimes. I don't imagine he's very pleased with your being here, but he's senile if he thinks putting you in substandard quarters is going to drive you away. I'll talk to him. There are VIP guest quarters on base—"

"Thank you, sir, but that won't be necessary," Alex interrupted before he realized he was doing it. The old man meant well, but the rank of major didn't warrant special treatment. He himself disliked people who used connections to get perks they weren't entitled to, and he didn't plan on being one of them. "Where I am is fine. I don't expect to spend much time there, anyway. It's also very convenient to—"

"But not an appropriate way to treat a field-grade officer. Besides, your act of heroism yesterday merits recognition." He rose, walked briskly to the door and opened it to the sound of a vacuum cleaner, which stopped immediately. "Sera," Alex heard the general say, "would you ask Mrs. Tiers to join us, please?" He turned back into the room, this time leaving the hall door open.

Alex became aware of subtle sounds off in the distance. The muted ticking of a clock in the hall, the distant chatter of children's voices. He'd caught a glimpse of kids and horses by the barn behind the house when he was driving up.

Tiers resettled himself at his desk and started to lift his mug to his lips, but returned it to the desktop without sampling the dark brew. "Now that I know about your saving Emily's life at the pool yesterday, we can use it as our cover for this visit. And, of course, since we have met, your stopping by periodically to visit a nostalgic old veteran will draw no particular attention."

The general's gaze shifted to the open doorway, the strong lines of his aged face softening. "Ah, there you are."

Alex turned and immediately rose from his chair.

Wearing bright-red slacks and a red checked, long-sleeved cotton blouse, Barbara Tiers walked into the room. Her pale, delicate-featured face, framed by snowy-white hair, was all smiles.

"Babs, dear, this is Major Huston, the young man who rescued Emily yesterday."

She went directly to him, hands outstretched, palms down. "Major Huston, how very nice to meet you. Rika's told me so much about you."

Charmed by her warm greeting and baffled by the name he still didn't recognize, he accepted her hands and wondered if he was expected to kiss her on the cheeks continental-style. Damn, but he felt as if he were in some kind of play and didn't know his lines.

"I can't thank you enough for saving Emily's life." Still holding his hands, she tugged him down to her level and kissed his cheek.

Alex's face grew warm and for the first time in his life he didn't know what to say. "I, uh... Is—"

If he felt unbalanced before, now his world was spinning. Saved Emily's life? At the pool? Light finally dawned. "Is...uh...Emily your granddaughter?"

"Great-granddaughter," Barbara replied, with a

proud smile that had her eyes twinkling fondly. "Of course you've met our granddaughter, Rika."

"Mrs. Philips?" At last, Alex connected the dots. Mrs. Philips, Rika, was the Tierses' granddaughter. "We never did get formally introduced," he said with a nervous grin. "I'm afraid I owe her an apology, though. I was a bit abrupt with her."

General Tiers slapped him on the back. "I'm in your debt, Major. Babs," he said to his wife, "why don't you take the major out to the barn and have Rika show him around." He turned again to Alex. "You must stay for lunch, Major."

"That's very nice of you, sir, but I—"

"See you in a few minutes, then." The general retreated behind his desk.

"This way, Major," his wife said sweetly.

She led him down the hall, through a big country kitchen that smelled enticingly of Mexican spices and coffee. "I really can't—" he started.

"I must say," Barbara commented, unmindful of his incipient protest, "you don't look anything like Rika described you."

That silenced him. So the woman in the bikini had talked about him. "Oh? And how did she—"

"She was right about one thing," the general's wife rambled on. "The gray hair is quite distinguished."

Not quite sure how to react to the statement, he asked, "Do your granddaughter and her family live here with you and the general?"

She glanced up at him, her clear blue eyes jubilant. "They live in Lansing, Michigan, but they spend several weeks with us every summer."

Alex wanted to inquire further about Mr. Philips,

but they'd already reached the barn. He could hear childish chatter inside. They stepped into the semi-darkness of the big sheet-metal building.

"Gram, we didn't go on our trail ride this morning 'cause Mommy had something she had to do, but we're going this afternoon after lunch, and—" Emily stopped short when she realized someone was with her great-grandmother.

"Emily, dear, you remember Major Huston. He's the man who pulled you out of the pool yesterday."

The girl lowered her head in embarrassment. She'd apparently been given a good talking to about the incident.

"Hi, Emily. Going trail riding, huh? Sounds like fun."

"Hey, Em," a boy called out from somewhere among the stalls, "where's the currycomb you said I could use?"

Emily seemed relieved at the distraction. "In the tack room," she replied, and darted around Alex to join her friend.

The sensation of a presence to his left instantly diverted Alex's interest.

"Hello, Major," Rika said, a smile in her quiet greeting.

In a flash he took in all of her: the soft brown hair, the contours beneath her white blouse, the tan riding pants clinging seductively to slender hips and thighs. She extended her hand. His breathing hitched. The sound of horses snorting and children giggling seemed to recede, and for a moment the space between him and Rika Philips virtually crackled.

"Ms. Philips." He took her hand and felt his heart

begin to race at the sensation of her warm skin slipping into his palm. "It's nice to see you again."

"Rika, Major Huston will be having lunch with us," Barbara said. "In the meantime, why don't you show him around, then come up to the house."

Alex locked eyes with Rika, his fingers still curled around hers, heat suddenly concentrating in another part of his anatomy.

"I really don't..." he began, only half-conscious he was enunciating words, "...have time to—"

"Gram, I think the major probably has other things to do." Rika shifted from her grandmother to their guest. "May I have my fingers back now?"

"Oh, uh." He released her hand and managed to find his tongue. "I'm afraid she's right, ma'am. Your invitation is very generous, but I really have to get back to the base." Was that a look of disappointment he saw in the granddaughter's eyes? "To buy a new uniform," he added.

"You do seem to have a problem meeting Air Force dress standards, don't you?" Rika muttered, giving a cursory glance at his stained uniform trousers.

The old woman screwed up her mouth indignantly. "You've got to eat, Major. Skipping meals is very unhealthy. As a dietitian I'd expect you to know that." She turned, clapped her hands and instructed the children to run along to the house for lunch, then left her granddaughter and Alex alone in the barn.

"Dietitian? What was she talking about?" He cocked an eyebrow at Rika for enlightenment.

"Food lab...dietitian," she reminded him.

"But I..." he stammered. He couldn't very well

tell her the food lab was a front and he was no expert on nutrition.

He thought he saw a smirk on her face and wondered what she was thinking. She placed her hand on his forearm, adding further to his sense of alarm. "There's no use fighting," she observed sympathetically. "She'll get what she wants. Gram always does. And if Gramps is on her side…" She shrugged. "The only possible course of action, Major, is tactical retreat."

"Call me Alex, please."

"Only if you call me Rika." She smiled, and he was sure the spring that was already wound tight inside him was going to snap. "Let me thank you again for what you did yesterday, Alex."

He gazed deep into her eyes. "I'm glad I was there to help, Rika."

They both allowed the moment to linger, then she moved down the aisle of the barn, letting him trail along.

"She's quite a character, your grandmother," he remarked. "I like her."

Rika started to slide a heavy stall door along its tracks. He interceded and pushed it for her, then stepped aside for her to enter. She clucked at a dappled gray mare as she approached it, then lifted one of its front feet for inspection.

"She seems to have taken a shine to you, too." Rika examined the hoof, set it down and straightened her back. "You're wondering if the Gracie Allen-Rose Nyland act is for real." She laughed softly. "Only when she thinks it's to her advantage."

"What about your grandfather?" Alex asked. "Is he an actor?"

Rika watched him close the stall door, then moved down the line. "When he needs to be. They're like a violin-cello duet, one light and trilling, the other rumbling and mysterious."

Alex enjoyed listening to her voice, liked the comfort zone that seemed to settle around her when she talked about her grandparents. But the senior generation wasn't his main interest. He wanted to know more about Rika Philips, one particular aspect about her life especially.

"Your grandmother says you live in Lansing, Michigan, and visit here every summer. What about your husband? Does he come down with you?"

CHAPTER FIVE

RIKA SHOT HIM A GLANCE. "Emily's father is a commercial real-estate broker in Detroit. He puts in eighteen-hour days and makes bushels of money, which he enjoys having more than friends and family. Besides, I don't think he'd be very welcome here." She entered the next stall and rubbed the nose of the bay gelding that came to greet her. "If you're asking me if I'm married, Alex...Emily's father and I are divorced."

"I'm sorry," he muttered.

"Don't be." She shrugged, her nonchalance not totally convincing. "I'm not."

After two years of divorce she still harbored the guilty suspicion that she should have tried harder to make the marriage work. But what? Clay was a full-time workaholic and part-time womanizer. Nothing she had done or said had been sufficient to change either of those personality traits. The more money he accumulated, the more obsessive he became about hoarding it. Even the stingy child support payments she'd been awarded in their divorce were always late. As for his women, he seemed to be generous enough with them.

"Tell me about yourself," she prompted, both to change the subject and to see if she could refresh her memory about where she'd met him. "I know you're an Academy graduate, a command pilot—"

"And a native Texan."

Her brows went up.

He chuckled. It was a rich sound with a certain self-deprecating quality she found unusual in a jet jockey and strangely, uncomfortably appealing.

"Native by accident," he informed her. "The only reason I was born here is that my father happened to be stationed at Kelly AFB in San Antonio. A year later we moved on, and a year or two after that we made another permanent change of station."

"I'm a second-generation service brat." Rika ran her hands along the horse's flank to its hindquarter. "I know the feeling. My father was on active duty. We relocated every couple of years. I remember getting sick every time we moved."

"What did your father do?"

She lifted a hoof and, pleased with its condition, let it drop. "He was an Air Force test pilot."

She raised her head in time to see Alex's face light up. "Exciting job."

"Until I was eight." She circled around to the other side of the animal and repeated the process. "Then my mother convinced him to quit and settle down."

The light went out. Apparently, the idea of settling down didn't appeal to Major Huston.

"In Michigan?"

She nodded, controlling a sudden urge to laugh. He made it sound like Devil's Island. "Dad went to work in the family business there."

He stepped aside to let her pass, but he was close enough for her to feel the heat radiating from his strapping frame. He slid the door closed. "What business is that?"

She faced him before answering. "Grocery retailing."

His eyes dulled as disappointment turned to derision.

"Quite a change of pace," he said soberly, "from flying state-of-the-art experimental aircraft to counting canned goods."

Let him jeer if he wanted. She'd considered the four years that followed the best of her young life. Her mother, who'd always been affectionate and very protective, seemed to blossom in a lighthearted way Rika had never seen before. It wasn't until years later that she realized how worried her mother must have been until then—knowing her husband's work put him in constant physical danger; continually afraid when she kissed him goodbye in the morning it might be the last time she'd see him alive or in one piece. Her father had relaxed after he resigned from the Air Force, too. Her parents appeared happier, and the three of them spent more time together as a family.

She saw a quizzical expression on Alex's face and realized he'd just said something.

"I asked if they still live there." He eyed her with curiosity.

A cold vise tightened in her stomach, and without realizing it, she lowered her voice. "They were killed in a plane crash when I was twelve. Ironic, isn't it? Mom was so worried about Dad being a test pilot, and then they were both killed in a commercial plane crash on their way to pick me up from my summer here with her parents."

"I'm sorry." His voice was low, intense. He circled his fingers around her arm, cupping her elbow. The sensation was warm, intimate and unexpectedly consoling. "I didn't mean to make you sad."

She cracked a smile, embarrassed by the moisture gathering in the corners of her eyes. "It was a long time ago." She swallowed the sudden knot in her throat. "Thank heavens I had Gramps and Gram."

He trailed alongside as they moved down the aisle to the tack room.

"You were lucky," he said, and watched her cringe at the way bridles and brushes were tossed on footlockers. "You had two people who loved you and were there for you."

There was something in the way he said it that made her pause. Disappointment? "Weren't your parents?"

He picked up a headstall and at her nod hung it on a hook by the door.

"My parents divorced when I was nine," he said. "My father was an NCO in the Air Force. Naturally, we moved around a lot. More than average, I guess. I went to three different schools for the first three grades. Dad was sharp, well liked by the bigwigs and being groomed for the top enlisted billet, Chief Master Sergeant of the Air Force. My mother grew to hate Air Force life. We'd hardly get settled in, make friends, and she'd have to pack us up all over again. She complained that Dad was TDY so much we never got to see him anyway, so what was the point of moving to begin with."

Rika covered an open can of saddle soap and put it in a drawer. "Then they split up," she said, spinning around to face him, "and you saw even less of him."

He cracked a smile. "Actually, I think it was just the opposite. There was certainly more quality time. I spent a few weeks of summer break with him every year. He'd take leave for part of it, and we'd do things together. You'd expect with all his TDYs he'd hate traveling, but he always took me places. The Grand Canyon. Yellowstone. The first time I saw Washington was with him. We visited the Capitol, the White House, the Smithsonian. He was stationed at Wright-Patterson one year, so I got to spend days on end in the Air Force museum there."

He was obviously very proud of his father. "Where do your parents live now?" she asked.

"Mom's in Florida. I see her once or twice a year. Dad died a month before I graduated from the Academy." His voice unexpectedly thickened. "He always said he wanted to pop me my first salute when I got commissioned."

"Oh, Alex, I'm so sorry."

He grimaced. "As you say, it was a long time ago." He picked a riding crop from the floor and clipped it on a rack beside others.

"We better go back," Rika said softly, "before the kids eat everything in sight."

She walked beside him along the crushed limestone path to the house. "Do you mind if I ask you a question?"

"Try me."

"The other day at the pool when you said parents had an obligation to protect their children—you were right, of course—you seemed unusually... The expression on your face was like you were somewhere else."

She looked up and saw the same faraway daze. It lasted only a moment.

"I was," he said.

They were almost to the back door of the house. He paused and turned to her, hands in his pockets, eyes downcast.

"I was about Emily's age, maybe a little older. Dad and I were visiting a friend of his who owned some property outside San Antone. The family had an aboveground concrete stock tank we were allowed to use for swimming, but only when an adult was present. Mr. Rancil, the owner, came with his son and me, but he was called away to the phone. Instead of making us get out of the water until he returned, he told us to be careful and left. His son got a cramp a few minutes later and drowned."

Rika's mouth fell open. "My God, that's terrible."

"I didn't even realize he was in trouble. He'd been fooling around on the other side of the tank. When he went still, I thought he was doing the dead man's float."

Rika put her hand on his wrist. "Alex, I'm so sorry. It must have been terrible for you."

"It took me a while to get over my fear of the water." He smiled, brightened his voice. "Eventually, I even qualified as a lifeguard."

THE PATIO WAS a broad, canvas-covered expanse of flagstone surrounded by half walls of creamy brick topped with planters. Alex had no idea what the colorful trailing flowers were, but he liked the loving care they represented. Barbara was at the far end, watering them with a sprinkling can, when he and Rika approached.

"Where are the children?" Rika asked her grand-mother.

"Mrs. Sanchez next door invited them over for lunch. Emily decided that playing with the puppies would be more fun than being around a bunch of adults."

The general appeared, and the four of them sat at the glass-topped table while Sera served the first course.

"What do you do in Michigan?" Alex asked Rika between mouthfuls of cheddar-rich tortilla soup.

"I work for a newspaper."

He had a sudden urge to reach across the table, take her hand and run his fingers along the soft ridges of her palm. "I'm sure you don't run the presses."

Her chin hovered over her bowl as she took a spoonful of soup. "I'm a reporter for the *Michigan Sun.*"

Reporter. Alex didn't like the sound of the word. He glanced at the general, but the old gentleman seemed intent on his steaming soup. "For the family section, human interest type stuff?"

Rika's eyes narrowed and her lips curled. "If you're suggesting I give out the latest recipes for bur-ritos or calamari canapés, you're way off the mark. I'm an investigative reporter."

"Ah." It wasn't the most pithy or intelligent com-ment he could have made, he realized, but it would have to do. The last thing he wanted was to get in-volved with a reporter, especially an investigative re-porter. He definitely didn't need a Jack Anderson publicizing his moves or second-guessing his conclu-sions.

Barbara perked up. "Several months ago she did a

series on the plight of the homeless, and just recently she got an award for uncovering a bribery scandal involving—''

"An award?" Alex's silvery brows shot up. "A Pulitzer?"

Rika snickered. "Don't I wish. Not a Pully. Not yet. Maybe someday. A more realistic goal right now is an Associated Press Award. The AP has categories for various-sized papers. The *Sun* fits in the medium class."

Alex poised a generous piece of corn tortilla over his bowl. "So are you working on a story at the moment?"

She grinned. "I'm always working on something."

"Here in Coyote Springs, Texas?" He gazed off into space. "What could it be?" He brought the fingertips of his left hand to his temple in mock concentration. "Let's see. Is someone trying to corner the Russian thistle market?"

"Russian thistle?" Barbara asked in mild alarm. "Is that one of those new terrorist weapons?"

Rika considered Alex beneath her long eyelashes and gave him an amused smirk. "Russian thistle is another name for tumbleweed, Gram."

The general's wife appeared momentarily baffled. "Really?" She addressed her husband. "Did you know tumbleweed is also called Russian thistle?"

"Babs," the general said sharply, "your soup's getting cold."

"Yes, dear."

"Well, if it's not the tumbleweed cartel, what could you possibly be working on?" Alex inquired, tilting his bowl away from him for the final spoonful of soup.

Rika edged her nearly empty bowl back slightly. "Can't tell you."

Sera removed their dishes and replaced them with large colorful taco salads.

Alex picked up his fork. "Not willing to divulge what your big scoop is, huh?"

Rika speared a wedge of avocado and held it to her lips. "Can't."

Sera moved around the table, topping off iced-tea glasses.

"Don't you just love intrigue?" Alex asked Barbara.

The old woman looked from him to her granddaughter, then ate a nugget of grilled chicken.

"I'm always on the alert for a blockbuster," Rika informed Alex, then fixed him with a Cheshire-cat grin. "As a matter of fact, I recently ran across a lead at the base that's stirred my interest. 'Mysterious Major Appears at Wolf Pack,'" she sang out.

Alex sputtered violently, his fork clattering against his plate. Did she know about the problems at the lab?

Rika regarded him curiously. "Did I hit on something?"

He brought his cloth napkin to his mouth. "No, I did. A piece of lettuce went down the wrong way."

He picked up his iced tea and was taking a long gulp, when Emily exploded, all out of breath, from around the side of the house and ran to her mother's side. Hands fluttering, she shouted, "Mommy, can I have a puppy? P-l-e-a-s-e. Micki's mom says I can. They have six, and they have to give them away because they can't keep them all, and she says I can have one, and I picked—"

"Whoa! Hold on a minute." Rika raised her hands

in front of her and leaned back, then gazed at her daughter. "Slow down."

"A puppy, huh?" Alex lowered his glass, grateful for the diversion.

Barbara's blue eyes read him. "Do you like animals, Major?"

"Who couldn't like a puppy?" He swiveled back to the girl. "What kind of dog is it?"

Emily was delighted to tell him. "Micki's mom says it's a mutt, because the mommy and daddy dogs weren't the same breed. Charmer is a big collie, and the daddy…well, they think it was a Austrian shepherd."

"An *Australian* shepherd," Rika corrected.

The general pushed back his plate. "Probably the one that lives with those people in the ramshackle house down the road," he grumbled. "Their dog is always running loose."

"I bet the pups are pretty, though," Alex countered, smiling at the girl.

"Especially the one I want," she bubbled, pressuring her mother with pleading eyes. "Can I have him, Mom? Huh? Can I?"

"I don't think—"

"Did you have a dog when you were a child?" Barbara asked Alex.

"I'm afraid not," he answered sadly. "I always wanted one, but—"

"How come you didn't have one then?" Emily asked, her expression serious.

Alex leaned back into his chair. "Well, you see, my father was in the Air Force, and we moved around quite a bit, so having a dog didn't seem like a good idea." At least, that was the excuse his mother used.

After the divorce, when he lived with her and they didn't move around anymore, there had been other excuses.

"Keeping a pet under any circumstances is a lot of work," the general contributed. "They've got to be fed and groomed and trained."

Emily wasn't deterred. "I'll feed him and brush him every day, and he'll be good."

Alex could remember making the same promises. Hoping and always having his hopes dashed.

Rika pursed her lips, clearly unhappy at the prospect.

"Have you got a name for this little guy?" Alex asked, convinced Rika's dilemma wasn't whether to agree but how to say no.

"I'm going to call him Scamper," the girl announced. "Micki's mom says he scampers all over the house."

"Great," Rika mumbled. "And probably chews everything in sight."

"Micki's mom says he doesn't have any real teeth, just little baby milk teeth, so he won't chew anything."

"Yet," Gramps muttered.

Emily bounced up and down excitedly. "So I can have him? I'll go tell Micki's mom." She bolted toward the kitchen door.

Rika reached out and snagged the waistband of her shorts, pulling her back. "Just a minute, young lady. I didn't say you could have him."

"Your mommy's got to think it over first," Alex explained. "Having a dog is a big responsibility."

"Exactly," Rika agreed. "After all, who's going

to take care of him when I'm at work all day and you're in school?"

Alex wasn't going to let her off easily. "Do you live in an apartment or a house?"

"A house, but—" Rika responded automatically, before apparently remembering she didn't have to answer to him.

"With a nice big backyard," Barbara chimed in, earning a warning scowl from her husband.

"Well, then," Alex concluded with a grin and a tilt of his head, "the problem's solved."

"Just a moment, Major." Rika shot him a stabbing glance that suggested the bite she wanted to take out of him wouldn't be with milk teeth. Keeping her tone level but forceful, she said, "This is my decision, not yours. I'll thank you to butt out."

"Oops, sorry. You're right." Alex brought his hands shoulder high, palms out, and withdrew farther into his chair. "Didn't mean to step on toes."

Rika's tight lips and scathing glare made it clear she didn't believe him.

"But, Mommy—"

"We'll talk about this later, Emily," Rika insisted. "Not now."

"But Micki's mom says she's going to have to send them away if somebody doesn't take them."

"I'm sure that won't be for a while yet. We have plenty of time to decide." Rika's features softened and she gave Alex a saccharine-sweet grin. "Maybe the major would like one."

Emily's eyes widened. "I know the one. Scamper's brother. He's not as big," she noted apologetically, "but he's cute. I call him Ruff, 'cause he likes to bark a lot."

"Sounds like a perfect watchdog," Rika noted with a crocodile smile.

Alex grinned back at her appreciatively.

"Ruffian." He let the name play on his tongue. "I bet he would make a very good watchdog." Dramatically, he shook his head as he addressed Emily. "But I have a bigger problem than your mom has. I don't even have a backyard. You see, I live in an apartment, and keeping a little puppy locked up inside all day wouldn't be very nice."

"Oh," the girl replied dejectedly.

"Why don't you go and play with the pups," Alex suggested, "and give your mom some time to think about it." He hesitated a moment, then brightened, inspired. "In fact," he drawled, "I have a better idea. Why don't you bring Scamper over here so everybody can meet him. I bet when your mom sees him, she'll love him as much as you do."

"Major..." Rika's tone vibrated as she slowly enunciated his rank.

Emily's face glowed at the suggestion. "Okay," she agreed, and before anyone could say another word, she had dashed off the patio.

"Emily," Rika called out, "we have the ride this aftern—" but the girl had already disappeared.

"Major..." Rika repeated, her brows lowered in disapproval.

Alex chuckled. "I know. I'm not playing fair. Once you see the little rascal, you won't be able to say no." He lowered his voice seductively. "And your daughter will love you for it. Trust me."

Barbara sat quietly, her clear blue eyes shifting between her granddaughter and her guest. The general's cautious frown relented for only the time it took him to wink at Alex.

AFTER LUNCH, Alex said his goodbyes and departed for the base. The general left for the golf course. Barbara, wearing her wide-brimmed straw hat and toting her flower basket and pruning shears, returned to the garden. Her prizewinning peonies required exceptional TLC in the harsh, alkaline soil of West Texas. Before taking the children on their promised trail ride, Rika stepped into her grandfather's study.

She'd brought her laptop from Michigan, but it was two generations out of date, slow and limited. The general had one of the latest models, with more bells and whistles than Rika could fathom. Another of those ironies. No one expected a man of his age and background to be so well versed in bits and bytes. In fact, he knew more about hardware and software than anyone she'd met. She smiled fondly. The old geezer was a geek.

He'd given her permission to use his setup on numerous occasions, so it wasn't as if she were going behind his back, she rationalized, as she clicked past the screen saver. He never turned the system off, and had it backed up with an uninterrupted power source as protection against electrical spikes and power failures. She signed on using her own password.

Access to government Web sites was remarkably quick and easy. She called up Coyote AFB, read its short history—it had been a flying training base in World War II—and checked on the units currently assigned to it.

Aerospace Food Laboratory. Mission: To perform high-level theoretical evaluation and analysis of nutritional requirements associated with space travel and long-term operations in a weightless environment.

It didn't tell her anything she hadn't already heard. Next, using her special password, she connected with the computer at the *Michigan Sun* and searched its huge database for the food lab. This time she came up with nothing. It obviously wasn't a newsmaker. She entered the name Alex Huston. Bingo!

Major Alex Huston, 34, Air Force Academy graduate with a Ph.D. in aeronautical physics and metallurgy from MIT; test pilot for the stealth F-117/Nighthawk fighter and the newer F-22/Raptor.

Test pilot? She remembered having told him about her father being a test pilot and how it had worried her mother. His only comment had been that it was "exciting work." The sparkle in his eyes had dimmed when she said her father had quit to go into the grocery business.

Two strikes against you, Major: jet jockey AND test pilot.

She read on. Major Huston had appeared last fall before the Senate Select Committee on Technology Proliferation. He'd been one of several military officials who'd testified about the dangers of selling certain types of technology to foreign interests, warning such transfers could severely compromise the U.S.'s lead in certain classes of weaponry.

Of course! That was where she'd seen him—or his

broad back. In the crush of spectators and reporters she hadn't gotten a good view of his face, but she hadn't forgotten his deep baritone voice.

Rika rested her head against the high back of the leather chair, her wrists dangling from the armrests, her mind spinning. What the devil was going on? Her grandfather had attended the hearings. Did he meet Alex there? Why hadn't he said anything about knowing him? Why all this secrecy?

She stared at the picture on the screen. Major Huston was standing in front of a long table, one hand raised as he took the oath. What would an officer with his impressive scientific credentials be doing at Coyote Air Force Base? Why had he shown up suddenly at the food lab? For that matter, did the food lab really exist, or was it only a sign on a door?

A smile worked its way across Rika's face. She was definitely onto something. She had three of the five essential elements of a news story: who, where and when. Now all she needed was the what and why.

A warm excitement hummed inside her. *Major Alex Huston, USAF, you've piqued my curiosity.* Professionally speaking, of course. Time to delve deeper. She put in a call to her boss in Michigan.

IT WAS CLOSE TO THREE when Alex broke away from the Tiers household. He'd managed to avoid being alone with Rika after lunch, knowing in doing so he was denying her the satisfaction of ripping his head off for maneuvering her into considering the wiggly ball of fur Emily had brought over from Micki's house. He was just putting off the inevitable, but he was also taking delight in her flashes of outrage at him. Those green eyes were mesmerizing and challenging, even when they were angry.

He felt a little guilty, too. Being a single parent couldn't be easy, and he had interfered, making it harder. But every kid deserved a puppy. If he ever had kids, he'd make sure they had pets.

His first stop when he returned to the base was at the Q to change clothes. Civvies, this time. He was running out of uniforms. He inserted the key in the lock, opened the door and walked in. Automatically unbuttoning his shirt, he stepped over to the closet, opened it and froze. It was empty. He surveyed the room. The bed he'd left rumpled was neatly made, but maid service would have taken care of that. He went into the bathroom he shared with the room next door. All his toiletries were gone.

He strode back to the bedroom. There on the miserable excuse for a writing table was a piece of paper. He picked it up: "Major Huston, please come to the billeting office."

"Damn straight," he muttered. He rebuttoned his shirt, pocketed his key and stormed out.

It wasn't yesterday's young female airman at the desk this time, but a male staff sergeant. Straining for patience, Alex barked, "I'm Major Huston. What's going on?"

The man, probably around thirty, had a slightly pockmarked face and receding hairline. He lowered the computer run he'd been reviewing and rose instantly to his feet. "Oh, yes, Major. You've been moved into the VIP quarters."

"By whose order?"

"The base commander called about an hour ago and instructed us to relocate you to the Cactus Suite."

Alex knew he should feel pleased; obviously, the general had "requested" the quarters reassignment. He should, but he didn't. The idea of people touching his possessions without his permission always bothered him. When he was a kid, his mother had routinely gone through his things, checking to see he didn't have drugs or alcohol or other no-nos. He couldn't blame her. As a single parent she'd been extremely conscientious about ensuring her son didn't get into trouble. But the snooping had made him feel soiled, as if his mother didn't trust him.

Then came the Academy. Inspections had been a way of life there, too. Again, he didn't blame his superiors for doing their jobs. There had been just enough incidents, enough infractions of the rules, to prove them justified. The constant surveillance and lack of privacy, however, had inevitably left him feeling violated.

"Where is this Cactus Suite?"

The sergeant opened a drawer, removed a plastic key card and placed it on the counter between them. "Right across the street, sir. The door on the right. It's our best. I hope you enjoy it."

Alex took a deep breath. "Thanks," he mumbled as he turned toward the exit.

The suite was classy. Alex couldn't deny it. From the outside the building looked like all the other two-story wooden structures, but the inside had been completely rehabbed. He entered a living room, complete with a wet bar. The walls were tastefully papered, the floors thickly carpeted. The lighting was subtle and indirect; the furnishings new and stylish. Across the room he found a narrow hallway, which led past a kitchenette on one side and a large, sparkling bathroom on the other. His toilet articles had been neatly laid out on the long faux marble counter. The bedroom was lush, with a king-size bed, double dresser and a broad writing table facing a heavily draped window. The closet had mirrored doors. Inside, his clothes were neatly hung. They took up hardly a fifth of the space available.

Alex sat in the easy chair across from the bed. If Colonel Eckert was displeased before with his coming to the Wolf Pack to investigate a missing drone, how much more annoyed was he now?

With a shrug and a chuckle, Alex removed his uniform, took a quick shower and put on a pair of casual slacks and open-necked sport shirt.

He was just about to leave, when the phone rang. He picked up the receiver. "Hello."

"You're not an easy man to get hold of," a soft, very feminine voice crooned.

CHAPTER SIX

"JUSTINE? It's good to hear your voice, babe."

He had no trouble conjuring up an image of the sexy model with whom he'd spent some very pleasurable hours over the past year. Long legs, red hair, amber eyes and stacked. Although for some reason another image presented itself, too. Light-brown hair, jade-green eyes, full soft lips, bikini top, bikini bottom. Damn.

"Have you already left Vegas?" he asked. "Where are you? Will you be getting here tomorrow or Saturday?"

She chuckled at the litany of questions. "I'm sorry, honey, but I can't drive your Jag out this weekend."

Letdown, a definite letdown.

"Have you had trouble with it?"

"Your precious car is fine," she assured him. "Is that all you think about?"

He laughed. "Not exactly."

"Where were you last night? I tried to call you."

"At work." He sighed audibly. "Stuck in a windowless building, reading boring papers."

"Poor baby," she commiserated sarcastically. He could imagine her wrinkling her perfectly shaped nose at the idea of sitting still with an inanimate object like a piece of paper. "They been keeping you busy, huh?"

"You don't know the half of it." Then, with a wry smirk, he added, "So busy I'm already running out of uniforms."

Justine snickered. "That's all right, sweetheart. When I get there, you won't need any clothes."

A small groan slipped from his throat, and from the sexy giggle he heard at the other end of the line he knew exactly what she had in mind. The notions it aroused were also frustrating. Phone sex wasn't exactly what he needed.

"How come you can't make it out here this weekend?" he asked.

"My agent booked me for a special shoot in Palm Springs. It's something I can't pass up."

"Of course not." He understood work and career. Justine was in the chorus line at the Grand Hotel, but she also modeled for national fashion magazines and, of course, aspired to get into the movies. "When do you think you'll be able to make it? I miss you."

"I miss you, too. It might be a couple of weeks."

He was hoping this investigation would be over by then. "I'm not sure if I can stand being without you that long."

"Or your car," she said with a snort. "What are you driving out there, or do they ride horses everywhere?"

"I have seen a few horses." And a horsewoman. "As for transportation, let's just say it's not up to the style to which I've become accustomed."

"That explains why you miss your car. How about me. Do you miss me?"

"Like a thistle has down."

"Huh?" The line went quiet. "What does that mean?"

What, indeed? he asked himself. He'd never used the phrase before and wondered where it came from. Except maybe his discussion with Rika about tumbleweeds.

"I'm just all prickly for you," he ad-libbed seductively.

There was another moment of silence before she rewarded him with a full-throated laugh.

"Either the sun is different, there's something in the water or you've met someone new," she said with amusement. "I've never known you to be poetic. Whatever it is…it might turn you human yet."

He pulled the phone away from his ear and stared at it. He wasn't the gushy type, but he'd never thought of himself as inhuman or cold. The accusation stung.

"I think," he replied, feeling uncomfortable, "I've shown you my most human side."

There was a soft chuckle from the other end. "You're good in bed, Huston. I never said you weren't. But…"

"But what?" He didn't like the turn this conversation had taken; nevertheless he wasn't about to back off from a challenge.

"We suit each other, Alex," she answered. "Let's leave it at that."

He should feel relief. He didn't. "So you're going to hurry here, right?" He deepened his voice. "I wish I could show you how much I miss you."

"I think I've got the picture." Justine tittered. "Hold that pose."

"We're talking major discomfort here," he confided in hushed tones. "But I'll do my best. How long will you be able to stay?"

"Probably not more than a couple of days. Do you know how long you're going to be there?"

"Can't say for sure. We'll just have to play it by ear."

"That's as good a place as any to start, I suppose. Body-part-wise, I mean," she murmured. "In the meantime, you better get some sleep. I'm going to need you well rested when I show up."

IT WAS AFTER 0800 by the time Alex arrived at the AFL the following morning. He went through the checkpoint, then used the electronic security card he'd been issued the day before to get into the building proper. The surface hangar had been converted to office space. Entrance to the belowground labs required passing through another checkpoint, this one also guarded by an armed sentry. As he walked down the wide corridor, Alex noted the institutionally framed Air Force lithographs lining the walls.

The minuscule office he'd been given contained a battleship-gray metal desk, a telephone, a computer with access to the base network and a two-drawer safe. There was still considerable data in the voluminous classified files Lacy had given him to evaluate, and he had yet to interview the people who had been on the flight line when the drone disappeared. They could wait. He had something else to take care of, something that had been eating away at him for more than a year. He turned left and opened the glass door into the director's office.

Lacy was handing a folder to his secretary when Alex entered. The colonel turned to watch his visitor come in. Surprise, then mild distress, crossed his tanned face. "Good morning."

"Good morning," Alex replied pleasantly. "I thought we might talk—if you have the time."

Lacy paused and nodded. "Come into my office." He took a step toward the door. "You want something to drink?" He motioned to an undercounter refrigerator tucked into the corner, a coffeemaker on top of it. "We can make a fresh pot, if you like, or we have soft drinks."

Alex watched Goodie lick his lips the way a man thirsty for something stronger than a soft drink might. "No, thanks. I'm fine."

Lacy barely shrugged. "Hold my calls," he told his secretary, and continued into his office.

Alex followed, closing the door behind him. As expected, the director took the seat at his desk, putting himself in the power position. Weighing the dynamics of the situation, Alex wandered around the room, examining the customary "I love me" wall, the proud accoutrements of a busy and productive career. There was Lacy's Bachelor of Science degree from the University of Wisconsin. He'd majored in biology, changing his specialty to physics in his graduate work. His master's was from Stanford, where he'd also earned his Ph.D. On both sides of the academic credentials were framed awards: diplomas from government courses and schools; certificates of recognition; plaques, some serious, others jocular, acknowledging his various tours of duty. Mixed among them all were autographed photographs of generals, congressmen, diplomats and other well-known personages, many with encouraging comments addressed to him by his first name.

"I haven't had time to fully digest all the materials in the folders Brassard gave me," Alex said over his shoulder. He studied a personally inscribed picture of the current Air Force Chief of Staff when he was still a two-star general. Alex turned. Lacy was sitting upright, or perhaps uptight, staring straight at him, elbows on armrests, fingers curled around the ends. "I have to tell you, Goodie, I'm impressed."

Instead of taking the chair closest to the desk, Alex settled onto the couch at the far end of the room, establishing even more distance between them. Placing one ankle over the other knee, he stretched his arms across the back of the sofa and reviewed what he'd gleaned of the project to date. He did so with scientific dispassion, refusing to allow his judgment to be tainted by jealousy. In fact, he saw the program's achievements with a mixture of envy and admiration. The concept had been his brainchild, the fruit of his thought processes. He should have been the one to nurture its maturation. Yet, in a professionally detached way, he couldn't help being proud of the progress his former colleague had made. Alex had never questioned Lacy's competence as a scientist, which made his purloining the design all the more stunning and disturbing.

"You've done well," Alex observed, "found a winning combination of talented people. Your chief scientist, Brassard, seems exceptionally well organized."

Lacy showed not a flicker of emotion. Alex found the cold reserve strangely unsettling. He'd expected Goodie to preen at the remark. Aloofness seemed out of character.

After a lingering silence, the man behind the desk commented, "You appear surprised."

Alex stroked a hand across his chin. "Not really.

You were always a good scientist, a keen observer—'' he paused briefly, putting emphasis on his next words ''—a team player. That's why your hijacking this program—''

"Hijacking?'' Lacy repeated the word in a vicious undertone. "You seem to think MADAM was all your idea. It wasn't. If you recall, we spent many hours discussing it. I contributed as much to it as you did.''

Did he? Alex asked himself. That certainly wasn't the way he remembered it. "The idea was mine,'' he noted, but without the challenge of insistence. "I posited the basic concept, gave structure to—''

"The design would never have gotten past first base without my solving the technical details for you.''

You can get a lot accomplished if you don't care who gets credit for it was one of his father's favorite maxims. It put the emphasis on what counted—results; but humility could be a bitter pill to swallow.

"You made a difference,'' Alex agreed. "I was willing to give you full credit for your contrib—''

"I recognized you as a major contributor to the central hypothesis,'' Lacy snapped before Alex could finish.

Yes, there had been an acknowledgment in Lacy's project proposal—one line thanking Major Alex Huston for his help and assistance in developing the underlying theory. The statement had been cleverly couched to sound generous on the one hand and charitable on the other.

"I would have invited you to be part of the team,'' Alex said. "Why didn't you extend the same courtesy to me?''

"Believe me, Alex, I gave it serious consideration, but it would have been overkill." Lacy spoke with apparent calmness; however, Alex could hear the weaseling desperation in his voice. "There were more creative and productive things you could have been doing with your time. Dogging my efforts wouldn't have done either of us, or the project, any good."

Alex suppressed most of the anger he felt, but he couldn't prevent irony from coloring his words. "So keeping me out was really to give me other opportunities."

"Exactly," the man behind the desk responded with an eager nod. He rested back, looking pleased—and perhaps relieved—that Alex might actually be buying his explanation.

Alex studied him, noting the tiny beads of sweat dotting his forehead, the gray hairs beginning to salt his temples. They'd been colleagues, friends, pals who shared similar interests and goals. Alex had enjoyed Goodie's company, envied him his family, his pretty wife and beautiful twin daughters.

He and Goodie were less than six years apart in age, years Alex had never considered any more significant than their one-grade difference in rank. Maybe he should have.

Alex had been a fast-moving major on his way up; Goodie, already a senior lieutenant colonel, sweating out selection for full colonel. Had he seen this project as his last, best chance of being promoted? The "up or out" system put a premium on ambition and advancement—oftentimes at the price of competence. Goodie's stealing MADAM hadn't worked. He'd been passed over for the coveted eagles of rank. He'd get another chance at them, but failing again, his career would be over, and he'd be forced to retire. Had he, like many other senior officers, neglected to plan financially for the future, so that now, as his children approached college age, he found himself unable to provide for them? In desperation and panic, had money motivated him to sell out the project he'd lied and cheated to establish?

The telephone rang. Lacy scowled at it for a moment, then, with what might have been relief, lifted the receiver.

IT WAS JUST BEFORE NOON when Rika drove onto base and turned down the narrow road leading to the lone hangar at the far end of the disused runway. She'd figured out her approach—an article, maybe a series of articles, on space-age nutrition. Stories about food were always popular, especially if they incorporated ways to lose pounds without having to work at it. Surely the "diet of the future" would be high on energy and low on calories. Maybe she could incorporate a few "out of this world" recipes from the Aerospace Food Lab, as well, recipes that would taste good and be fat-free.

The hangar was surrounded by chain-link fence topped with barbed wire. Rika frowned, yet her pulse quickened. The security seemed excessive for a lab working on food. On the other hand, if they were doing more than cooking up stellar brownies…

She went to the wooden guard shack, noting the sign that identified the facility as a restricted area and warned that the use of deadly force was authorized against gate-crashers.

"Hi," she said brightly to the two military sentries on duty. They stared back blankly. "I'm Rika Philips, here for my appointment with Colonel Lacy.'' They remained mute. "He should be expecting me," she elaborated. "He's going to give me a tour of the facilities." She dug into her purse and took out her press card. "I work for the *Michigan Sun* and we're doing a series of articles on—"

The senior of the two noncoms, a technical sergeant, glanced at her card politely but without enthusiasm. "Ma'am, nobody's told me anything about your visit."

Rika did her best dissembling. "The notification should have arrived today."

John had promised to fax a letter of introduction and request for cooperation to the director of the Aerospace Food Laboratory, Coyote Air Force Base, Texas. The only number she'd been able to give him, however, was for the base Public Affairs office. It was anyone's guess where the document might have ended up—or if anyone had even gotten around to reading it yet.

"I'm sorry, I can't let you in, ma'am," the NCO informed her.

"Maybe the colonel's secretary forgot to give it to him, or he just didn't get around to telling you." They didn't budge. She allowed a touch of patient irritation to creep into her voice. "Perhaps if you call Colonel Lacy? This is probably just some bureaucratic snafu."

Should she invoke her grandfather's name? Under other circumstances it might open doors. In this case, she had the distinct feeling it wouldn't, and when word got back to Gramps—and it would, she had no doubt—she'd really be in hot water.

"I'll call him, ma'am, but I don't think there's any mistake. We don't give tours to reporters."

Rika raised an eyebrow. He picked up the phone and pressed a button.

It wasn't Lacy who came out of the building a few minutes later but Alex. He crossed to the guard shack in a few efficient strides. The set of his jaw told her he wasn't happy to see her.

Why was she surprised to see him? It was because of him she was here. Yet his looming presence made her suddenly uncomfortable. What the man did for a uniform—wet, dry, clean or stained—was downright sinful. The close quarters of the guard shack made her disconcertingly aware of his height, the broadness of his shoulders, the way his deep chest tapered to narrow waist and hips.

"Major, this is Ms. Philips," the NCO informed him. "She's a reporter with the *Michigan Sun*."

Alex stared at her. "What are you doing here?" he demanded.

"I—" She started to open her mouth and realized she didn't know what to say. She'd figured on bluffing her way with Lacy, getting at least a quote, maybe even a statement or, better yet, an interview. She hadn't counted on Alex showing up.

"She says she's supposed to get a tour of the facilities," the guard said helpfully.

"A tour?" He knit his brows, his piercing eyes never leaving her. "That's out of the question."

She felt perspiration break out on the back of her neck. "You…uh…should have received a letter or a form or whatever it is you're supposed to get from my editor—" She was stammering. She never stammered.

He stared her down. "We didn't, and it wouldn't have made any difference if we had. We don't give tours.'' He wasn't having trouble getting his words out.

"Darn," she said, trying to sound resigned. "This was going to be a feature article for the *Sun,* a two-page spread. I was even hoping I could get a couple of recipes.''

His face went blank, then she saw the corners of his mouth twitch and it struck her that he was enjoying her discomfort. She had the distinct impression Major Huston was doing his damnedest not to laugh in her face.

"I thought you said you didn't do food articles," he reminded her, tongue in cheek, eyes glittering.

"Yeah, well...not normally.''

He gave her a crocodile smile. "I'm sorry, Mrs. Philips,'' he said softly. "We don't make burritos or calamari canapés here.''

Good grief, the man had the memory of an elephant. She straightened. "My boss is going to be really disappointed.''

He curled his hand over hers sympathetically. "You won't get fired, will you?''

His concern was touching, but if he suppressed the guffaw that was bottled up much longer, his face was going to crack.

She pulled her hand out from under his. "Thanks for your time...and courtesy, Major.''

She could feel him watching her as she slunk away to her car. "I'll get you for this," she muttered, and started the van.

BARBARA CAME IN from her afternoon session in the greenhouse, where she'd been setting flats of seedling tomatoes and squash for fall planting. The phone rang. She let Sera answer it and had just reached the hall on her way upstairs to wash up, when the house-keeper sang out that the call was for her.

Barbara picked up the receiver by the staircase. "Hello."

"Babs? Henrietta. He was just in. Again. Major Huston." She sounded almost breathless. "Ordered three more sets of uniforms. Special-ordered them, actually. We don't normally carry sizes for a man built the way he is." She emitted a pleasant little sigh of awe. "If he's going to be around awhile, though, maybe I should."

"We'll have to work on that," Barbara told her, wishing her friend would get to the point. Henrietta had an annoying habit of veering off on tangents. "In the meantime—"

"He's also going to the Log Cabin for dinner," Henrietta blurted.

This was useful news. "This evening?" Barbara's interest was definitely piqued now. "When and with whom?"

"I don't know who with, but I'm pretty sure it will be tonight. When he was getting ready to leave, he asked me for the name of the best steak house in town. I told him my favorite was the Log Cabin."

"He said he was going there?"

"Well, he didn't invite me along, but I'm pretty sure he was. Of course, I'm a married woman, but if I wasn't—"

And thirty years younger. "Did he say what time?"

"No. He mumbled something about happy hour."

Barbara's mind raced. It was Friday, which meant happy hour at the club ran from 4:30 to 7:30. Much too long, she thought. Used to be only one hour. Ironically, the deemphasis on alcohol in recent years had prompted the last club officer to extend ''the social hour'' in the hope of luring in more people. Dumb. If they didn't want cheap drinks for one hour, they certainly wouldn't want them for three. Oh, dear. Her mind was wandering again.

She thanked Henrietta for the call and hung up. What to do?

She shook her head gleefully. It's a no-brainer, you old fool.

RIKA WAS SURPRISED when her grandmother suggested they all go out to the Log Cabin Steak House that evening. Gram enjoyed lunching during the week with her friends at the city's small assortment of sandwich and tea shops, and there was the years-long tradition of brunch after church every Sunday. But her grandparents normally avoided the crushing crowds on Friday and Saturday nights, even though the general's social status inevitably got them quick and efficient service. Gram was up to something.

Rika offered to drive, but to her chagrin, her grandfather declined. Nathan Tiers may have been an outstanding officer and pilot, but he was a terrible driver. His foot was on the gas, off the gas, on the gas... Rika felt her stomach lurch dangerously. Fortunately, their destination was on the near side of town, so the trip took only a few minutes.

They stopped for a traffic light across the street from the restaurant. She scanned the parking lot. It appeared that for once her grandfather's luck had deserted him. Not a single empty space in view. He'd have to drive around back. Then, just as the light turned green, a car backed out of a spot right in front of the door. Rika rolled her eyes in disbelief.

"Gramps, have you been holding out on me?"

He glanced over at her, baffled by her question.

"Is there a patron saint of parking spaces you pray to that you haven't told me about?"

"What do you mean, Mommy?" Emily asked.

Rika grinned. "Haven't you ever noticed that whenever we go somewhere with Gramps he always manages to find a parking space right in front of the entrance?"

"Oh, Mommy. That's because he's a general."

The adults all laughed.

"I just wish it were true." He got out of the car and opened the rear door of the Cadillac for his wife.

Clutching her handbag, Barbara surveyed the cars around her.

"Looking for someone, Gram?" Rika asked with a teasing casualness.

"It's crowded, isn't it?" was all she said.

"Are we going to have onion rings?" Emily begged.

"I don't see why not," her great-grandfather assured her.

Emily deferred to her mother, her expression begging for confirmation.

Rika chuckled. "Yeah, onion rings and French fries if you want." She might as well enjoy all the forbidden foods they were going to indulge in tonight. There was certainly no sense trying to reason with a man who had been eating sausage, bacon and fried eggs every morning for nearly eighty years.

People were lined up to be seated when the group entered the waiting area that spanned the front of the building. The tantalizing smells of deep-fried onions, potatoes and sizzling steak that hung in the air didn't help Rika's still-queasy stomach.

While her grandfather advanced to the reservations desk to have his name put on the waiting list, Rika swept the busy room for a familiar face. Coyote Springs was one of those places in which it was practically impossible to go anywhere without running into someone you knew.

The sight of gray hair and broad shoulders caused her heartbeat to suddenly accelerate. Great. Just what she needed, another encounter with Major Alex Huston. She was consoled by the knowledge that the heat rising to her cheeks was indubitably hidden by the egg on her face from her rather inept charade at the AFL earlier that day.

He was sitting at a table against the back wall with a man she didn't recognize. Strange. Alex had mentioned at lunch that he didn't know anyone in this part of Texas. Of course, it could be someone from base showing him around, she supposed.

Alex raised his head, saw her, and for a moment their eyes locked. She read shock, pleasure, then discomfort in his gaze. Not exactly normal reactions, she thought. What was going on?

"Oh, my," Barbara chirped. "Isn't that Major Huston over there?"

Rika glanced at her grandmother to confirm she was only feigning surprise. The old woman had the eyes of a hawk and the cunning of a fox, she reminded herself.

"What a coincidence running into him here," Rika exclaimed dramatically, her heartbeat definitely irregular.

"Isn't it?" her grandmother agreed, apparently unmindful of the note of sarcasm in her granddaughter's remark.

"General Tiers, sir," a male voice called out pleasantly. Rika turned to see a man in a suit, undoubtedly the manager, shake her grandfather's hand. "Good to see you, sir. We'll have a table for you in just a moment."

Rika only half listened, her interest riveted elsewhere. Alex led his companion among tables and people to the cashier's counter, where he handed him the dinner check and a large bill. Who was the guy? She didn't recognize him.

Military for sure. She could tell by his haircut and the way he wore his clothes. Even in sport shirt and chinos, the edge of his belt buckle was in precise alignment with his shirt and trousers, and nothing bulged from his pockets. She managed to get a glimpse of his feet. His loafers were polished to a mirror shine.

Alex stepped over to join Rika and her family.

"My, what a surprise seeing you here, Major," Barbara gushed.

He reached out and took her hand. "It is indeed. A very pleasant surprise, too." He spoke to the old woman, but Rika didn't miss the sidelong glance or the amused gleam in his eye.

"Micki's mom says I can have Scamper as soon as he's old enough to be wormed," Emily informed him happily.

Releasing Barbara's fingers, he smiled down at the girl. "I think you mean weaned. I'm glad to hear it." He winked at her. "But then, we still have to convince your mom, don't we?"

"Yeah." The girl gave him a conspiratorial grin. "Are you going to have dinner with us?"

"I wish I could." He patted his narrow waist. "But I just finished eating a huge steer, and I haven't got room for even a blade of grass." He turned to the general, who'd just walked up beside him. "Good evening, sir." They shook hands.

His head angled, he finally greeted Rika with a slight bow. "Hello, Rika," he said softly. "How nice to see you again today."

He reached for her hand and sandwiched it between his own. She should pull out of his grip after the humiliating way he treated her at the AFL.

"Rika stopped by to see me at the food lab this morning," he told the others. His eyes were playing with hers, waiting to see what her response would be.

She managed to maintain just enough presence of mind to keep her mouth shut. She also noticed her grandfather's raised brow and the simpering smile on her grandmother's lips.

"If you'll come this way, General," the manager interrupted, "your table is ready."

Gratefully, Rika reclaimed her hand and allowed herself to breathe.

"Sure you can't join us?" Barbara asked, obviously disappointed that he'd already eaten and apparently oblivious to the dynamics between her granddaughter and the major.

Alex grinned crookedly at Rika even as he answered the general's wife. "Thanks, maybe another time."

"Can you go riding with us on Sunday?" Emily asked.

"What a splendid idea!" Barbara perked up, and

Rika instantly wondered if her grandmother had put Emily up to the invitation. "You can stay to dinner afterward."

"I don't know…"

"I'll let you and Rika work out the time. We usually eat early on Sundays, around five." With that she tucked her arm under her husband's and followed the maître d' to their table. "Come along, Emily."

"Your grandmother can be very persuasive," Alex said quietly.

"You mean manipulative."

He held her gaze. "If you'd rather I didn't…"

She leaned back. "And disappoint Emily?"

"We certainly can't do that." The sounds around them seemed to fade into a velvety hum. "When?"

She was strangely mesmerized by his lips forming words. "About one. That'll give us time to…"

"Oh," he said, "we definitely don't want to run out of time."

"Coming, Alex?" the man who had been sitting with Alex called out as he brushed by.

"Be right there, Mike," he mumbled over his shoulder without actually taking his eyes off her. "See you Sunday, then. Around one o'clock."

Rika nodded, turned, paused, glanced back, then continued on to where her grandfather was standing at a table, holding a chair for her.

She joined her family, then immediately excused herself to go freshen up. Whether the butterflies in her stomach were the aftereffects of the general's driving or the major's magnetism, she couldn't say. All she knew was that she needed a moment to collect her wits.

The ladies' room was at the rear of the building,

down a narrow hallway that had an outside window. It was by pure chance that she caught sight of Alex climbing into a large motor home with his friend, a friend he hadn't bothered to introduce.

Rika watched the oversized vehicle lumber out of the parking lot, her investigative instincts stirred. Whatever he was up to, she intended to find out.

CHAPTER SEVEN

"WHERE IS EVERYONE?" Alex asked Emily Sunday afternoon as she escorted him to the barn.

"Saddling up," the girl replied. "Mom says to bring you."

The eight-year-old was wearing a T-shirt that said Cowgirls Rule, jeans and cowboy boots.

"Do you and your mom go riding in Michigan?"

"Naw. We don't have horses up there."

He was curious. "How do you and your mom usually spend your weekends?"

"Sometimes, when the weather is nice, we go out on a boat."

"Your mom owns a boat?" Journalists apparently made a better living than he thought. "That must be fun."

"It's not ours. Mom says we can't afford a big boat. Or even a little one. It belongs to a man she knows."

"What kind of boat is it?"

"He's got two. One's for sailing. The other is just for fun. That's the one I like."

So Rika had a rich boyfriend who liked to take her out sailing. The idea shouldn't shock him, but after the way she'd spoken of her ex, it did. Did they go out on the lake at night? he wondered. He tried to imagine her stretched out on a sloping deck, with moonbeams accentuating her feminine curves. Remembering her lounging at the pool, he didn't find it difficult. Would her eyes be misty green in the moonlight?

"Who is this friend of your mom's?" he couldn't keep from asking—though he felt like an intruder doing so.

Emily shrugged. "His name is Mr. Smith, but I'm allowed to call him Uncle John."

John Smith? Now, that's original. John Smith, indeed.

"Mommy works with him, and sometimes on weekends we stay at his house."

Stay at his house? This sounded more serious than dating.

He would have asked more questions, but he saw Rika leading a horse out of the shadowy recesses of the building to the hitching post near the corral gate.

"You two better get a move on," she called out, "if we're going to be back in time for dinner."

He couldn't help feasting his eyes on her pastel blouse and the slim sweeping curve of her jeans while she tied the horse to the rail.

Rika swiveled toward him. Folk wisdom said any man looked good in a uniform, but not every man could do for clothes what Alex Huston did.

The fitted, snap-button, canvas-colored shirt emphasized the breadth of his chest. The long sleeves, rolled up to just below the elbows, accentuated the deepness of his tan as well as the power and strength of his forearms. Her appreciation slid down to his stonewashed jeans. They were new and a little stiff, but she could easily imagine them molding themselves in time to the narrow contours of his hips, the hard muscles of his thighs, and... Heat rose to her face.

"I like your boots." She tried to sound light-hearted, though her heart was beginning to thrum erratically.

He hooked both thumbs in his belt loops and slouched on one hip. "Goin' native, ma'am," he drawled, and tipped his brand-new Stetson. "Where are we riding to?"

"I thought we might go down by the river. It's cool and shady there."

Emily led a huge black horse out of a stall and came toward them. "His name's Dark Thunder," she told Alex. "Mommy says a man your size needs a big horse."

Rika took the halter rope from her daughter. Another girl brought out a saddle blanket, and a boy struggled with a heavy western saddle. Alex quickly relieved him of it.

"How many are going on this trail ride?" he asked.

"Six, plus you and me," Rika answered.

It didn't take more than a few moments of watching Alex try to saddle the sixteen-hand gelding for Rika to realize he knew nothing about horses or their tack. She wondered what his reaction would be if she tried to assist him. Her ex-husband never admitted to not being able to do anything and everything. Clay always regarded suggestions as interference.

"Can I help you?" she asked, expecting Alex to automatically reject her offer.

He assumed a very serious expression. "I'd appreciate it."

She moved over to his side of the horse. "Lift the saddle a minute." She rearranged the blanket, helped him reposition the heavily tooled, western saddle, then tightened the cinch.

Other horses were lined up along the corral and hitching post; children gathered, waiting for the adults.

"Everyone," Rika called out, "this is Major Huston. He's going to be riding with us this afternoon."

Alex felt half a dozen pairs of eyes pinned on him.

"This is Cindy Roberts," Rika said, placing her hand on the shoulder of the redheaded girl who'd delivered the saddle blanket. "And her brother, Dale." He was taller and huskier, his hair closer to auburn. Alex shook his hand. Rika introduced the other two girls: Micki Sanchez, who was olive complected and raven haired; and Lottie James, whose platinum-blond hair and shy demeanor contrasted with her friends' in every way. Finally, Rika presented ten-year-old Shawn Mullens.

"Planning any cannonballs off your horse today, Shawn?" Alex teased.

"No, sir." The boy hung his head.

Alex laughed and ruffled his curly hair. "I'm glad to hear it."

"No one's going in the water today," Rika assured him, then shouted, "okay, let's mount up."

Alex dawdled, fiddling with the reins and pretending to check the cinch, in an attempt to buy time so he could observe how the others were mounting. A couple of the girls led their horses over to a set of wooden steps, which they used to get a foot into the stirrup. The big boy, Shawn, reached his hands up, grabbed the saddle horn and, with unexpected grace, pulled himself onto the saddle without using the stirrup at all.

Rika, unfortunately, was on the other side of his horse, so Alex wasn't able to watch her mount, though he did see her long, slender leg swing over the animal's rump and settle onto the shiny curve of the western saddle.

She peered down at him. "Is something wrong?"

"No…uh, no. I was just checking the strap."

"You mean the cinch?" she asked with a grin.

"Uh, yeah, the cinch." He made a futile attempt to slip his hand between it and the horse's belly. "Seems to be okay," he commented.

He started to lift his right foot to the high stirrup, paused in self-conscious awareness of his mistake and lowered his leg. He saw Rika pressing her lips together, trying to disguise her amusement. He bit back the epithets going through his mind—idiot, jerk—reversed his stance and raised his left boot to the leather-covered stirrup.

Once he'd hoisted himself up to the saddle, he settled into it and glanced over at her.

"That's a relief." She nudged Sandy forward. "I was afraid there for a minute you didn't know one end of the horse from the other."

The young people started toward the gate that opened to a wooded area.

"Hey, wait up. Don't go so fast." He rocked his torso ineffectively, trying to get the horse to move forward.

The children stopped and gaped at him, wide-eyed with shock.

"You guys are going to have to help me," he said humbly. "I don't know much about riding." No sense pretending otherwise.

"You don't?" Micki Sanchez asked, amazed that

you could be a grown-up and be unfamiliar with something as elementary as riding a horse.

"Nope. The last time I was on a horse was when I was six—and I fell off." He noticed Rika's surprised expression under the shade of her cowboy hat, as if he'd shocked her as much as he had the kids.

"Didn't you get back up on it right away?" Micki asked.

He hung his head dramatically. "I was too scared."

"My daddy says whenever you fall off a horse, the first thing you should do is get right back on," Dale Roberts informed him.

"Even before brushing yourself off?"

Dale appeared slightly confused for a moment, then relaxed when he saw the grin on Alex's face. "Well, you can dust yourself off first," he agreed, "but then you have to get back on right away. Otherwise you'll always be afraid of horses."

"Your dad is absolutely right," Alex confirmed.

"Are you afraid of horses?" Lottie James asked. "Is that why you don't know anything about riding?"

"I guess I used to be, but a man's got to do what a man's got to do." It wasn't as if he had any choice. This ride hadn't been his idea, and if he had his druthers, he wouldn't be on this horse now. He reached forward and patted Thunder on the neck. "It's just that I haven't ridden as much as you have." He looked at the six-year-old, in her red jeans, purple boots and green shirt. "You ride really well."

"I've been riding since I was a little kid," the girl informed him. The others screwed up their faces in "give me a break" expressions.

"I hope you all will help me. When I do something

wrong, let me know, because that's the only way I can learn to do things right.''

"The first thing,'' Rika said, observing the way the youngsters seemed to be drawn to him and he to them, ''is to pronounce it as one word.''

He stared at her. ''Huh?''

"It's not you all,'' she explained. ''It's y'all. Unless you want to sound like a Yankee.''

He stiffened his back. ''Hey, who're you calling a Yankee? Remember, I'm a native Texan.''

"You are?'' Shawn asked.

"Yep. Born in San Antonio, Texas, home of the Alamo.''

"And the Spurs,'' Shawn added.

"You like basketball?'' Alex asked.

The two of them starting trading opinions about the Spurs' last season.

"Okay,'' Rika interrupted, ''let's move out. Dale, why don't you take the lead. Just walk. Don't trot until I tell you to.''

The husky towhead seemed uncertain whether he wanted to go in front of the group or remain a part of it. Then, perhaps realizing that being a leader was an honor, he reined his horse into position and waved his arm with a big ''wagon ho'' signal for the others to follow.

"The second thing,'' Rika prompted Alex, ''is to use your legs to get the horse to move forward. You don't have to kick him—just touch his flanks with your boots.''

"Like this,'' Micki Sanchez said, and squeezed her short legs against the sides of the saddle, prompting her horse to step out.

Alex did as instructed and Thunder moved ahead.

"See, it's not so difficult." Rika's praise was mild, but she was favorably impressed. He actually appeared to be trainable.

They passed through the gate, leaving it open. Rika brought up the rear, watching to make sure everyone was safely in place. Alex was in the middle, the kids maneuvering to be next to him.

Well, she mused to herself, Gram said taking him riding with us would give me a chance to see how he gets along with children. Now I know.

Alex began to relax in the saddle, letting his hips sway with the rhythmic stride of the animal. They rode for half an hour, the kids hanging close, asking questions about a thousand things: his uniform, the planes he flew, where he'd been. The life he described wasn't always as exciting as it sounded, but he did nothing to destroy the illusion.

Patiently, each of them gave him advice about riding. Kids love to play teacher, he realized. Getting the chance to "teach" an adult had to be even more thrilling.

He didn't lose awareness of the woman trailing behind him, though. It was just as well she wasn't in view, he decided. It would be hard to concentrate on all the pointers from the kids if she was sitting astride her bay mare in front of him. Not that his imagination had any difficulty conjuring up the shape or movement of *her* hips rocking gently in the saddle.

Damn, but she had a way of stimulating his imagination and making him uncomfortable.

"Dale," Rika called out as she came up beside Alex, "lead everyone in a trot to the rock and tree. We'll take a break there. Major Huston and I will catch up."

They were on a crest. The children kicked their horses into a quick trot down the slope.

"They're great kids," he said.

"They seem to like you, too." She gathered up her reins. "Willing to try a short trot?"

He shifted his eyes from side to side and groped behind himself on the saddle with his left hand, then his right.

"What are you doing?" she asked, brows raised in confusion.

"Looking for my seat belt."

She hooted. It was the first time he'd heard her uninhibited laughter and he realized he liked the sound—more than liked it. He had a sudden awareness of wanting to be a part of the joy bubbling from inside her.

He seldom considered his bachelor status limiting. On the contrary, it allowed him freedom to come and go as he pleased, to associate with or get away from people at his option. Being with Rika and her family, though, was making him see another dimension of life, one he wasn't sure he understood.

"Try to sit in the saddle when the horse speeds up, but if you can't, rise and fall in it with every other bounce. If worst comes to worst," she instructed, "just stand up in the stirrups."

"You sure you want me to do this? Once I get started I may not be able to stop."

She looked at him curiously for a moment, as if unsure there wasn't a hidden meaning in his words. "Just pull back on the reins and sit hard in the saddle."

He firmed his mouth and nodded subtly. "I'll give it a try."

She rode ahead, and he paused for a moment to watch the liquid motion of her round hips swaying as the brown horse skipped forward. He drew up his shoulders in a shudder of erotic frustration. Hmm. Sitting hard in the saddle wouldn't be difficult at all.

Thoughts of her vanished instantly when he kicked Thunder into a trot. It seemed the gelding was galloping at breakneck speed and he was about to fly without a plane. Till the instinct for survival took over. He tightened his knees, only to find the animal racing even faster. Meanwhile his butt was getting the worst spanking he'd ever endured. He remembered to stand up, but it helped only a little. Thunder seemed to have his own idea where they headed, and it wasn't toward his friends.

"Ride 'm, Major," he heard off in the distance amid a chorus of cheers and laughter.

"Pull back on the reins," another voice, Rika's, called out over them.

He tried to follow instructions, but as he tugged one rein and then the other, the horse veered from side to side. With each wild zig he felt his hold zag. Just a matter of seconds, he told himself, before he was launched onto the hard-packed earth or—with his current luck—into a cactus patch. The image brought determination. He put a stranglehold on the saddle horn.

Out of the corner of his eye he saw Rika gallop up beside him, reach over at an impossible angle and snag Thunder's reins.

"Whoa," she commanded.

The horse stopped so abruptly Alex catapulted forward, nearly injuring certain body parts. He lifted his face off the animal's neck as dust billowed up around them.

"You all right?" she asked calmly.

He closed his eyes, breathed raggedly through his nose, expanded his chest in relief and exhaled. "I've got this terrible pain," he acknowledged.

"Where?" Alarm colored her voice, giving him a foolish pleasure.

"My pride," he stated meekly. "I think I've bruised my pride."

Her laughter this time was like a warm blanket on a cold night. Yes, he definitely wanted to snuggle into it.

The group waited a few yards ahead. As Alex and Rika approached, the kids slid off their horses with youthful agility and tied their mounts to short, bushy mesquites.

"Loosen the cinches," Rika instructed, as she threw her leg over the back of the saddle and dropped herself smoothly to the ground. She peered up at Alex, who hadn't moved. "Ready for a break?"

"Whatever," he replied with feigned indifference, and dismounted, feeling clumsy, bowlegged and decidedly stupid.

Rika opened her saddlebag and distributed apples to the kids. "Save the cores and feed them to your horses," she told them as they wandered off, crunching happily.

She held out a shiny red apple to Alex. "Want one?"

He looked around, up and down. "I'm not sure, Eve. Will it get me in trouble?"

A glint sparkled in her eye. "You'll never know until you bite, Adam."

To see her smile, to hear her laugh—yes, he'd bite. He took the apple.

"Besides," she added as his fingers grazed hers, "I got it from Gram's refrigerator, not a snake." She picked up Sandy's reins.

"Who was the guy you were with Friday at the steak house?" she asked over her shoulder before bracing the bright-red fruit between her teeth so she could tie her horse to a low branch. "I didn't think you knew anybody here."

Alex ran a hand down Thunder's neck. "That was Mike Lattimore, an old friend of mine who's passing through."

"He's on active duty. Is he here for the same reason you are—this AFL business?"

His hand slowed at the question. "What makes you think that?"

She answered with a sigh of irritation. "Come on, Alex. I've been around the military all my life. Don't you think I can recognize a GI when I see one?"

They leaned against a hip-high outcropping of stone near the water's edge.

"No comment."

The best defense is a good offense, he reminded himself. "My turn for a question. Who's Uncle John?"

Rika slowly transferred her attention from the surface of the river to him. Her demeanor was one of confusion at first, then mirth swept across her face, making her eyes crinkle and her lips curve. "Who told you about John?"

"Emily mentioned you sometimes stay with him at his house."

Her smile deepened into a taunting grin, and Alex felt his face grow warm.

"Is that what she said—that I stay with him? Or did she say *we* sometimes stay at his house?"

"Well, she …could have said it that way, I guess."

Her prolonged apple-eating grin was making him more uncomfortable than he cared to admit.

"Why, Alex Huston," she murmured sweetly, "I don't think I ever noticed those green specks in your eyes before."

"I just wondered…"

She chuckled audibly now. "John Smith is the owner and editor of the *Michigan Sun,* the paper I work for. Everyone calls him Uncle John." She beamed at Alex with mischievous eyes. "As for sleeping at his house…he has a lodge on the lake where he's invited Emily and me to spend weekends." She paused for emphasis. "The lodge has ten bedrooms and they're usually all full—with family and other guests. He takes us out for rides in his sailboat and his motorboat. We water-ski. He even has several jet skis for people to use."

A soft "Ah" was Alex's only response.

Rika bent down to dip her hands in the water to wash away the stickiness from her fingers, then stood up again. "By the way, Uncle John is more than ten years older than Gramps, has been happily married to the same woman for almost seventy years, has six children, eighteen grandchildren and I forget how many great-grandchildren." She lifted a wet hand and patted him on the cheek. "I think there are a couple of great-great-grandchildren, too."

"Hey, I just asked," he muttered.

She searched his eyes very intently. "Have you ever been married, Alex?"

"What?" It wasn't a question he'd been expecting, not here and now, anyway. "Why do you ask that?"

"You obviously like children and get along well with them. I just wondered why you don't have a bunch of your own."

He didn't like being interrogated. His marital status was no one's business but his own. He shouldn't have to defend it.

"I don't have time for a wife and kids," he all but snapped. "I put in long hours at work, sometimes dangerous work. It wouldn't be fair to them."

"The way your father was unfair to your mother and you?"

Telling her about his parents had been a mistake. He never discussed his growing up with anyone. Why had he mentioned it to her?

"For your information," he retorted, "my folks didn't break up because of my father's job but because my mother couldn't accept she wasn't the center of his universe."

He expected her to challenge him, point out that other people managed both careers and families. She obviously did. She was also divorced, he reminded himself. But instead of pursuing, she backed off.

"Maybe the green I saw mirrored in your eyes was just the reflection of the trees," she said. "Your eyes really are a pretty Air Force blue."

Rika started to climb the bank toward the horses, but he snagged her arm. His warm, firm touch stopped her dead in her tracks. A scissor-tailed flycatcher fluttered through the trees. A woodpecker tapped a staccato tattoo. The scent of musky aftershave filled her nostrils. She looked down at his hand, at sunbeams dancing on his skin. They made his silver-blond hair sparkle.

She said not a word as her gaze rose and locked onto his. Beautiful didn't begin to describe the depthless color of his eyes or the desire she saw in them.

''You might want to check a little closer,'' he muttered huskily.

His mouth came down on hers. He wasn't hesitant as he wrapped his arms around her and pulled her tightly against his hard torso. She surrendered willingly to his embrace, brought her hands up to entwine her fingers behind his neck. Their bodies met, chest to chest, hip to hip.

The summer sun was nothing compared with the searing fire that spread through her as he pressed his demand. His tongue probed her lips and parted them. She welcomed him with demands of her own, challenging, taunting, taking. He tasted of apple and sex and heat and pleasure. His hand cupped her breast while his thumb teased the rigid nipple. He deepened the kiss. She tightened her hold, hungry for more.

The wanton intimacy of his kiss expelled the world around her. There was no daylight or nighttime, no earth or water or sky or air. Just her body and his, locked, inseparable, consuming each other in feverish bliss.

He broke off the kiss and gazed down, his eyes filled with pleading, his hands bracketing her face with a gentle strength that had the power to wilt all resistance. Any instinct to fight gave way to the impulse to surrender. It had been so long since a man had held her. So long since she'd allowed herself to be possessed. Her heart did a somersault in her chest.

She closed her eyes and let herself wallow in the flood of warmth his firm embrace ignited.

She was breathless when at last their lips parted. Still she leaned against him, unwilling to give up too soon the sensation of his manhood pressed against her.

"We should be getting back," she whispered raggedly. "It's getting late."

He tilted her chin with the side of his finger. "I think it might already be too late."

A remnant of logic wanted to protest that they hadn't been out that long, but she knew the time of day wasn't what he was talking about. She ought to make light of his comment, chide him for getting things mixed up, but she was the one who was confused. She didn't need her life complicated by a man, but, oh, at this moment she wanted this man more than she had ever wanted anyone in her life.

She released her hold on his shoulders and let her hands course down his chest, feeling the warm mass of thick muscles. He flinched.

Her head shot up in confusion, then genuine delight. "You're ticklish!"

She trailed her fingers along the sides of his rib cage and watched him squirm. "Ooh." She chuckled with cruel mirth.

He backed away. She darted after him, reaching out to torment him. He grabbed her wrists and was drawing her close, when two girls bounded through the woods and stood, mouths open, gawking at them.

Extricating herself from Alex's possessive grasp, Rika turned to her daughter. "Ready to start back?" Casually she bent down to pick up the piece of apple she'd dropped.

"I guess," Emily replied, regarding her mother suspiciously.

"Here, let me give you a hand," Alex offered Rika, pretending it was what he'd been doing when the girls appeared.

Slipping out of his gentle grip, she stepped into the bright noontime sunshine and called to the kids. "Let's mount up."

She walked over to her mare and fed her what was left of the apple core. Alex followed and started to do the same.

"Horse bites hurt," she observed as he clutched his core with the tips of his fingers and began to bring it up to his horse's muzzle.

Quickly he dropped his hand and cast her an inquiring glance. Thunder snorted.

"Hold your hand out flat with the apple in the palm." She demonstrated. "You don't want your fingers between the horse's teeth and his snack. They look too much like carrots."

He did as instructed, then carefully tugged on each of his fingers. "All present and accounted for."

She smiled thinly first, then burst out into a chuckle before tightening the cinch on her mare.

Alex followed Rika's lead, then climbed into the saddle.

She asked Shawn to lead the pack this time. Instead of retracing their steps, however, they took a different route. Alex rode beside her, both of them quiet.

They arrived at a creek.

"Single file," Rika called out. "Don't stop. Keep moving and keep your horses' heads up."

Shawn reined his mount over to what was obviously a commonly used crossing, a spot where the steep banks of the stream were trampled into gradual slopes. The gelding barged into the gently flowing current. The clear water came up to the animals' knees. On the far side, the boy moved to a ledge overlooking the channel and watched the others cross.

Finally, it was Alex's turn. Nothing to it, he told himself. Keep the horse's head up and don't stop. He nudged Thunder forward and felt a moment's trepidation as the horse stepped into the now-muddy stream. He reached the other side feeling proud of himself and was just going up the bank, when he heard splashing behind him.

"Oh, no, you don't," Rika vowed in a strident voice. The sudden yelling and screaming of the kids jolted Alex. He turned in his saddle in time to see her horse stall in the middle of the stream and paw the murky water. The mare started to kneel.

"Get up. Get up." Rika kicked furiously and pulled back on the reins. "Get up, you cantankerous witch." With a contented snort, the horse rolled over in the clay-red creek.

Rika was in trouble.

CHAPTER EIGHT

REFLEX ACTION had Alex returning Thunder to the watercourse. Without thought or hesitation he plunged into the creek just as Rika stepped out of the stirrups.

Mindful of the weight and power of the flailing animal, she backed away from the clumsy horse, but not quickly enough to escape the splash and tidal wave the mare produced. Before she could turn, the front of her riding pants and most of her shirt were soaked with muddy water.

Alex rode up behind her. Withdrawing, Rika nearly stumbled against Thunder's shoulder. Alex bent forward and stretched out his left arm as a lifeline, but she rejected it with a shake of her head and signaled him to give her room. Sandy continued to roll like a child slapping the surface of a mud puddle, then, with a great grunt and tensing of muscles, bounced to her feet. Rika moved forward, but before she could grab the horse's reins, Sandy shook herself like a shaggy dog, sending monster drops of dirty water flying. In the moment it took Rika to recover from the spray, the mare turned tail and trotted downstream, where she climbed the bank and disappeared into the tall weeds.

Rika stood, obviously seething, her jaw clenched,

her upraised hands tightened into fists at the cloppety sound of her mount's retreating hoofs.

Struggling knee-deep through the reddish-brown water, Rika made her way to the far bank where the children sat atop their horses, watching. No one said a word. Alex followed her to dry land and dismounted.

"You all right?" he asked as he approached.

"I think I got bruised in the same place you did," she commented wryly. She looked at him, her expression forlorn. "My pride hurts."

Without even thinking, he wrapped his arms around her and chuckled endearingly. "It'll heal."

The sensation was electrifying—this man's big, warm body pressed against her, the deep timbre of his voice reverberating in her ear as if it were a part of her...as if it belonged there. She coiled her arms around him, encircling his strong back, and snuggled into his chest before she fully realized she was doing it.

"You scared me." He cleared his throat. "I was afraid..."

"I'm fine." She could feel his heart beating and the tension in his hard muscles. She glanced up and realized how very close his lips were. She and Alex stood motionless, then those lips brushed hers. She closed her eyes.

"Definitely too late," he murmured.

"Hey, Mrs. Philips, Sandy's getting away. You want me to go after her?"

Rika's eyes popped open. For a timeless moment she'd forgotten all about her horse and the children, and where they were. Struggling to regain composure, she unwound herself from Alex's hold and pivoted around to the kids.

"No sense chasing her, Shawn," she said, and wondered if they could hear the tremor in her voice. Nervously, she yanked on the woven cord at the base of her neck and retrieved the hat that had fallen down her back. She positioned it carefully on her head. "She'll go home on her own."

The kids tittered.

"What's so funny?" Alex asked. His lips had barely touched Rika's, but to the children it probably qualified as a kiss. Not him, though, not him. Nevertheless, he shouldn't have done that in front of them.

Hand covering her mouth, Cindy snickered, "You look like you wet your pants."

Startled, Rika turned to examine Alex. Two muddy-red splotches clearly outlined where her breasts had pressed against his new western shirt, and there were long wet streaks from his crotch down the inside of his thighs where her legs had slipped between his.

He looked down at himself, glanced up at her, certain she could see the immodest thoughts going through his mind.

"Sorry," she said with a contrite smile, and found she wanted to kiss him on the cheek.

"Yeah...well...um."

Her gaze slipped once more to his pants, and she immediately realized it wasn't the damp marks that had him stuttering with embarrassment but the bulge.

"You can ride with me, Mommy," Emily called out, innocently oblivious of the exchange of awareness between the two adults.

Temporarily speechless, Rika managed a tiny coughing sound, then turned back to her daughter. "You and Micki ride together on her horse, and I'll take yours."

While Alex helped the girls get settled on Rainbow, Rika walked over to a boulder, her tooled leather boots making squelching noises. She tugged them off and poured out streams of brown water, rolled off her thick cotton socks and wrung them out.

"At least when I go swimming fully dressed," Alex teased lightly, "it's in nice clean water. You really ought to get out of those messy clothes."

She stuck her tongue out at him but couldn't keep the music from her voice. "There's a limit to how far *I'll* go, too, Major."

He chortled. She sneered. And they both broke into laughter.

"Fortunately, we're not too far from home," she commented a minute later while she forced soggy socks and clammy boots back on. Alex gave her a leg up onto Emily's pinto and handed her the reins. She avoided eye contact, but she was very conscious of his hands on her leg.

"Don't let me slow you down," he insisted. "You and the girls ride on ahead. I'll follow with the boys."

"You don't mind?" she asked.

He only grinned. "You really do need to get out of those wet clothes and boots. Go on. We'll keep an eye out for Sandy in case she dallies and catch up with you at the house."

Alex was lying when he said he wouldn't mind letting her go ahead without him. He wanted her by his side. More, he wanted her in his arms again. He stood and watched the girls move out at a brisk trot.

The gentle breeze ruffled his damp clothing and cooled his skin, but the sight of the woman riding away continued to stir his blood. He closed his eyes for a second to clear his mind and regain control, but he just couldn't distract himself with Zen contemplation of the sound of one hand clapping, or the peace of transcendental meditation. Rika Philips was getting to him.

Sighing, he climbed onto Thunder's back.

"Okay, you guys," he said jovially to his two companions. "Now's the chance for you to give me some serious lessons on how to ride this hayburner."

THE SUMMER SUN baked down, making Rika's wet clothing feel like a Turkish bath. Every movement in the too-small saddle threatened to chafe her skin and rub her raw. Confident of the riding skills of the girls with her, she rose in the saddle and set a loping pace, checking to make sure the double riders were able to keep up. For them it was a lark, and she relaxed with the knowledge they were safe. But what about her?

It wasn't the first time she'd fallen off a horse. Technically, she hadn't even fallen or been thrown; she'd merely stepped out of the stirrups. Maybe she could have handled Sandy better, but that was water under the bridge. She smiled. Muddy water. Very muddy water.

Things happen, she reminded herself.

Unexpected things.

Things that have nothing to do with horses or riding.

Scary things. Like having a man put his arms around you and realizing you don't want him to let you go. Things like feeling his lips brush against yours and wanting to taste more of him.

She thought she'd buried the need for a man so deep no one would ever find it, including herself. Apparently, she'd been wrong. Alex Huston had exposed her hidden pool of wants and needs and was stirring it up. The mud on her clothes and skin was nothing compared with the muddy feeling churning inside her.

Taking the most direct route, the barn was only a few minutes away. Rika and the girls had hardly dismounted, when Barbara appeared, a frilly white apron wrapped around her tiny waist.

"Back so soon, dear," she greeted Rika, then stopped. "What happened to you?" She searched the group. "And where're the major and the boys?"

Rika couldn't help but smile at her matchmaking grandmother's concern. "He'll be along in a few minutes. Has Sandy shown up yet?"

"Sandy dumped Mommy in the creek..." Emily chattered as she slid off the back of Micki's horse to the ground. "And she ran away...and the major hugged Mommy...and he kissed her."

Rika knew her cheeks must be bright red. She turned to loosen the girth on Buttercup, but not before she saw her grandmother's eyes widen and an approving grin quirk the corners of her mouth. Barbara's expression begged for more details, but wisdom kept her from asking too much—at least in front of the children. Rika knew the kind of subtle grilling she'd be in for later.

"Where's he now?"

"Major Huston and the boys are right behind us." Rika searched the trail. "Somewhere. They should be here in a few minutes."

"Good," Barbara said decisively. "That'll give you time to clean up and change. We're dining on the patio."

"Emily, put Buttercup in her stall," Rika instructed her daughter, "then you and the girls can go up to the kitchen for lemonade."

While Emily complied, Rika sat on a bench and once more pried off her boots and socks. After kicking her feet in the air to dry them, she put on an old pair of tennis shoes her grandmother brought from the tack room.

"Shouldn't he be back by now?" Barbara asked worriedly.

"Relax, Gram. He's not an experienced rider. I told them to take it nice and slow."

The sound of horses' hooves brought both women to the open barn door. Three riders approached at an easy trot, Alex in the lead.

"I thought you said he didn't know how to ride," Barbara commented.

Her grandmother wasn't an equestrian and obviously didn't understand the nuances of good form. Alex's style had improved since they'd gone out an hour earlier, but it still wasn't exactly smooth. There was no denying, however, that he made a damn good impression in the saddle. A grin swept over Rika's face. He'd find aches and pains tomorrow where he didn't even know he had muscles.

Better not think about his muscles, especially under her hand or pressed against her body, but willpower couldn't quell the frisson of delight skipping through her.

"He has a lot to learn," she said, trying to sound casual, yet maddeningly unable to take her eyes off him, helpless to repress the memory of his lips taunting hers.

"I suspect he's a quick study," her grandmother remarked as she stepped into the broiling sun and approached the riders.

"Major Huston," she called out cheerfully, "I must say you look like something the cat dragged in."

He dismounted. "And when she saw what it was, dragged it out again." He loosened the cinch and started to lead the black gelding to his stall, when Rika found her voice.

"Did you see Sandy? She hasn't come home yet."

Just then the mare trotted into the barnyard, caked with mud. She gave no resistance when Rika snagged her reins. Rika rubbed the nose of the bay mare, who seemed very pleased with herself. "It'll take me forever to get the tangles out of your mane," she complained to the horse. She unbuckled the cinch and Alex lifted the saddle, then set it down on a hitching rail.

"No," she corrected him, "please take it into the barn so the sun doesn't dry it out. I'll have to clean and oil it."

He complied without question.

Rika found it impossible to concentrate on the tasks at hand. Her mind was too preoccupied with Alex's kiss and the passion his touch had kindled. How many times had she told herself she didn't need a man complicating her life? Yet here she was, fantasizing about a gorgeous hunk like a lovesick teenager heartthrobbing over a rock star.

Rika led Sandy to the wash rack and hosed her down—to keep busy, she decided. She didn't want to be idle in Alex's company. Up at the house she would have nothing to do but sit on the patio, sip a cool drink, gaze at him and remember what it felt like to be swept into his arms, to taste his kisses, to breathe in the scent of his skin as his body touched hers.

The children reappeared.

"I have to go home now," Micki announced.

The others echoed the comment and climbed expertly onto their horses.

"Thank you, Mrs. Philips," they called out in turn.

"You're welcome. Be careful on the way back."

"Bye, Major," came the second chorus.

"Bye." He waved to them. "Thanks for your help today."

"You're welcome," one of them answered for the others.

Rika and Alex stood side by side a moment, watching them ride away.

She finished washing Sandy and left her tied to a hitching rail to dry, then went to the barn. Alex had already cleaned the mud off the saddle and was rubbing it down with Neatsfoot oil.

Barbara reappeared in the doorway. "Did you enjoy your ride, Major?"

"Very much." He winked at Rika. "Your granddaughter says my trot is getting better and pretty soon she's going to teach me to lope."

Alex wasn't sure if Barbara was familiar with the terms or had any notion of the meaning he was associating with them. But she definitely hadn't missed the exchange between him and her granddaughter.

"We'll be along in a moment, Gram," Rika assured her.

"Dinner is almost ready, so please don't dawdle."

"I'll make sure she doesn't," Alex promised her.

The tiny woman gave him a quick, satisfied nod and walked toward the house.

"I don't need a warden," Rika announced, not quite sure if she was irritated or amused.

"How about a friend, then?"

Even in the dim shadows of the barn she could feel his eyes on her. He tipped her chin with the crook of his finger and she went still, unable to advance or retreat. "Let's get the rest of the tack put away," she finally snapped.

Alex grinned as she jerked away. Yep, it was getting to her, too—the pull, the irresistible attraction.

AFTER DINNER, Emily asked permission to go over to Micki's house and play with the puppies. Rika was still undecided how she would handle the issue of letting her daughter get one. Rika certainly didn't dislike pets—she'd had a cocker spaniel when she was small and later a mutt called Flash. Caring for a dog in her present circumstances, however, seemed more than a little problematic.

"Have a good time," she told her daughter, "but I want you home by eight. We need to wash your hair tonight."

Emily darted to the door.

"And be careful riding your bike over—" The kitchen door, though, had already slammed.

Rika helped Sera clear the table, but her grandparents' chief cook and housekeeper was never comfortable with people in her kitchen, so Rika took the first opportunity to slip out to the garden. The sun was waning, casting the colorful world of her grandmother's green thumb in mellow golden light. Rika noticed the two men, each with a snifter of brandy in his hand, were sitting in wicker peacock chairs on the veranda outside her grandfather's study.

There was no direct path between where she was in the garden and the veranda. She had to detour around a low wall and raised flower bed and take the narrow walk that hugged the side of the house, or go inside and join them through the French doors. Would they welcome her, or be annoyed at a woman interrupting their "men's talk"?

She was about to turn the corner of the building and find out, when she heard her grandfather's question. It stopped her cold.

"HOW IS YOUR INVESTIGATION going?" The general rotated the cognac in the palm of his hand.

"Not fast enough." Alex raised his own snifter and inhaled deeply of the liquor's tangy aroma.

"Getting stonewalled?" The old man sounded concerned.

Alex shared his apprehension. "Not really." He sipped and wondered if he had missed something at the lab. "At least I don't feel I am. Lacy's given me full access to all his files, and they seem to be complete."

He'd gone over hundreds of pages of documents, some of them nearly pure science. Reading between the lines, he'd seen competence, even a certain amount of daring, in the work Brassard had performed at the technical level. He'd also felt a twinge of envy for the civilian scientist who had been able to deal with what Alex had anticipated handling himself.

"I went over to the flight line where they flew the bird," he continued. "Didn't find anything that looked even remotely suspicious." Which hadn't surprised him. Lacy's people would have policed up the area as a matter of routine.

Tiers sipped his drink without comment.

"I've also talked to the military and civilian personnel on base who were involved that day," Alex went on. "They substantiate everything Lacy's told me. If there's a conspiracy to hide something, it's damned well organized."

"How about the people downtown?"

"I have the names of all the members of the High Flyers. We're running background checks now, even on the ones who weren't present that day, to see if any of them has a criminal record. I need to be careful about interviewing them, though. I don't want to tip our hand."

The old man agreed. "I suppose you've worked out a cover story?"

Alex nodded. "I'll have one of my sergeants talk to them, keep it low-key. They'll say we're checking on the loss. Headquarters is concerned about liability. The model took off from Air Force property and might have done some damage when it went down. They'll also hint that officials are reviewing whether to allow the club to continue to use base facilities."

"Think it'll work?" The general didn't sound very convinced.

Alex savored the fumes rising from his bulbous glass before answering. "They'll buy the liability part. Everyone's afraid of lawsuits these days, but the stealth design of the drone made it stand out. If its uniqueness didn't raise questions then, our inquiry into it now is bound to."

"Difficult situation."

Alex didn't detect any sympathy, just a statement of fact.

"Speaking of stories—" Alex sampled his brandy "—Rika came out to the AFL Friday."

"I wondered what your comment at the restaurant the other evening was about. What did she want?"

"Fishing for a story on space-age food, or so she said. She didn't get one." Alex chuckled at the recollection of how he'd had her stuttering. "Don't worry, she won't be back."

The old general eyed him. "Good." He swirled the spirits in his snifter. "Did you get the photoreconnaissance you ordered?"

"Received the first batch of film on Friday. My people went over it with a fine-tooth comb. Zip. But that's about what I expected. An object that small could be retrieved by hand and hidden in a pickup truck very quickly. If we'd had coverage immediately before and immediately after the flight, we might have found something, but with nothing on which to base a comparison…" Alex didn't bother to finish. The general undoubtedly knew the sophisticated capabilities of various digital surveillance processes that could penetrate shadows and camouflage. Unfortunately, the coverage Alex had ordered had been too little too late.

A short silence ensued while the two men sipped their afterdinner drinks.

"I hate to add fuel to the fire," Tiers finally said, "but there was an incident out in California yesterday—"

"You mean the so-called buzz bomber? Yeah, I saw the intel message on it in the read file this morning."

Some crazy publicity seeker had flown a model airplane into the stadium at Candlestick Park near San Francisco during a baseball game. It had crash-landed in the outfield, doing no damage. Park security quickly carted it away and almost as quickly apprehended the nut who'd radio-controlled it in. The *Chronicle* mentioned the incident on the second page of the sports section. The AP hadn't bothered to pick up what appeared to be a minor interruption in a routine, uninspired game. That was because they didn't know the rest of the story. The aircraft had been carrying an internal payload of several sticks of dynamite. Fortunately, the detonating mechanism malfunctioned as a result of the crash. The FBI had immediately been brought into the case, but so far the kook was remaining mute about his reason for the incident.

"I know what you're thinking," Alex said. "The newspaper described the plane as looking like a motorized hang glider. They didn't recognize it as a stealth design. It was about the same size as our drone, too."

The general's brow wrinkled. "Are you sure it wasn't ours?"

Alex nodded. "I went through my sources and checked. It was made of balsa. Not very well, either."

"That's some comfort."

"You think this might have been a trial run for something bigger and more spectacular?" Alex had had the same itchy feeling when he was reading the report and following up on it.

"I received a back-channels message last night—" which meant it was an unofficial, personal communication from the Pentagon "—asking about your

progress," the general said. "They're concerned this
incident was a dress rehearsal—"

"For a more spectacular terrorist attack." The po-
litical-party conventions were coming up, followed by
the national election and the inauguration of a new
president in January. Alex polished off the last
mouthful of his brandy. "Which means I'd better find
out who has it, and what the hell they're planning to
do with it—fast."

RIKA BACKED AWAY. She wasn't supposed to have
heard this, and she felt a twinge of guilt for allowing
herself to continue listening. But how could she not?
Her hands suddenly shaking, she slipped quietly from
the corner of the house and returned to the garden,
where she slouched numbly onto the concrete bench
facing the birdbath.

She stared at the bees hovering around the roses,
aware of, but not quite hearing, their buzz. Somehow
she had to make sense of what she'd just learned.
Forcing herself to mentally rewind the tape, she re-
played the conversation she'd overheard.

Her grandfather had asked Alex about an investigation, not an inspection. Which meant he wasn't
checking to see if everything was being done by the
book. Something had gone wrong. Obviously, too, the
lab did more than develop space-age food—if it did
that at all, because Alex had talked about everything
but food. The High Flyers. A missing drone. Stealth
technology. Photoreconnaissance. Then there'd been
the mention of a terrorist attack. What was the incident in California her grandfather had referred to?
Also, what did it have to do with Alex's being here?
And why would a long-retired general be involved?

Rika didn't scare easily. She'd done stories on some fairly dangerous characters, yet the cloak-and-dagger aspect of this situation, exciting as it was, also spooked her. Was Alex in danger? Was her family at risk simply by association?

"You were definitely wrong about one thing, Major Alex Huston," she told herself. "I will be back at the AFL. Just you wait and see."

How could she learn more? She didn't know a darn thing about model airplanes or drones, but didn't one of Emily's friends, Shawn, build models? Was he a member of the High Flyers? Kids loved to show off the things they made. If she asked to go to one of his club meetings, she could get to know the other members and find out what they flew. Most hobbyists were more than happy to discuss their projects.

"Rika, dear, what are you doing out here all by yourself? I thought you'd gone to join the men after dinner."

"Just thinking, Gram."

Barbara sat beside her, her hands folded neatly in her lap. "Are you all right? You look like you've had a brush with an iceberg."

Rika couldn't suppress a grin. She'd never been very good at hiding her moods and emotions from her grandmother. Gram might play the ditsy old woman sometimes, but a fool she wasn't.

"In West Texas in August?" she jested, and flapped her elbows as if seeking relief from the pervasive heat. "An iceberg right now would be more than welcome."

Barbara studied her. "He's nice, isn't he?"

Rika didn't have to ask who she was talking about. "Emily likes him, too."

"Gram…" Rika drawled in a warning tone. She wasn't ready to share the jumble of emotions that were doing somersaults and cartwheels inside her, not even with her grandmother. How could she, when she had so many questions, so many doubts, not only about herself, but about Alex, about what he was doing.

"Give him a chance, dear." Barbara rested a hand on Rika's. "Give yourself a chance, too. Finding the right man—"

Treat it light, Rika told herself. Act as if it's just another of Gram's matchmaking adventures. "*You* may think Alex Huston's the right man, but *I* don't."

Her grandmother's response was soft and sympathetic. "I think he's a good man." She squeezed Rika's hand with her cool bony fingers and looked at her granddaughter with the compassionate eyes of a wiser generation. "But what I think isn't important. It's how you feel about him." She smiled sympathetically. "It's scary, too, isn't it, the way he makes you feel?"

How could she possibly explain to Gram that she was afraid the man she was attracted to might be involved in something even more dangerous than being a test pilot—catching spies and apprehending terrorists. "It's complicated."

"The relationship between a man and a woman always is," Barbara commented. "Yet, in the end, it comes down to a simple matter of trust."

I trusted a man once, Rika mused, *and look where it got me. Trust doesn't work if it only goes one way.*

Rika gave her grandmother a hug.

They were returning to the living room as the general and Alex emerged from the study. Barbara asked

if anyone wanted coffee and was receiving polite re-
fusals, when the front door burst open and Emily shot
into the room.

"Look, Mommy, see what I have."

A fur ball of white, russet and black squirmed in
her outstretched hands. "Micki's mom says I can
have him."

Rika felt a moment of panic. "Emily, I didn't say
you could have the puppy. I told you I had to think
about it, and we had to talk."

"Isn't he darling?" Barbara crooned, and went
over and petted the adorable animal's small head and
floppy ears.

Determined not to be manipulated, Rika refused to
soften. "You'll have to take him back."

"But, Mommy—"

"No buts, young lady."

Emily plopped down on the floor by her great-
grandmother, her face distorted by a pout. She cud-
dled the animal against her chest. "If we don't take
him, Micki's mom is going to have to get rid of him,"
she sniveled.

Did she know what "get rid" meant? Rika didn't
want to think about it.

Alex squatted beside the girl and petted the dog's
head. "He's a cute little bugger, all right."

Rika shot him a stern "stay out of this" look, but
it did no good. He avoided her by concentrating on
the creature that was trying to gnaw his finger.

"Maybe if you let your mommy hold him," he
suggested.

"Yeah, Mommy—" Emily jumped up, dangling
the animal at arm's length "—you can pet him.
You'll see he's really nice."

"May I hold him?" Gramps asked from his seat by the cold fireplace.

Emily brought the tiny critter to him and placed it on his lap. He stroked its back, then examined its paws. "Going to be a good size," he commented. "Aren't you, Scamper?"

"Traitor," Rika grumbled. She came over to her grandfather's chair and bent to touch the eager creature. The dog inched forward and licked her hand.

"Still sending him back?" Alex asked, one eyebrow raised provocatively.

"I didn't say he wasn't cute," she allowed grudgingly, wishing she could wipe the silly grin off his face. "I just don't know how we'll take care of him."

Gramps put him down on the floor. "We can set up a box for him in the kitchen."

"I'm sure Sera will love that."

"I can keep him in my room," Emily volunteered.

"No, you cannot. He stays in the kitchen."

She caught the satisfied grin on Alex's face and realized she'd just conceded victory. Damn him.

Scamper moved to the middle of Gram's favorite Chinese silk carpet, the one she had purchased in Japan fifty years earlier, and proceeded to relieve himself.

"Oh, great. That's why we can't keep a dog," Rika intoned to her daughter. "Go get some paper towels from the kitchen. Hurry."

"Now, dear," Barbara chided, "Scamper isn't the first dog this old carpet's welcomed. I'll bring some baking soda."

Rika narrowed her eyes. "Collaborator," she mumbled.

"I'll see about a box," Gramps said as he rose and left the room close behind his wife.

Her grandparents' calm acceptance helped keep Rika from screaming, though she still didn't know how she would housebreak a growing pup back in Michigan or keep it from barking while she was at work all day. She looked at Alex, who'd grabbed a handful of tissues from the box on an end table.

"You're in trouble, Major. Big time."

He cupped a hand to his ear. "I think I hear the cavalry charging over the hill right now," he informed her as Emily and her great-grandmother returned with cleaning materials.

CHAPTER NINE

IT WAS MORE than an hour past Emily's usual bedtime when Rika finally tucked her in. She descended the stairs to find her grandparents and their guest standing in the hallway.

"I'm so glad you were able to join us today. You're welcome anytime, anytime—"

"Say good-night, Babs," Nathan prompted in her ear.

"Oh. Good night, Major."

The old man wrapped his arm around his wife's slender shoulders and together they mounted the broad staircase.

Alex and Rika migrated to the front door.

"Your grandparents are incredible," he said. "Imagine after all their years... Did you see the twinkle in his eye when he told her to say good-night, and the way he held her?"

"Gives you reason to hope, doesn't it?" She seized the doorknob.

From behind her, Alex asked, "What do you think is the secret to their success?"

Curious where he might be going with this discussion, she spun around and studied his face. The question wasn't frivolous. His expression was serious. "Gram says it's trust."

He scratched the back of his neck, unconvinced. "I

never heard my mother accuse my father of being unfaithful," he said, studying her nose, lips, chin. "But their marriage sure didn't last."

There was no reason to whisper, except he was so close she didn't seem to have breath for more. "If it's not trust, what is it?"

He lifted a hand and stroked her cheek, a feathery touch. "Trust is part of it," he murmured. "But there's bound to be more."

She opened the door. "Like what?"

He stood beside her, bewitched by the satiny flow of long brown hair, while she checked the door lock to make sure she could get back in.

Placing a hand on her shoulder, he turned her to face him. "Are you asking me to solve the riddle of the ages—what is love?" His tone was light, but there was earnestness beneath it. "I don't have an answer, Rika." He traced her jawline with the side of his finger. "But I hope I'll recognize it when I see it."

Before her legs became too rubbery to support her, she stepped outside. The catch clicked.

The moon overhead cast the Mediterranean fountain beyond the portico in silver and gold. Its splashing sounds suited the warm night air. The wind had relaxed to a gentle breeze, bringing with it the floral scents of her grandmother's garden.

Crickets chirped. An owl hooted.

Suddenly, all she could think about was Alex's kisses earlier in the day. But they had been in sunlight. Moonlight and night sounds made the prospect of a kiss here too intimate, too...seductive. She shifted away from him and strolled over to a waist-high planter filled with trailing rosemary.

"Did your parents love each other?" She stroked

a branch and brought her fingers to her nose. The rich spicy aroma was intoxicating.

Alex leaned against a pillar, the tips of his fingers tucked in the tops of his western-cut pants. ''In their own ways, I guess they did, but not enough to stay together.'' He fell silent, as if reviewing old memories, old arguments. ''Mom says she loved Dad, at least in the beginning, but she got tired of competing with his job for time and attention. She insists to this day that she didn't divorce him as much as she did the Air Force.''

Breaking off a delicate tip of the aromatic plant, she offered it to Alex. ''Did he love her, do you think?''

He held her hand and sniffed, closing his eyes in dreamlike appreciation of its scent, then let her go. ''I'm sure he did. He never failed to ask me about her when we talked on the phone or when I went to visit him. He wanted to know what she was doing, how she was, who and what was new in her life.'' Alex's features grew somber. ''He kept pictures of her in his wallet and in his quarters, as though she was still his wife.''

''How sad.'' Rika moved over to a hibiscus trained on a narrow trellis. ''Yet he refused to give up his career for her.''

''He was dedicated to his work,'' Alex explained, ''just as your grandfather is…was.''

He moved alongside her, broke off one of the red bugle blossoms and placed it next to her ear. Their fingers touched as she guided the stem into her hair.

''Giving it up would have been like throwing away a part of himself,'' Alex continued. ''If he did that, he wouldn't have been the man he was. He would no longer have been whole.''

''Your mother couldn't see that?''

Alex shook his head. ''She never understood the difference between a job and a profession. As an NCO Dad wasn't making a lot of money. He didn't have the prestige of being an officer. She couldn't see the point of his putting in all that time, time away from her and me.''

Rika almost said she felt sorry for his mother because she sounded like a very unhappy woman. Maybe a selfish one, too. ''I guess it takes a special person to be a service wife.''

''Spouse,'' he reminded her. ''There are career military women now, too.''

She half turned and sneered at him. ''Are you calling me a sexist?'' There was laughter in her question.

He grinned. ''Hardly.''

''Anyway,'' Rika continued, leaning against the planter, ''not everyone is cut out for the hardships of being married to a person in the military. Gram watched Gramps go off to three wars, never knowing if he was going to come home, or what he might be like when he did. But she waited and treasured the times they had together. My mother knew what she was getting into when she married my father.''

Alex crossed his arms over his chest and settled beside her, close enough to touch her. ''Still, she made him leave the Air Force,'' he pointed out.

''Made him?'' Rika wondered if he had any idea what the word *compromise* meant. It hardly seemed a word he would have learned from his parents. ''She asked him to, Alex. It wasn't an ultimatum. He could have said no, and she would have accepted it.''

"Unhappily, I'll bet," he concluded.

Rika tilted her head to one side. "Mom would have been disappointed certainly, but *unhappy* is too strong a word. She loved him—whether he was flying airplanes or stacking groceries."

"My mother wasn't the accepting kind." He paused. "Are you the accepting kind, Rika? Could you be married to a military man and let him 'do his thing' without being jealous?"

The reminder of the past threatened to sour the placid mood that had set in. "I didn't like Clay's long workdays," she said, "but I tolerated them. That isn't why I left him, Alex, if you really want to know." She took a deep breath, her voice hardening perceptibly. "I divorced him because of other women. It wasn't that I didn't want to trust him, but that I couldn't." She pushed away from the planter and faced him. "Infidelity goes beyond tolerance. I can't love a man who is unfaithful to me. I will not allow myself to be a victim, Alex."

Her outburst surprised her as much as it did him. She'd told herself the anger was past. Obviously, it wasn't forgotten, and it still had the power to hurt.

To prove she was in control, she didn't resist when he hooked her hand with his and brought the tips of her fingers to his lips. It was a consoling gesture, one of sympathy, one she hadn't anticipated. His eyes held hers, and her heart seemed to stop. He pulled her closer, slid his hands down to her shoulders and held her so their lips were barely an inch apart. His arms enveloped her. Warmth flowed through her.

"You're beautiful, Rika. The most beautiful woman—" His mouth suddenly covered hers, his tongue eager, aggressive, wanting, needing. It touched hers. She should stop him. But she didn't. Her mind might be telling her one thing, but her body wasn't listening. Her heart was pounding too hard.

STELLA BROWN OCCUPIED a cubicle in the rear of the sprawling single-story *Coyote Sentinel* building one block from city hall. She and Rika greeted each other like old friends, bought themselves soft drinks from the soda machine outside the ladies' room and returned to Stella's paper-cluttered workspace.

"I went to the AFL last week, but they wouldn't let me in," Rika said, struggling to suppress the memories of her encounter with Alex there. "I'm trying to find out something about the lab."

Stella threw back her head and took a long, satisfying swallow of Orange Crush. "If you do, I wish you'd pass it on to me. I've been working for months to get information on that mysterious lab. No one wants to talk about it."

"How about PA?" Rika asked. The purpose of government public affairs offices was to control information, not broadcast it, but even their denials were occasionally useful.

"Gobbledygook," Stella said. "They acknowledge there is an Aerospace Food Laboratory whose mission is the development of foods and supplements for space travelers, but they won't give any details. All questions get a wishy-washy 'I'm afraid we don't have that information available at this time.'"

"Surely you could find someone willing to talk about it," Rika argued. Every organization had its loudmouths and disgruntled employees.

Stella twirled her soda can. "As a matter of fact, there was a new airman on base a few months ago.

He commented to a friend of mine at a bowling alley that he worked at the lab in hangar number seven at the end of the runway. The next day, when I tried to contact him, I was told he'd been transferred to another base.''

''Just like that?''

''Amazing how fast the bureaucrats can do their jobs when they want to, isn't it?''

''Were you able to locate him?''

Stella chuckled ironically. ''For all the good it did me. They shipped him out to Saudi Arabia.''

Rika stared wide-eyed at her fellow journalist. ''That seems rather drastic for telling someone where your duty section is.''

''I thought so, too, but the people in the personnel office on base insisted his transfer had been in the mill for some time. Of course he was a volunteer for the assignment.'' She twisted her mouth in disbelief. ''If he was supposed to go to Saudi, why send him here to begin with and then move him out overnight?''

''Good question.'' Rika thought a moment. ''What do you suppose is the significance of hangar number seven?''

Stella's hazel eyes glowed cynically. ''You mean beside the fact that the only other hangars on base are numbered one and two, or that old number seven is supposed to be the top of an underground factory?''

Rika paused, her brain trying to process what she'd just heard. ''Did you say an underground factory?''

Stella's face lit up with the delight that comes from being a step ahead of a colleague. ''It's only rumor, you understand, but one that's been around for years. The story goes that the building you see on the flight line is only the tip of the iceberg, a facade for a much-bigger facility that runs nearly the length of the runway. Legend has it that in the closing days of the World War II, the Wolf Pack was one of the places where scientists worked on the new jet-propulsion systems. Another version is that the atom bomb was born here.''

A food lab in an underground factory, maybe even a nuclear facility? Rika was getting that skipped-beat sensation in her chest again. ''Do you believe it?''

Stella shrugged. ''I ask myself that question every time I go out to the base. All I know is, considering some of the weird characters they've got running around there, anything's possible.''

''Like who?''

''Lacy, the AFL director, for one. He's pleasant enough. Does all the obligatory social things you'd expect an officer in his position to do—Boy Scouts, community fund-raisers, that sort of thing, and he's got a real nice family. Still, there's something…devious about the guy, you know what I mean? Seems like he's always looking over his shoulder.''

''Have you checked his background?''

''Got his biography from the Public Affairs office. An egghead. Nothing unusual.''

''Who else?''

She laughed. ''They're all a little…strange, but then I guess eccentricity goes with genius.''

''At least that's what they'd like us to believe. Who in particular?''

''Pascal Brassard—they call him Brassy. He's Lacy's chief scientist. The absentminded-professor type. Sweaty palms. Rumpled clothes. I wouldn't be surprised to see him wearing two different shoes, or at least socks.'' She laughed. ''He's probably brilliant.''

Rika took notes.

''Then there's Keith Nelson, the deputy director. Career civil service. Been there for years. I buttonholed him one day at a newcomers' reception. Talked about the lab or tried to. At the end of almost an hour I realized he hadn't told me a thing. Guy ought to be in the diplomatic corps.''

Rika wrote down his name, also.

''The person you really want to talk to,'' Stella insisted, ''is old Mrs. Franklin over on Chestnut Street. She remembers when the base was being built.''

''Thanks, I'll do that.'' But first there was someone else she had to contact.

ALEX WAS BOTH pleased and puzzled when Rika called him at the AFL and invited him to lunch. He remembered all too clearly the way she'd kissed him back the evening before. He was beginning to understand the line about parting being sweet sorrow.

Of course, there was also the matter of the puppy, he reminded himself. Maybe she wanted to chew him out about meddling with her private family life. He sobered. She'd be right, of course. His interference had been wrong. Pitting mother against daughter was hardly the way to win either of them over. He avoided thinking about what he was winning them over to.

He met her at the Prairie Wolf Inn. The nostalgic strains of ''The Tennessee Waltz'' were being piped in through ceiling speakers. A waitress took their drink order. Two iced teas. Alex was about to reach for her hand, when she stated, "I finally figured out where I've seen you before."

No mention of kisses or puppy dogs. "Oh? And that was?"

"In Washington," she replied a little smugly. "I was there last year covering a story. So was Gramps."

The buoyant feeling in his chest began to sag. He had a sneaky suspicion he knew precisely where. Under other circumstances his rubbing shoulders with the political aristocracy, the country's movers and shakers, was something he could capitalize on. "I get up there now and then. It's a beautiful city."

"In parts." Her fingers unrolled the napkin, releasing flatware. She spread the starched white cloth in her lap.

"Was it at the Pentagon? It's a big place, but you could have seen me there."

She arranged her knife, fork and spoon neatly beside her plate. "No, I spent all my time covering a couple of hearings on Capitol Hill."

He had a sudden premonition he wasn't going to like what she said next. The twisted smile on her lips as she gazed at him wasn't so much aloof as self-satisfied.

"You testified before the Senate subcommittee investigating technology transfers to nonallied and unfriendly countries."

She was more than pleased with herself, he decided. He flashed her a grin. "I suppose you were profoundly impressed with what I had to say."

Her eyes never wavered from his. "Actually, I don't think you said anything profound at all, or anything your audience hadn't heard before."

He turned down his mouth in an exaggerated pout. "And I tried so hard to wow them."

She allowed him a soft, ironic chuckle. "I was much more impressed with your credentials."

The waitress arrived with their drinks, then rushed off to serve other customers.

"So tell me, Alex—or should I call you Dr. Huston," Rika went on, "what is a fighter test pilot with almost three thousand hours in the cockpit of high-performance aircraft and a Ph.D. in aeronautical physics doing at a food lab in the middle of West Texas?"

He lifted his glass, poised it at eye level and smiled over it. She'd done her research. He was impressed, but not encouraged. He took a slow sip of the cold drink, letting its tang play across his tongue. How much more did she know about him, and where might she be going with what she knew?

"High performance and good nutrition go hand in hand, especially in this fast-paced society." Spreading his fingers around the sweaty glass, he studied her. Her playful "I've got a secret" expression had changed.

"I need to talk to you about something."

He reached across the narrow table, tapped the backs of her hands and lowered his voice to a seductive murmur. "That you love me to distraction, can't live without me, want to run off with me and make mad, passionate love?"

She didn't even crack a smile. "None of the above."

"There's still time." He withdrew his hand. Obviously, banter wasn't going to work. "So what do you have to tell me?"

She realigned the silverware before again meeting

his eyes. "I overheard you and Gramps last evening on the veranda."

Alex didn't move. He had no amorous comeback for her this time. At least he managed to swallow the profanity that rose to his lips. "What exactly did you hear?"

"Everything. About your mission, the food lab, the High Flyers club, the missing drone, the terrorist threat."

Don't panic, he admonished himself. She heard what you said. That doesn't mean she understood its significance. "Was your grandmother with you when you were spying on us?"

"No!"

He wondered if the alarm in her instant denial was at the question or at the word *spy*. "Have you told your grandfather?"

She bowed her head, at last dropping her gaze, and started twisting her glass. Then, apparently realizing she was acting defensively, she shifted in her seat, squared her shoulders and again faced him eye to eye.

He rested back in his chair, putting symbolic distance between himself and her, and lowered his hands to his lap, as if not touching the table meant breaking contact with her, as well. He kept his voice subdued, objective. "The question is, what are you going to do with this purloined information?"

"I didn't steal the information, Major," she shot back. "I didn't break into someone's office, didn't bribe or blackmail anyone for it. *You* gave it to me."

His blood pressure was building. Patiently, he said, "The question remains. What are you going to do with it?"

"Use it," she declared defiantly.

His voice was inclined to rise, so he consciously subdued it. "Use it?" he muttered. Damn it, he was beginning to sound like a parrot. "How?"

Background music switched to Hank Williams's classic, "Your Cheatin' Heart."

Rika ran a fingernail along the rim of her glass. "I'm an investigative reporter, Alex. My job is to find news and report it."

His mind raced with the implications and complications of a media leak on Project MADAM. He'd accused Lacy of laxity in security. His own culpability now seemed greater. How could he have screwed this up so badly? How could this temporary duty assignment to Coyote Springs, Texas, be turning into such a catastrophe? Ruined uniforms were insignificant compared with this. The greater price could be his career. It could also cost him his freedom.

"Rika," he said with a dispassion he didn't feel, "we need to talk about this."

"I agree."

"But not here. Not now." He picked up his menu. "Shall we order?"

She regarded him with a combination of awe and aggravation. She'd just announced a coup, the inside scoop on a story that could be a blockbuster, and he was brushing it off as if it were a mere distraction to ordering lunch. Surely she hadn't misunderstood what she'd heard. Maybe she was blowing everything out of proportion.

Or was he just playing cool? She watched the way his fingers momentarily drummed at the edge of the laminated folder in his hands. His brow was smooth, not furrowed in worry. He raised a steady finger to his pursed lips, apparently intrigued by the choices the bill of fare offered.

Cool, she decided, was too mild a word to describe his aplomb. *Sangfroid.* Yes, that was better. Cold blood. Jet-jockey nerves. He raised his head suddenly as if to ask her something and caught her staring at him. Panic rippled through her.

"Figured out what you want?" He slanted an innocent smile at her.

There was something scary about the way he goaded, and at the same time unnervingly stimulating.

She selected a seafood salad. He opted for a club sandwich.

He asked about Emily's school. She was a good student. Recently, she'd become interested in gymnastics, and Rika was worried about fitting it into their busy schedules.

The clatter of a food cart announced the arrival of lunch.

"By the way," she said as she dribbled pineapple-walnut dressing on her salad, "you owe me for a pair of running shoes."

He cocked his head. "Excuse me?"

"Scamper, the cute little puppy you're so fond of, chewed up one of my sneakers last night."

He raised a triple-decker triangle of sandwich. "I'll put it on account against the price of a dress uniform."

She stopped in midmotion.

"Then there's the uniform pants that got stained—"

"Don't push it, Major." She laughed and gathered lobster on her fork. "Maybe we can call it even."

He gazed at her, unwilling to give in so easily. "We'll see."

The discussion returned to life in Michigan. In addition to working full-time, she was involved with the Brownies and was on the board of the local symphony, organizing programs and putting out publicity. A very busy lady. With a medley of Willie Nelson and Kenny Rogers tunes for backdrop, Rika talked about the coming symphony concert season. There would be the usual classics, the three Bs—Bach, Beethoven and Brahms—but the new conductor had also scheduled twentieth-century composers: David Diamond and John Corigliano.

"But you're not interested in this," she concluded after keeping him spellbound for the entire meal. True, he wasn't particularly interested in long hair, and the only Diamond he'd ever heard of was Neil, but if she liked it, it must be good, and he was always willing to learn.

"Keep talking. I love the sound of your voice. Especially in the dark."

"You haven't heard my voice in the dark."

"I can only hope."

"In your dreams, Major."

"Yeah, there, too."

Alex called for the check, which Rika insisted on paying since she had invited him. She permitted him to leave the tip.

He took her by the elbow when they stepped outside and steered her toward his car. Time to go to plan B.

"What are you doing? My van's over there."

"We're going for a ride."

He didn't want to think of her being afraid of him,

but in that moment he saw she was. "Relax, Rika. I'm not kidnapping you, but we need to talk—privately. I'll bring you back as soon as we have this matter settled."

No need to explain what matter. Out of the corner of his eye, he caught the nod and the pensive expression. She wasn't frightened, but she was worried.

Ten minutes later, he parked at a lay-by of the narrow road that ran the length of an earthen dam. At night it probably offered a lover's view of the dark lake to the right and the twinkling lights of the little city to the left. In front of them now was only parched, sun-bleached scrub.

Alex slipped the gearshift into park but left the engine running so they could have air-conditioning. For a minute his hands remained outstretched on the steering wheel, then he took a deep breath, exhaled and rotated to her.

"Rika, this story...you can't do it."

She said nothing, but from her stiff posture he could sense her bracing for battle.

"You can't do it," he repeated. "You don't know what you've got, and idle speculation and half-truths... You could jeopardize national security."

She blinked slowly, as if collecting herself, praying for guidance or maybe patience. "If anyone's jeopardized national security, Major Huston, it's you."

He unsnapped his seat belt and swiveled in the narrow seat to face her, the most beautiful woman he'd ever seen. He kept his voice low, afraid he'd shatter the tenuous thread of civility between them. "You're right. I screwed up and screwed up badly."

She turned slowly to him, her face blank with

astonishment. She obviously hadn't expected so bold
an admission.

"But you still can't do it."

"I'm a reporter," she reminded him. "I'm dealing
with a story."

"Are you telling me a story is more important than
the security of our nation?"

Her voice hardened. "The truth is more important
to the well-being of our nation than your secrecy. It's
called a free press, Alex. Without it there's no freedom, and without freedom there's no safety."

He looked at her profile against the stark-white
daylight. A lock of hair had fallen loose. He ached to
caress its softness and tuck it behind her ear. He
wanted to feel the warm curve of her flesh with his
lips.

"Noble words." His voice sounded husky. He
wondered if she could hear the tremor in it. "Do you
have any idea what they mean?"

It was her turn to release herself from the belt and
shift in the seat. She glowered at him, eyes piercing,
lips tight. "Get off your high horse, Major. As you
said, you screwed up. So don't try to put the responsibility for a security leak on my back. If this project
is so damn secret, why were you discussing it over
cognac and cigars outside Gramps's study?"

Alex could feel his temper heating up, partly, he
told himself, because she wasn't being reasonable;
mostly, he had to concede, because she was right.
They had fouled up. What he had to ensure now was
damage control.

"Your grandfather had an expectation of privacy
in his own home," he told her, trying not to let his

frustration show. "He trusted you not to spy on him. Apparently, his trust in you was misplaced."

"He knows who I am," she flared, but the hurt, even more than the anger, told him he'd found her Achilles' heel. "I'm a reporter—"

"Who will sacrifice anyone or anything for a story," he snapped back. "Including your own family. Do you have any idea what this story will do to him when people find out General Nathan Tiers, war hero and military genius, leaked a sensitive government program?"

Her eyes grew big with horror. "How dare you!"

She gaped at him with fury and bitter anguish contorting her face. Turning stiffly away, she peered out the side window. Even from across the seat Alex could feel the tension in her body, the confusion and shame. Did he see a tear glisten in the corner of her eye? Don't cry, he nearly pleaded. He hated himself at that moment, knowing he'd brought this pain. Desperately, he wanted to reach out, pull her into his arms, beg her forgiveness.

"This isn't getting us anywhere," he finally said. "You've got a job to do. I respect that. I have a job to do, too. I hope that you'll respect mine, as well."

She didn't move, didn't acknowledge she'd heard him, but he knew she had.

"Go off half-cocked with speculation and misinformation, Rika, and you'll probably sell a lot of newspapers, but it won't do you, the country—or your grandfather—any good. A false story can harm us as much *or more* than the truth. Eventually, you'll be found out and made to look like an incompetent, or worse yet a stooge."

She stiffened. "That sounds like a threat."

He refused to retreat. "It's a reflection of reality. You want a journalism award? Fine. Come by it honestly, without endangering the reputation and lives of good people."

"Good people like you?"

It took all his willpower to keep his voice level and low. "Think of me however you want, Rika. Just remember this isn't about you and me. It's about something much bigger."

Her eyes darted away for a split second, then returned their hostile glare at him.

"Despite what you seem to think," he continued, "I believe very strongly in freedom of the press. I also believe it has an obligation to be responsible and truthful. Getting a prize based on half truths and lies is an abuse of that freedom, and it's not worthy of you."

A vicious smile bowed her lips. "You're good, Huston, you know that? Very good. Maybe you should have stayed in Washington."

She was trying to insult him, but he wouldn't give her the satisfaction of taking offense. "Will you back off?"

She had such beautiful eyes. He had fantasies about them softening and melting as he held her in his arms, making them glaze over in the throes of passion. They were hard now and strangely frail in the way they reflected disappointment and disillusion. They'd both miscalculated, he realized, both underestimated each other.

"If I have bad information, straighten me out," she insisted. "Tell me about this MADAM, about how the drone disappeared, and how it all ties into stealth technology."

So she wasn't bluffing. She had overheard their conversation. "All I can give you is deep background—without attribution," he relented, "at the strictly unclassified level."

"How do I know I can trust you to tell me the truth?"

He let the moment linger. "You don't."

Again he experienced the satisfaction of seeing her blink in astonishment at his bold admission. He watched her weighing the choices.

"Okay," she finally yielded. "Deal. But you lie to me, Major Huston, and all bets are off."

"You divulge information that I tell you is off-limits, Ms. Philips, and I'll have you arrested for violation of the Securities Act."

She almost flinched at his harsh tone, then a conspiratorial smile softened her features. "You're on, Major."

"Shall we seal it with a kiss, Rika?"

"I think a handshake is traditional." She extended her hand. "Alex."

CHAPTER TEN

BECAUSE SHE'D SEEN herself in a position of power, Rika had expected her lunch with Alex to go very differently. She'd been so wrapped up with her career as an investigative reporter she hadn't foreseen the repercussions her big scoop could have on her grandfather. It had taken Alex to point out her ethical problem.

He dropped her off at her car and drove away without a backward glance, abandoning her to a gnawing feeling of self-reproach.

Her grandfather was getting ready to leave the house when she arrived home. "I'm on my way to my monthly meeting of the board at the country club," he told her when she asked if they could talk. "Is it important?"

"It won't take long," she responded, grateful that the pain of her admission wouldn't drag on. Rika sat in the chair at the corner of his desk. "I've done something you're not going to be very happy about, Gramps."

He smiled sympathetically. "We all do things we're not proud of from time to time." When Rika didn't respond, he added, "Now, why don't you simply say it and get it over with. Chances are I've done something equally stupid at one time or another." He folded his hands on the desk in front of him. "I've had a lot more time to practice than you."

She took a deep breath and braced herself. "I overheard your conversation with Alex on the veranda last night. You were talking about a special government project."

The general didn't pull back in horror or even shake his head.

"And you intend to write an article on what you heard." It wasn't a question but a statement, one that sounded completely neutral. He could have made it a biting accusation.

"No." The word came out too quickly, too defensively. "I thought I was going to. Gramps, this could have been the big story I've been looking for."

With the barest nod, he asked, "What's changed your mind?"

"Alex. Major Huston." She hung her head, more ashamed than she imagined she could be to admit it had taken a stranger—or near stranger—to bring her to her senses. "He turned the tables on me." She had to admire his skill. "He admitted he shouldn't have been discussing the project where anyone could overhear. Then he made me see I couldn't report it because it would bring disgrace on you and ruin your reputation."

"The only one who can disgrace me is me."

He was such a proud man, proud in the good sense of the word. A gentleman who considered his word his bond; a warrior who believed that to act with fidelity and integrity was his sacred duty. If she followed through with her story, his reputation could be sullied by lies and innuendo, by distorted truths and vicious rumor. She couldn't let that happen.

The room grew silent. Rika could hear the muffled ticking of the clock in the hallway and her own heartbeat.

"Gramps, you know I would never do anything to hurt you," she said to fill the uncomfortably silent void.

"Nevertheless you have a tiger by the tail and don't know how to let him loose." He half closed his eyes and let his head drop, but only for a moment.

He rose from his seat. "Now I'm off to a meeting of the board—spell that b-o-r-e-d." He pushed back his chair and came around the corner of the desk. Clasping both her hands in his, he said, "We'll talk about this later."

"Gramps…"

"Later, sweetheart." He walked past her and out the door.

ON HIS WAY BACK to the base Alex wished there were some way he could spare General Tiers the news that his granddaughter had eavesdropped on their conversation. The success or failure of this mission could depend on what she chose to do with the information she'd learned.

Alex adjusted the air conditioner to max and directed the vents to blow into his face. He should never have agreed to give her background information. He should have told her unequivocally that the story was off-limits, that she couldn't report it. If he'd put his foot down and ordered her to leave the matter alone… No use. She wouldn't have listened, much less obeyed. His hands were tied. He had no choice.

Damn it, Rika. He slammed his palm on the steering wheel. Why couldn't you play by the rules? Why did you have to listen in?

Alex saluted the guard at the gate as he entered the base. He'd become very fond of Nathan Tiers in the short time he'd known him, and now their special bond would be shattered. Even if the old man didn't hold him totally responsible for the situation, he would lose respect for the way Alex had handled it.

He pictured Rika, the soft glow of her light-brown hair, the tanned smoothness of her complexion and, most of all, the incredible beauty of her green eyes. He'd seen them laugh, and he could still feel the merriment they filled him with. He'd watched them smolder with longing and passion when he brought his lips to hers. Even now, the recollection of her feminine fragrance sent a tremor to his gut and a twitch to his groin. Then he recalled the last time he'd looked into her eyes and beheld the uneasiness, the uncertainty and guilt troubling them. Damn. He turned onto the narrow road that led to hangar number seven, certain he wouldn't want to be in her shoes when she had to answer to her grandfather.

Alex greeted the sentry on duty, crossed to the main building, swiped his pass across the electronic reader and entered the AFL. At his desk he stared at the folders piled up there. Dammit. He had to inform the general.

Sera answered the phone. "I'm sorry, sir. He just left for a meeting, but he said that if you called, to ask if you could come to see him this afternoon around five."

Did he already know? Had Rika beat him to the punch?

"Tell him I'll be there."

THE HOUSE on Chestnut Street was small, inconspic-
uous and white. Rika parked her van in the narrow
driveway and walked to the front door. Landscaping
was minimal—a few evergreen scrubs, a trimmed but
spotty lawn. She rang the bell, noting the clapboard
siding could use a fresh coat of paint.

A delicate, gray-haired woman in a turquoise linen
pantsuit opened the door.

"Mrs. Franklin? I called a little while ago. I'm
Rika Philips."

"The general's granddaughter." She swung the
door wide and invited Rika inside. The living room
was faded, feminine and cluttered with dusty knick-
knacks, framed photos and mementos of trips to Cor-
pus Christi, Florida beaches, London, Paris and
Rome. Rika wondered if the woman had actually
gone to those places or if the tourist trinkets had been
gifts from children and grandchildren.

A window air conditioner struggled but kept the
room only moderately cool. Rika sat on the lumpy
couch in front of double sash windows, while Mrs.
Franklin settled across from her in an overstuffed
chair with worn lace doilies on the armrests.

"I was hoping you might be able to help me on a
feature story I'm planning to write about Coyote Air
Force Base," Rika began. "I understand you were
here when it was being built."

"Indeed I was, more than sixty years ago now, but
I remember. Used to be ranch land. Belonged to
Frownin' Frank Duthrow. Deeded it to the Army for
a dollar. His girl, Elsie, and I went to school together.
That was before the war, of course. We called it Coyote Field back then. It was a flying training base, you
know."

Rika listened with a sense of relief. Mrs. Franklin appeared to be at least eighty and moved with a deliberate slowness, but her mind seemed clear and perceptive.

"I've heard there's an entire factory assembly line under hangar seven. Is that true?"

The old lady didn't bat an eye at the question. "Could be. My father worked construction during the war. Said they were digging the biggest damn hole he ever did see, but when I asked him particulars, he clammed up tighter than a drum. Refused to say another word about it."

"Why was that? Do you know?" Rika asked.

"The war was going on by then, and everybody was real closemouthed. Posters were plastered all over the place, warning people that 'loose lips sink ships.'" She cackled. "Not many ships around here, then or since. Of course, later I began to hear rumors."

"About the factory?"

She nodded. "A few people wanted to say we had something to do with developing the bomb, but I didn't believe it. Do recall strange noises coming from the base at night, though. Later, I realized they were jet sounds."

So they had been working on jet propulsion. "How long did they use this underground facility?"

The old woman gazed at her with piercing blue eyes, her wrinkled lips thinning in a subtle smile. "I reckon they're still using it."

The statement, made so confidently, jolted Rika. What did this woman know that she wasn't telling? Then, in a flash, the answer came. The government had been closing hundreds of installations all over the country in the past decade.

"Why else keep open an out-of-the-way Air Force facility that doesn't have an operational runway," Rika speculated out loud, "unless it has something no other place can offer? Or would cost too much to duplicate?"

The woman awarded her a satisfied grin. "You'd be amazed how many people never put two and two together."

"I'M NOT PLEASED with the situation," Nathan Tiers intoned late that afternoon to the two people sitting stiff-shouldered across the desk from him. "I can't lay the blame on either of you, however. As the senior person, it's my responsibility to make sure things are done properly, and I failed to do so."

"Maybe we can compromise," Alex offered. He wasn't sure if his proposal was wise or strictly legal. He understood only that he had to try to bridge the gap that threatened to destroy people he'd grown fond of in a short time—and save his mission.

"What kind of compromise?" Rika demanded.

The general studied him, waiting for an explanation.

"I told Rika," Alex went on, watching her, wondering what her reaction was going to be, "I would give her unclassified background information. As you know, sir, this is a delicate situation. What I tell her, even though totally unclassified, can lead to her drawing certain conclusions, which may or may not be sensitive."

The conundrum was an old one. Individual pieces

of information could be unclassified, but assemble them in a certain fashion and they became classified.

"What do you have in mind, Major?" the general asked.

Alex addressed Rika. "I'll make a deal with you. I'll brief you on our mission and allow you to ask questions. In exchange, I want you to tell me what you know or suspect. If the conclusions you draw are classified or could entail a security leak, I'll inform you and ask you to respect those boundaries."

She snorted. "It sounds like a win situation for you and a lose situation for me." But she didn't say no.

"Not really. I promise I'll tell you the truth one way or the other. You may not be able to publish all you learn, but at least you'll have the satisfaction of knowing what you do write will be accurate."

He could see her weighing the proposition in her mind. This was a dilemma for her, too. The very concept of censorship—which was what he was proposing—was totally anathema to journalists and reporters.

"It's a reasonable request," General Tiers said as he leaned forward and rolled a fountain pen between his fingers. The observation wasn't a command that she agree to the offer, so much as a way out.

"When can I get briefed?" she asked.

"Tomorrow," Alex said. "After duty hours. I don't want Lacy or any of his people there if I can avoid it."

MATHILDA LIVINGSTON had worked at Coyote AFB for over fifty years, retiring only last year following the sudden death of her husband. She was also a member of Gram's bridge club and a valuable source in her "old girl" network. When Rika mentioned she was considering an article on the history of the base, Gram pointed her in Matty's direction.

Her residence in the University Heights area was more impressive in size than Mrs. Franklin's modest house in the old part of town. The lawn looked professionally maintained. Only the pink flamingos seemed out of place.

"Hello, Mrs. Livingston," Rika said when the door swung open. Her grandmother's friend was wearing a matching blue polyester blouse and slacks, a beaded necklace dangling from her rhinestone-trimmed eyeglasses.

"Come in. Come in." She backed up, swinging her arm in invitation. "You look just like your mama, you know that?" She closed the door and led Rika into the living room. "The same beautiful green eyes and—"

"So I've been told," Rika responded quickly, hoping to get past the subject. Even after twenty years, being compared with her mother still made her uncomfortable.

"Come on out to the kitchen. I've got some peach tea."

Five minutes later, they returned to the living room with oversized plastic glasses of fruit-scented iced tea.

"Gram tells me you are the best-informed person around here," Rika began. "That you really keep your eyes and ears open."

"Try to," Matty replied proudly before taking a healthy swallow of her drink.

Rika placed hers on the coaster at her elbow. "I'm working on a story about the base," she explained, "and thought you might be able to help me with background information. The Public Affairs office—''

Mrs. Livingston compressed her lips and waved her head in rejection of the idea. ''They won't tell you what you want to know, only what they want to tell you. Besides, most of the young kids who work out there don't have a clue about what's going on, anyway.''

''Exactly. I was hoping you could give me a little of the human interest—''

''There's nobody around anymore who remembers,'' the woman said, cutting her off. ''People were closer then. The Air Force used to be like a family. Nowadays people don't know one another 'cause they don't talk to one another. It's all computers. New employees don't even recognize the people they work with.''

''It's a fast-paced world out there,'' Rika observed.

Henrietta raced on. ''Folks these days would rather stand in line to fiddle with one of them automatic banking machines in the hot sun than walk into a nice air-conditioned lobby and talk to a real live teller. Machines over people.'' She snorted derisively. ''Then they fly into a rage when the gadgets don't do what they expect. Can't reason with a machine.'' She smirked. ''Or grab it by the scruff of the neck.''

''What can you tell me about the Aerospace Food Laboratory?'' No sense in mentioning that she'd tried to crash the place and been rejected, or that she had an appointment to see it this evening.

''The AFL.'' Matty picked up a figurine on the end table beside her and examined it, apparently unhappy with the dust on it. She fingered it clean. ''They sure like using acronyms and abbreviations. It becomes a separate language after a while. Alphabet soup.''

Rika wondered if she'd ever be able to get the old lady to stick to the point. ''What can you tell me about it?'' she repeated.

''The lab?'' Matty replaced the statue and settled back in her chair. ''Supposed to be developing space food, but if you ask me, I'd say there's something else going on out there.''

''Like what?''

''UFOs.''

Rika boggled. ''UFOs?'' *Uh-oh, I may just have walked in on the Mad Hatter's tea party.* ''Really?''

''You know about the Roswell incident in 1947?''

''About flying saucers and space aliens?'' Keeping a note of incredulity out of her voice was hard.

''Mind you, I'm not saying I believe in any of that stuff,'' Matty said emphatically, ''but in '47 and for ten years after that, I worked in the billeting office. I was only a teenager when I started, of course, but I met just about everyone who came here on temporary duty, officer, enlisted or civilian. I'm pretty good at remembering names and faces, and I can tell you this.'' She leaned forward and lowered her voice. ''All those people you hear about who were involved in that secret program came here, as well. I didn't know who they were then. Nobody did. But years later, when the story broke about Project Blue Book, I had no trouble recognizing their names and faces. No trouble at all.''

Was it true? Rika asked herself. Could Coyote AFB have been associated with what was going on at White Sands and Alamogordo? Was that how the rumors started of the atomic bomb being developed here?

"How long did they stay?"

"Some of them were only here overnight. Some stayed for days, even weeks. Most of them were here more than once. They weren't just passing through, I can assure you. They were here for a reason."

"What about the people who work there now? What about them?"

Henrietta settled back in her worn La-Z-Boy rocker. "You got a couple of hours?"

ALEX CALLED RIKA at the Tierses' residence at 4:00 p.m. and confirmed their seven o'clock briefing was still on. He'd meet her at the AFL guard shack. His curt, businesslike tone didn't offend her, though secretly she'd hoped he might invite her to dinner first. It annoyed her that she wanted him to.

She understood how angry he was—at himself as well as at her—and realized with a stab of regret that he might always be. In his mind, she'd betrayed her grandfather and was using him. Get over it, she wanted to tell him, but wasn't sure that in his place she would herself.

If the way a man touched a woman, the way he kissed her, was any indication of how he felt about her, Alex Huston felt something more than outrage for her. And if a woman's reaction to a man's touch and his kisses were signs, she felt something for him, too. Alex's father had placed work before family. Alex apparently bore no grudge. In fact, he seemed to idolize his dad. Like father, like son? How could she expect Alex to put her above his work, when he had made no promises, offered no pledges?

He might have been guarding Buckingham Palace at seven o'clock, the way he stood at parade rest, his hands clasped behind his back, his feet spread shoulder width. He refused to make eye contact as she walked toward the perimeter fence. On her drive to the base, she'd entertained the smug satisfaction of knowing she was going to breach the barbed-wire battlements of the AFL. Complacency quickly yielded to discomfort, however, as he escorted her into the guard shack.

She accepted a red plastic badge from the same sergeant who the previous week had refused her admittance, clipped it onto the collar of her powder-blue sanded-silk blouse and signed the visitors' log as required. Unfortunately, she was presented with a clean page, so she couldn't see who previous visitors might have been.

Alex accompanied her into the building, which was well lit and disappointingly ordinary. No exotic machines buzzing and whirling, no test tubes bubbling and vaporizing, just an ordinary institutionally carpeted corridor like hundreds she'd walked down in other office buildings. Of course, she had no way of knowing what might be going on behind all the closed doors or below her feet. Maybe that was where the people in white jackets and spiked hair crowed, "It's alive. It's alive."

They stopped in front of a single varnished wooden door with an electric sign overhead that flashed Briefing In Progress, Do Not Enter. Alex punched in a security code on a keypad above the knob, twisted the handle and pushed. Standing tall, his arm holding back the open door, he nodded for her to pass.

A man in camouflage fatigues came to his feet inside the long, dark-paneled room. It took Rika a moment's memory search to recognize the face—Mike, the man who had been with Alex at the steak house. After the door closed, Alex introduced him and announced, ''Sergeant Lattimore will brief you on the program.''

She noted he'd referred to her as Mrs. Philips, not Rika, and that he had given the NCO's first name as Michael. Apparently, this was going to be a very formal session. Was it standard protocol? Yes, but she'd also attended enough military briefings and news conferences to know it wasn't always that way, especially with small groups.

''Would you like some coffee?'' Alex asked.

''Please.''

He poured her a cup from a service neatly set up in the far corner, then sat opposite her at one end of a long conference table. She felt him watching her, not solicitously but warily. In her job she was used to distrust, even hostility, but the animosity she felt radiating from him threatened to push her back in her chair as far as she could go. He had her on the defensive, and she didn't like it.

Sergeant Lattimore took his position behind a podium to Rika's left, next to a rear-projection screen. He clicked a controller, and a full-color slide materialized. It welcomed her by name, identified the NCO as her briefer and the subject. The words were all superimposed on a muted picture of the main entrance to the base.

''Good evening, Mrs. Philips,'' he began his spiel. ''I'm Master Sergeant Michael Lattimore and I will be briefing you on the MADAM program. This briefing is unclassified. It will take approximately one hour.''

"There'll be a question-and-answer period at the end," Alex informed her.

He met her eyes, daring her to challenge him. His hostile glare put her back up and made her want to rebel, but being uncooperative would play into his hands and she refused to give him the satisfaction. Besides, there was nothing to object to. She nodded her understanding.

She had a pretty good idea what she was in for. The military briefing formula was three-part: tell them what you're going to say, say it, then tell them what you said. It had merit for long, complex issues, but for shorter subjects it tended to be boring, repetitive and condescending. She wondered if she was going to get the idiot treatment.

An overview slide came up, which Lattimore paraphrased. The real mission of the AFL, she learned, was to develop a means of detecting stealth aircraft and other weapons systems being deployed against the United States and its allies. There was no mention of space food, UFOs or alien visitors. Were they telling her the truth or was this some sort of diversion?

Alex was purposely staring at her, his laser-sharp eyes drilling into her from across the table, trying to make her squirm. She wanted to scream at him, but fighter pilots weren't the only people with nerves of steel. She forced herself to maintain a calm, dignified pose. Holding her breath underwater would have been easier.

The main body of the presentation was divided into three sections: radar, stealth and counterstealth. Rika sipped her coffee, which to her amazement was quite palatable.

"May I take notes?" she asked, and reached into her handbag for a steno pad.

"No problem," Alex agreed. "I will have to read them, though, before you leave."

She was tempted to object. If what they were presenting to her wasn't classified, why should her jottings be of interest? She also knew she wasn't going to win the battle if she chose to fight it. Plus, she had a trained memory. What she didn't put on paper she could still take with her in her head.

"Good luck trying to decipher my shorthand," she said indifferently, and uncapped her pen. "What about a tour of the facilities?"

"Out of the question." Alex replied so quickly she knew he'd anticipated the request.

She poised her ballpoint over her pad. "Will you at least confirm there is an extensive lower level to this building?"

He rested back in his chair, his muscular arms extended in front of him, fingers interlocked on the shiny surface of the table.

"We have something of a dilemma, don't we?" he asked. "I'm not going to show you around the building. Consequently, there's no point in talking about it. If I were to tell you there's no underground factory—or whatever you've heard is supposed to be there—you won't believe me. I can't prove a negative—that we don't have flying saucers or their debris, or cadavers of space aliens. You see, Mrs. Philips, I'm aware of the rumors about the base." He smiled thinly and without humor.

"At the same time," he went on, "if I were to tell

you there is a vast underground structure but refuse to describe it or let you see it, you're just as likely to think I'm lying.''

''I've never accused you of lying,'' she said, not as calmly as she would have wished.

''Good.'' He turned his head to the screen. The subject was closed. ''Sergeant Lattimore, would you continue, please.''

A ripe selection of words—*arrogant* and *insufferable* foremost among them—went through her mind. She bit her tongue.

The next several slides were a series of well-executed graphics depicting various aspects of radar technology.

''Radar,'' Lattimore explained, ''beams radio signals into the atmosphere. If they strike an object, some of the signals bounce off it and return to the transmitting antenna. Because we know where we're aiming the signals and by calculating the time it takes them to return, we can determine the range of the object. Using more than one radar in different locations or configurations against the same target allows us to pinpoint the object's position, its speed and size.''

Rika nodded. She knew this, but the review was worthwhile. Did that mean they were working on some new generation of radar? Maybe they weren't going to stonewall after all.

''Radio signals,'' the sergeant continued, ''only reflect off metal objects. The bigger the object, the easier it is to detect. A wooden glider, for example, would be essentially invisible to radar. Unfortunately, wooden planes aren't strong enough to withstand the G forces necessary for supersonic aircraft. Nor has anyone been able to develop a powerful-enough engine of materials other than metal.''

Rika thought about the pictures she'd seen of the flimsy wooden gliders that had carried troops behind enemy lines in World War II, especially during the D-Day invasion. Howard Hughes's monstrous Spruce Goose had been grounded forever after one, very brief test flight.

''Which brings us to stealth.''

She automatically straightened in her chair as Lattimore clicked to the next slide. It showed the F-117/Nighthawk stealth fighter-bomber. Its sleek, sharp-edged lines had a sinister quality that was both fascinating and forbidding.

She cut a glance at the major. His posture changed subtly when the jet flashed on the screen. His focus shifted from her to the familiar aircraft. There was a comfortable expression on his face that resembled affection. Rika nearly shivered.

''Stealth technology involves two components,'' the sergeant went on. ''The first is the design of the aircraft itself. You've probably noticed that stealth aircraft are very angular. There's a reason for this. The tubular shape of conventional aircraft means there're always some surfaces that will reflect radio signals. By flattening those surfaces, we severely limit the number of angles at which signals can be reflected.''

''But doesn't that also increase the size of the reflecting surfaces,'' she interrupted without thinking, ''and make the plane a bigger target?''

''Yes,'' Lattimore agreed, pleased by her observation. ''Which brings us to stealth's second component. The material of construction itself. While stealth aircraft are still made of metal, they are coated with a radar-absorbent material called RAM. This combination, shape and RAM, makes these aircraft virtually invisible to radar.''

''But what about the engines?'' Rika asked. ''Surely you can't coat them with this absorbent material, too.''

''We can minimize their radar signatures,'' Alex interjected, ''by positioning them behind RAM surfaces.''

It sounded so simple. ''So we have invisible aircraft,'' she concluded.

''Precisely. We know it's only a matter of time, however, before other countries, not all of them friendly to us, will be using this technology. What we must do now is stay one step ahead of them.''

Made sense, she thought. ''How?''

Alex nodded to Lattimore. The sergeant clicked to the next slide. Across the screen in large bold black letters appeared the word MADAM. Under it in more subtle gray tones were the words Molecular Anomalous Detection And Measurement. It certainly was a mouthful, and Rika had no idea what it meant.

''The MADAM program is designed to detect and locate aircraft and other flying objects in the atmosphere,'' the NCO resumed. ''The same range and triangulation techniques used by radar are employed in this system. The difference is that while radar detects the object itself, MADAM detects the molecular anomaly, the 'hole' the object creates in the atmosphere.''

Barely able to keep her mouth from hanging open, Rika looked at Alex. ''Find a hole in the atmosphere?'' she asked incredulously. ''How?''

CHAPTER ELEVEN

ALEX SMILED for the first time. "The details of how it's done are, of course, classified."

Rika struggled to put this new information in perspective. "You're saying MADAM can detect stealth aircraft even though radar can't see them."

"MADAM allows us to see anything and everything in the atmosphere above the surface of the earth."

"Wow!" And she meant it. "That means radar's become obsolete."

"Not completely," Alex responded. "It's the most economical way of detecting and tracking conventional aircraft under ordinary circumstances. MADAM is still experimental, but yes, one day this new system will replace radar altogether."

A whirlwind of questions buffeted through Rika's head. Before she had an opportunity to form one, Lattimore summed up his presentation and reminded her the briefing was unclassified.

"I'm impressed," she said, and was infused with pride for the man sitting across from her. He hadn't claimed any role in the program, but she had no doubt he was somehow involved in it—otherwise he wouldn't have been sent here to investigate. Not only was he a hunk, but he was a very smart hunk. A very smart hunk who knew how to kiss better than any man who'd ever kissed her.

Lattimore pressed a button and turned off the projection screen. With a nod from Alex, he sat a couple of chairs down from Rika on her side of the table, allowing Alex to establish eye contact with both of them.

"This project is still experimental," Alex repeated. "The concept has been proven on paper, but we still have to do low-level practical experiments to prove its viability. That's what Colonel Lacy and his people have been working on."

"Here at the food lab?" She let sarcasm creep into her voice. "If it's not Top Secret, can you tell me what 'food' really stands for?"

Alex let out a soft chuckle, the first noticeable reminder of his sense of humor. "Find Object On Demand."

"Cute," she said, and scribbled a note on her pad.

"If MADAM is successful," he pointed out, "it puts us two steps ahead of our potential adversaries. We know stealth technology has been compromised, but we also know it's expensive. That means its wide-scale employment is limited. If we can detect their 'invisible' aircraft, it means we can defend ourselves against them. That's step one. The second step is to keep them from getting MADAM. As long as we can remain invisible to the detection systems of our adversaries, stealth technology is still useful to us."

"Is it true the AFL has been flying special drones with the High Flyers from town in order to test this system?" she asked.

"Exactly."

"And now a drone has disappeared."

Alex worked his jaw. This obviously was a difficult subject for him to discuss. "Unfortunately."

"By accident or by design?" she asked.

"That's what we're trying to find out," he replied. "You can help."

"Me?"

"Looking into something of this nature can be very tricky," Alex reminded her. "We have to be careful the investigation itself doesn't compromise our position. That's not a problem on base. I have the authority to monitor the activities of government personnel, military and civilian, while they're on a military installation. Off base is another matter. That's where you come in."

So he was going to use her. Rika grimaced at the irony of the situation. She knew reporters, especially investigative reporters, were often seen in a negative light, even as evils to be tolerated, but evils, nevertheless. Now a man who had subtly but unmistakably indicated his repugnance for her work was willing to take advantage of her profession.

"How?" she asked.

Alex rose and restlessly paced the open area between the screen and the end of the table. "On 30 July, members of the AFL flew a stealth-technology drone on the base flight line with members of the High Flyers. The drone, which contained special instrumentation to assess the effectiveness of our tracking, departed its planned flight path and disappeared from sight. It hasn't been found. My people are asking club members who were there that day what they saw and what they think might have happened to the aircraft. The thing my team can't do, however, is monitor the activities of nongovernment personnel downtown.''

''But I can?''

Alex nodded.

''What are you looking for?''

He shrugged and rested an elbow on the podium. ''Suspicious activities. Anything that would suggest an individual might be involved in espionage, or susceptible to blackmail by somebody else in that capacity. As an experienced investigative reporter, I'm sure you know what to look for, and I have no doubt you have resources that go beyond the kinds of official channels I can use.''

Remembering the vulnerable situation in which she would place her grandfather by reporting what she already knew, she could hardly afford not to comply to protect the people and the country she loved.

''Do we have an ethical problem here?'' she inquired. ''Aren't you asking me to act as a government agent and in so doing making anything I discover inadmissible?''

''First of all, I'm not asking you to do anything illegal, like tap phones. Any information you come up with, you can, of course, write about. I have no way to stop you. Naturally, once published, it becomes public domain and information on which the government can launch a legitimate inquiry of its own.''

He was cutting it close, almost forcing her to report what she found. A good lawyer would argue, perhaps successfully, that if she simply passed information on to him, having been asked to uncover it, she was acting as his agent and therefore violating the subject's civil rights. She had no doubt he'd thought of that.

She also recognized that a big controversy over this could very well cost him his career. If he was willing to put his fate in her hands, the least she could do was return the trust.

"On one condition," she said. "I'll share with you what I find out about people downtown in exchange for your telling me what you find out about people here on base."

His posture stiffened, not much, but enough for her to realize he was uncomfortable. "I can't make that promise," he told her almost sadly.

"Then it's no deal," she replied adamantly. "I'll go with what I've got and see if anything else develops."

"Mrs. Philips," he said without raising his voice but with a force that brooked no opposition, "we had an agreement. I would furnish information in exchange for your cooperation."

"What you've delivered, Major," she reminded him, "is unclassified. I could have gotten it off the Internet."

"Hardly. It's also all I'm free to give you."

"As far as I'm concerned," she went on, ignoring his last statement, "I can report everything you've told me without compromising national security." She watched his eyes darken, saw the subtle tightening at the corners of his mouth.

"Need I remind you," he asked as he returned to the end of the table, "of the effect such a report would have on your grandfather's reputation?"

She straightened her back and thrust out her chin. "No, Major, you needn't. But let me reiterate that the things I've learned I've come by legitimately—and I thank you for helping me fill in the blanks."

He stared down at her. But if he thought the intensity of his blue-eyed gaze, the rumbling harshness of his words or the imposing mass of his wide shoulders and deep chest were going to intimidate her the way they had at the pool…he was wrong.

"Can I make a suggestion?" Lattimore asked quietly, breaking the tense silence between them.

"What?" they both snapped as they redirected their glares at him. Rika had the distinct impression the sergeant was biting back a smile.

"You both want the same thing—to identify whoever is responsible for what happened to the drone. On the government side, we're limited in what we can give you and how we use information we receive. On your part, Mrs. Philips, there are sources that you, no doubt, want to protect."

She nodded, not quite sure if he was getting them any closer to a solution.

"So share the results of your efforts that pertain to solving this problem," he said. "If either of you discovers someone is filing for bankruptcy, for example, let the other know. It's ultimately public knowledge. No sources are compromised. No civil rights are violated."

A long moment of reflection followed.

"Just the results of our investigations?" she asked. Lattimore nodded.

"What do you say?" Alex finally asked.

He wasn't begging her, but there was a plea in the question. To feel elation with her sudden position of power was unworthy of her, but she felt it, anyway. "I'll go along with that," she said casually, "if you will."

"Whew," Lattimore breathed. "Let's refill our coffee cups and get down to brass tacks."

OVER THE NEXT THREE DAYS, between loads of laundry, taking Emily and the other children to the base pool, horseback riding, getting the van serviced and helping her grandmother in the garden, Rika went downtown to research the High Flyers. The assignment could be a dead end, of course, a diversion Alex had concocted to keep her from what was really happening; however, she didn't think so. The compromise they'd worked out had been his idea, and her grandfather had later endorsed it. Alex Huston might deceive her, but not General Nathan Tiers. Even though he might distrust her, she was convinced of Alex's genuine respect for her grandfather.

Sergeant Lattimore furnished her with the names and addresses of the club's twenty-six members—not exactly a huge organization. He also identified the nine people who'd been at the base the fateful Sunday afternoon when the drone went missing.

Checking each of the names in the newspaper's morgue for the last year revealed little. In the official notices section, she found where they had bought and sold homes, received traffic tickets and made requests to the city council for the installation of stop signs or adoption of lowered speed limits on particular roads and streets. Nothing unusual or suspicious. Certainly nothing extraordinary or preferential.

In the interior pages of the daily paper, she learned of the weddings of their sons and daughters, the parties for charity they attended and sometimes hosted and the hobbies and volunteer organizations that occupied their spare time.

The High Flyers Model Club had been recognized by the city council and several state and national organizations for its inspirational and motivational work with youth and the handicapped. Again nothing seemed in the least relevant to the disappearance from Coyote AFB of a high-technology drone.

She checked official records at the courthouse. Since the paper was willing to accede to the base commander's request to not include unit designations, maybe it also conveniently omitted other information, like arrests or complaints against prominent citizens. Another dead end.

Except for one thing. The police had raided a floating poker game and craps shoot a couple of months earlier. Nothing more was published on the incident and Rika discovered the allegations were subsequently dropped. She did learn the names of the people who had been involved, however. Among them was Tilly Silvers, the base commander's secretary. Rika pictured the tall, lean, eagle-eyed woman wearing a dark-green eyeshade with a pair of dice in her clawlike hand. Seven come eleven.

"I ran across something curious," Rika said as she put her handbag on the hall table Friday afternoon. "Did you read about the gambling ring they broke up a couple of months ago?"

A gleam animated Barbara's face. "I believe I do recall something about it."

"Did you know Tilly Silvers was one of the people there?"

"Really? How curious. Have you had lunch, dear? Sera can fix you a sandwich."

Until then Rika hadn't thought about food, but at

the mention of it, she suddenly realized she was famished. They went out to the kitchen.

"If you want the straight skinny," Barbara said, spouting slang Rika had never heard her use before, "I know just the person you should talk to."

Rika bit into the avocado-and-bacon croissant Sera had fixed her. For a moment she allowed herself to be distracted by its smoky flavor. "That's what I need, Gram, the inside poop."

Her grandmother went to the counter, picked up the phone and dialed a number. "Henrietta? Babs. I thought if you have time today after work we might get together for a quick rubber of bridge. Yes, here. About five? Good. I'll see you then."

Before Rika had a chance to question or object, her grandmother hit the automatic dial button for the base operator.

"Glenda, this is Babs. How have you been? We missed you at mah-jongg last week. Well, of course. I hope he's feeling better. Glenda, do you think you can find Major Huston for me? No, I'll wait. Thank you, dear."

Rika nearly choked on a piece of tomato. Only Barbara Tiers could pick up the phone and get her party without knowing where he was. Rika sighed. If she had connections like that, the world of journalism would be warehousing awards for her.

"Hello, Major. Yes, everything is fine. But I would like you to come out to the house this afternoon, if you can. About five? No, I really would prefer not talking about it on the phone. I'm sure you understand... I'll see you then. Goodbye."

"Gram, I don't think he's going to be very happy

when he finds out you tricked him here to play cards. You don't even know that he can play the game.''

"The man is intelligent and civilized. Of course he's a bridge player. As soon as you finish, let's get the table set up.''

Rika laughed. She was looking forward to seeing his reaction.

"ANY LUCK?'' Alex asked Lattimore when he climbed aboard the van parked at the end of the flight line.

"Routine stuff,'' the sergeant reported. "Found a couple of things that might help. The lab sends its WAR, weekly activity report, to the base commander by unclassified E-mail every Friday afternoon. They include test-flight schedules for the coming week as well as accomplishments of the previous week.''

"Who gets the WAR besides the commander?''

"All his division chiefs.''

"So any base personnel, military or civilian, even if they aren't directly involved in MADAM, would know when something's going to be tested?''

"Yep. We're checking now to see if a copy of the report is being forwarded off base under a different header. It'll take us a while. The information could be buried in another message.''

Alex glanced at the stacks of transcripts accumulating on shelves. Each one would have to be analyzed to determine if it contained anything of value. People, even in high-security facilities, were notorious for thinking they could talk around information and not give it away. They had no idea how transparent their supposedly arcane allusions were.

Lattimore tossed him an amused grin. "Would you like to know what the old lady wants you for?"

It required only a fraction of a second for Alex to figure out who Lattimore was referring to. They were actively monitoring the lab, and the general's wife had reached him there. Naturally, they would have listened in. Her mysterious call had baffled Alex. He'd wondered if she was phoning on behalf of her husband or if Rika might somehow be behind it. "Do tell."

"Before she spoke to you she telephoned the clothing store on base."

Alex frowned. What did the clothing store have to do with this?

"To talk to Henrietta. Name ring any bells?"

Alex pictured the Amazon of a woman. "She runs the place."

"She apparently also plays cards, because Mrs. Tiers invited her to the house for a rubber of bridge at five o'clock this afternoon."

"The same time I'm invited. But why?"

"Can't tell you for certain," Lattimore said with a taunting lilt, "but I suspect they need a fourth."

A fourth? Who would be the third? Rika? The general?

Alex pinched his lower lip between thumb and forefinger. Bridge. He wasn't sure exactly what was going on, but he decided it might be wise for him to arrive prepared.

RIKA OPENED THE DOOR a few minutes before the hour and was surprised to find Alex standing there in western shirt, snug jeans and cowboy boots. The outfit brought back memories of a ride by the river, eating apples and stolen kisses. Suddenly, her knees went weak and her palms grew clammy. The man oozed sex.

"Hi," he said brightly as he stepped across the threshold without even giving her a chance to greet him. "Am I early?"

The grandfather clock in the hall struck five. "Uh, no. You're right on time."

Barbara Tiers appeared in the doorway of the living room. "Major Huston, how good of you to come, and on such short notice." The general's wife paused, taking in his attire with about the same degree of interest as Rika had shown. She didn't get a chance to say anything, however, before Alex stepped up to her and, bending, kissed her fondly on her cheek.

"I brought a little something." He held out a small package.

Barbara's eyes opened wide. "For me, Major?"

"For you, Mrs. Tiers. I was in a shop downtown, saw them and just knew you would enjoy them."

Utterly baffled, the old woman slipped off the silver ribbon and carefully unwrapped the gold paper. She looked dumbfounded as she stared at a black lacquered box. She opened it and found a double set of playing cards.

He smiled innocently.

Rika put her hand in front of her mouth to hide the wide grin tugging at her jaw. The expression on her grandmother's face was positively priceless.

"Why...uh...they're...I..." Gram speechless. It was a sight to savor. The doorbell interrupted her sputtering.

Biting her lips, Rika faded back toward the door and opened it. Henrietta, dressed in a bright-orange pantsuit, took one step inside and stopped dead in her tracks. "Oh, er, Major Huston!"

Rika sucked in her cheeks and pulled on her left earlobe, not hard enough, however, to discourage the grin bursting from within her. She didn't know how Alex had done it, but he'd managed to throw the two ladies completely off balance.

Alex caught her expression and gave her a wink before addressing the new arrival. "Henrietta! What a surprise to see you here."

He beamed down at the general's birdlike wife with an expression of the cat who just ate the canary. "Say, I have an idea. I was about to invite Rika out to dinner and maybe dancing later, but it's much too early. Since there are four of us, maybe we could play a rubber of bridge." He frowned. "I didn't think to ask. You ladies do play, don't you?"

Rika watched her grandmother recover, while Henrietta still had her mouth hanging open.

"Why, Major," Barbara said, and slipped her hand around his arm. "You're a man after my own heart. That's a splendid idea." She gazed up at him with an adoring smile. "You know, I just happened to have a card table set up in here." She steered him toward the open double doors of the living room. "Isn't that a funny coincidence?"

"It certainly is," he said, and patted her hand. "I have to warn you, though. I was pretty good at the Academy. Of course, that was some years ago, and I haven't played since, but they say it's like riding a bicycle—you never forget."

Barbara's sweet tone turned to sudden steel. "Well, son, you better get pedaling. You're up against a grand master here."

Alex held her chair. "I'm sure you can teach me a lot," he whispered in her ear.

"DID YOU TELL your grandmother what we were hunting for?" Alex started the engine of his car and rolled down the gravel driveway.

The question could have been an accusation, but Rika didn't detect any acrimony in it. She took her lead from his light tone.

"Nope. All I said was that I was thinking about writing a story on the model club because of all the good work they've done for disadvantaged kids."

"Could she have wheedled information out of your grandfather? She seemed to know precisely where to focus the conversation." He braked at the main road and looked both ways, then turned toward town.

"Maybe. It's more likely she managed to put enough pieces together on her own and figured I could use a little help."

"From a well-informed source." There was humor in his comment this time.

Rika couldn't help chuckling. She'd never heard her grandmother spread gossip, but the old dear wasn't above listening to it. "Gram refers to Henrietta as a keen observer of her neighbors."

This time he laughed. "Let me guess. The town being small, she considers everyone her neighbor." He was forced to slow down behind a wide-bodied dinosaur of a Cadillac poking along at twenty-five miles an hour. He pulled around the car, glanced in passing at the little old lady who could barely see over the dashboard and continued down the road, giving her a wide berth.

"I've got to ask," Rika admitted, "how did you know we were going to play bridge?"

"What? You want me to reveal my sources?"

He was baiting her, trying to see if he could make her grovel. Okay, she'd grovel. "How did you know?" she repeated.

He paused long enough for her to wonder if he would answer. "How do you think?"

She contemplated his profile and had the sudden urge to run her hand down his clean-shaven cheek. "You tapped our phone!"

He snickered. "No, and you needn't sound so offended. We're not tapping your line, but we are monitoring all the phones on base, so when your grandmother called Henrietta and invited her to play bridge—" He lifted his shoulders and let them drop.

"So you can listen in on private phone calls?"

"If one or both of the parties are on base, yes."

Alex turned onto the main drag leading to town.

"Where are we going? Were you serious about dinner and dancing?"

"Any objection?"

No. Yes. She liked the idea of sitting across from him; watching him eat; studying his face, his hands; gazing into his eyes. As for dancing with him, feeling their bodies moving together—she hadn't forgotten the tingling sensation he'd given her when he held her in his arms.

"No," she said, meaning going dancing wouldn't be wise. Except the question had been if she had any objection. Damn it. He was getting her all mixed up again.

Okay, she admitted, so she was attracted to him *physically*. She couldn't deny it. Judging by the way he looked at her, the way his hands and fingers and lips made contact with her hands and fingers and lips, he was attracted to her, too. But the attraction was *only* physical. Nothing more. The events of the last week proved that. She had to resist the impulses his body stirred in hers, because peering into his eyes seemed to draw Alex and her into a kiss, and when their lips touched, she wanted other parts of his body to touch hers, too.

"No," she said again, meaning a physical relationship would definitely interfere with the job they'd agreed to share.

"Good," he replied, and reached across the narrow seat to place his fingers over hers. "I thought we'd have dinner at the Ranch House, then go to the Cowboy Honky-Tonk next door. I hear they've got a great band."

His hand was large and warm and solid. The thought of it holding her close in a belt-buckle-polishing slow dance had heat blazing across her chest and puckering her nipples.

"We have a lot to talk about," she stated, and hoped he didn't hear the nervous anticipation in her voice.

CHAPTER TWELVE

THE RANCH HOUSE specialized in barbecued beef, ribs, chicken and sausage, all of which were served cafeteria-style. It was Friday, so the place was crowded. Fortunately, they seemed to have come in between the big waves of people, because after filling their plates, Alex was able to find a quiet table in a corner of the dining area.

"Your grandmother missed her calling," he said after disposing of their serving trays and sitting at an angle to Rika so they could both look out into the huge barnlike room. "She should have been a spy or a talk-show host. She has a way of eliciting information without ever giving the impression she's prompting."

Rika slathered butter on the end of a corn stick. "Gramps says she could coax Bible verses out of the Devil himself."

Alex laughed. "I believe she could." He broke off a piece of tender mesquite-smoked brisket with his fork. "Do you think Henrietta realized she was being pumped for information?"

Rika sampled coleslaw and considered the question. "I doubt it. She probably figured she was there to round out the fourth so Gram could further her matchmaking." Alex's fork stopped midway to his mouth, his blue eyes sparkling with an amused expression that seemed to ask how she felt about the notion.

The truth was, Rika was beginning to like her grandmother's meddling. That her grandmother's matchmaking didn't upset him surprised her.

"Besides," she added before Alex could make a comment on the proposition, "Henrietta obviously likes to talk. She would have found someone or something to gossip about even if Gram hadn't asked the first question."

"She'd probably still be chattering, too," he commented, "if we hadn't finally had to call it quits."

Emily had come home from Micki Sanchez's house, bubbling over with stories about the games they were playing and begging to be allowed to take Scamper and spend the night with her friend. When told she could, she dashed out to the kitchen with hardly a backward glance.

The general came home a few minutes later and reminded his wife they were attending a dinner at the country club at eight. Henrietta, realizing it was nearly seven o'clock, had bounced to her feet and barreled out, saying she hadn't gotten anything out for dinner and Harold was due home any minute.

Rika spooned up red beans and rice. "We learned more from her this afternoon than I was able to pick up all week downtown."

"Let's review," Alex suggested as he polished off the last of his German sausage.

"Well, we now know Keith Nelson, Lacy's civilian deputy, is involved in a messy divorce."

"That bit about Tilly Silvers, Eckert's secretary, playing the numbers is interesting," Alex offered.

"It goes beyond that." Rika told him about the

gambling raid Tilly'd gotten caught in. "But I didn't know she went to Vegas three or four times a year. The lady might be under severe financial strain if her luck's run out."

"It could leave her vulnerable," Alex agreed. "Especially since she has access to all the information floating through the base commander's office, including AFL schedules."

"You think she might be the leak?"

Alex shrugged. "I'll have my people check her background more closely."

Rika sipped iced tea. "Before Henrietta let the cat out of the bag, did you know about Brassard's background?"

"You mean his getting arrested for embezzling some twenty years ago? No. I wonder if he mentioned it in his security clearance."

"Would he have to if the charges were dropped?" Rika asked.

"If he was arrested and charged with a crime, he would. In fact, he should have included the information even if he was only detained."

"Maybe he figured no one would ever be able to check it."

Alex agreed. "Still, it raises questions. If he's willing to lie about a thing he could righteously claim to be innocent of, what other detail is he withholding? On the other hand, it might have been nothing more than a youthful involvement he'd prefer to forget. We'll have to see if there's anything more recent to suggest a pattern of questionable activities or associates."

"What else have we picked up?" Rika asked.

Alex pushed back his empty dinner plate and centered the small serving of peach cobbler that came with the meal in front of him. He scooped up a spoonful. ''Not much we didn't already know. Several people in the model club apparently have tempers bad enough to involve them into fisticuffs once in a while. You might check to see if other vices get them in trouble.''

He watched her nudge her plate away from the edge of the table and take a lazy sip of tea. ''You better eat your cobbler.''

''It looks good, but—''

''It is good,'' he insisted. ''So eat it. You're going to need every one of those calories for dancing, because, lady, I plan on whirling you around until you're dizzy, then holding you in my arms until the music stops.''

She regarded him under knitted brows, not quite sure how to react. She'd been about to give in to the temptation of the sweet dessert. Now she wondered if she should abandon it simply to show him he couldn't push her into something she didn't want to do—or did want to do. As for whirling her around...did he have any idea how off balance he already made her feel? Maybe the light-headedness was low blood sugar. Sure, that must be it. She pulled the shallow dish toward her.

''Hard-nosed investigative reporters,'' she commented as she picked up her spoon, ''don't get dizzy.''

A cunning smile swept across his face. ''God, I love a challenge.''

SHE KNEW she was asking for trouble when she let Alex take her hand as they crossed the busy parking lot to the entrance of the Cowboy Honky-Tonk. She'd sensed the tension, the magnetic pull, that special sexual awareness emanating from him the moment she'd opened the door at her grandparents' house that afternoon. Now the warm, gently insistent tug of his big hand threatened to melt every ounce of her resolve to resist his allure. Alex Huston was a dangerous man—dangerous because he made her want more of him.

The air was sultry inside the huge dance hall. The yeasty odor of beer competed with Chanel No 5, Brut and Stetson.

"I know now where everybody goes on Friday night in Coyote Springs, Texas," Alex commented as a hostess in skintight jeans and gold-fringed red shirt led them to a tiny table on the far side of the bandstand.

"Unless high-school football has started," Rika observed.

The bass vibrations thudding from the hardwood floor were mere echoes of the drumroll of Rika's pulse as she wrapped her hands around Alex's brawny arm. The room was crowded, but she wasn't aware of the people hemming her in, only of the compulsion to stay close to the man smiling down at her.

They ordered drinks. Dark beer for him, a frozen margarita for her. But he didn't wait for them to arrive before he invited her onto the dance floor. The ballad being played had a waltz beat. She wasn't surprised he knew how to dance. What did shock her was the momentary feeling of disappointment that his hold on her hand and hip was so light. It was absurd for her to have expected or wanted a tight embrace. They were dancing, after all, not propping each other up.

But propping up was exactly what she needed by the time the sixth number ended. His touch was buoyant, but not totally weightless—she was aware of each of his fingers just above her pelvis. He maintained a modest distance from her as he guided and spun her among the other dancers. Not so distant, however, that she didn't feel the firmness and heat of his muscles as she rested her hand on his broad shoulder. Modesty wasn't exactly on her mind, either, when the music stopped and their eyes met. In that fleeting second the noise of the room faded to a murmur, and the lights, already dim, seem to recede to vacant darkness around them. All she saw was the seductive gleam in his blue eyes.

He led her back to their table. The jukebox wailed, tinny and hollow sounding, as it tried to fill the musical void left by the band's break. They sipped their tepid drinks in silence, each self-consciously watching the die-hard dancers on the boards.

"You play a mean game of bridge," she commented, convinced conversation was what they needed to keep from gazing at each other and conveying decidedly wanton thoughts with their eyes.

"It was close there for a while." He rotated the base of his beer bottle but didn't drink. "Your grandmother's no slouch. She would have won, too, if Henrietta hadn't reneged on the last trick." The game had been a draw when they'd finally had to quit.

"Give her a rematch and she'll whup ya," Rika jested. "You're lucky Gramps wasn't her partner. You wouldn't have had a chance."

Alex laughed. "You're probably right."

The waitress came over and asked if they wanted another round. They were hardly halfway through the drinks they had, but Alex ordered cold replenishments anyway.

The band returned. Alex rose from his chair and extended his hand. Rika looked up and smiled, set her fingers in his palm and slipped out from behind the table.

The first number was a polka, followed by a Texas two-step and a lively fox trot. Rika waited, knowing it was coming—the grinding slow dance. She'd been looking forward to it, fantasizing about what it would feel like to have his body shifting intimately against her. All the time she'd worried about it, too, the way one obsesses about forbidden chocolate. Now it was here.

"Put your sweet lips a little closer to the phone," the singer crooned, and suddenly Alex's arms were enfolding her, drawing her against the solid contours of his body. Before she even realized she was doing it, Rika spread her hands on his chest and angled her head under the shelter of his chin.

Her nostrils inhaled the scent of the man as she listened to his heartbeat. Her eyes drifted closed when his fingers began gentle kneading contractions on her back. A fluttering restlessness filled her bosom. Heat built, simmered and settled lower. Thought drifted away until all that remained were the sensations of warmth and strength and sweet, tormenting desire.

She was jarred when suddenly Alex clasped his hands just below her shoulders and eased her away. His knowing smile melted her. The music had changed to a fast number. She hadn't even noticed.

"It's getting crowded in here," he murmured in her ear. "Maybe we ought to go somewhere more... private."

Her heartbeat picked up. She should say no, but the word wouldn't come out. All she could do was nod.

They slipped back to their table. Alex tossed some bills on it to pay for their drinks. His hand grasping her elbow, he piloted Rika to the door.

The night air was no cooler than the inside of the building, but it was fresher, the soft breeze caressing, stimulating. As they made their way across the parking lot, Alex bracketed the back of her neck with the fingers of one hand, while his arm sent heat waves coursing down her spine. He opened the car door for her and closed it after she got in, then went around to his side and climbed behind the wheel.

"Where are we going?" she asked, her voice shy and husky.

"I thought we might go to my place for a nightcap." He started the engine. With one hand on the wheel, he reached across the narrow seat with the other and squeezed her shoulder. "Is that all right?"

Her mind warned her against it, but her heart didn't listen. "Okay."

Alex grinned, his eyes grazing her. He shifted into gear and backed the vehicle out of its parking space.

Dimming his lights, Alex slowed the Ford as he approached the base guard shack. At the gate he reached into his back pocket, extracted his wallet and flashed his identification card. The sentry stepped out of the small building, glanced at the sticker on the windshield, noted Alex's upraised credential and waved him through.

Alex turned left onto the narrow road that led to his quarters. The night was dark, the street deserted. He pulled into the spot in front of his doorway and doused the lights.

"You've moved up," Rika noted approvingly. "VIP quarters."

"Thanks to your grandfather." Alex got out.

Crickets chirped. Their tinny, rustling sounds served only to emphasize his own agitation as he walked around the back of the vehicle. Rika hadn't budged. Was she having second thoughts? He opened her door, and to his immense relief she accepted his proffered hand without hesitation.

Touching the small of her back, he escorted her up the narrow walk to the paneled wooden door of the Cactus Suite.

Off in the distance a coyote bayed at the moon, a wailing complaint of loneliness and unrequited love. Its sadness heightened Alex's awareness of the woman standing silently by his side. Her aura was close enough to make his fingers unsteady as he inserted the key card and pushed the door open. He reached through, flipped on a light and motioned her to precede him.

She paused in the middle of the large room while he switched on a table lamp beside the couch facing an entertainment center. After walking over to the cabinet, he opened the door, ignored the TV and switched on the radio to a quiet music station.

"What would you like to drink?" he asked over his shoulder. "I can make coffee." He turned and his pounding heart almost stopped. She'd hitched her hip on the back of the couch, the soft light settling on her curves disconcertingly reminding him that he was a man and she was a woman. He took a deep, steadying breath. "There's decaf, and a variety of soft drinks. Or perhaps you'd like something stronger. They furnished me with a well-stocked bar."

"Maybe just some water." She smiled at the nervousness his babbling implied. "You haven't made me dizzy, like you promised, but all that dancing has given me a thirst."

And me a greater hunger for the feel of you. He detoured into the tiny kitchen for ice and a glass.

"You didn't sound especially pleased when you said Gramps got you these quarters," she commented when he returned.

"I'm very grateful now." He wouldn't have considered taking her to the shabby room overlooking the pool.

"But not then." She lifted an eyebrow. "Why?"

A woman who'd had the privileges of being a general's granddaughter thrust at her all her life probably wouldn't understand his answer. "I like to earn my perks."

"You don't think you deserve this?"

"I didn't say that."

He opened the bottle of spring water he'd snagged from the refrigerator, poured it and handed it to her. He watched her sip and felt his own mouth go dry as her lips puckered on the edge of the glass.

"Aren't you going to have anything?" she asked, her long lashes blinking slowly as she studied him.

He narrowed the distance separating them, curled his fingers around the upper half of the glass, letting his palm cover the back of her hand. "I'll share with you."

Gazing into her eyes, he brought the cool drink to his lips but only wetted them before prying the tumbler from her grasp. After placing it precariously on the end table, he nestled his hands on her hips and touched his forehead to hers. Violin music swelled in the background.

"I want to make love to you, Rika," he murmured, the deep rumble of his voice adding to the tumult already ravaging her insides. "I've wanted to from the first moment I saw you."

She raised her hands to his shoulders, felt the quiver of excitement beneath their hard mass, saw the pleading seduction in his deep blue eyes. Her knees turned to jelly, forcing her to tighten her hold.

He dragged his lips across hers, watched her eyelids flutter, and completed the kiss. He probed, sampled, tested, challenged. Her responses were tentative at first. Then his tongue met hers, and all hesitation evaporated. Her arms pulled him closer. With one hand slipping behind her back, he crept the other up from her waist, along her ribs to the side of her breast. He caressed it. Its fullness and warmth threatened to undermine his tenuous control.

The sensation of his hands skimming along her body had blood racing to places that were already too hot for comfort. She gave a soft mew as their mouths separated. The shadowed features of his face, the yearning passion in his eyes, made her body ache for more of him. Lacing her fingers behind his neck, she drew his face down to hers. This time she didn't wait for his tongue to prod but met it halfway, then plunged and taunted, toyed and savored. His elation was an erotic jolt, a sudden blaze, like brandy tossed in a sizzling skillet.

His embrace glided over her—insistent, yet incredibly gentle, as if he were afraid to fully possess, wary she would pull away. He needn't have worried. She didn't know when she'd passed the point of no return.

She only knew that it was behind her. There would be no retreat now. To confirm it she ran her hands across his chest, outlined its sculptured ridges. Snap by snap she opened his shirt, yanked it out of his waistband and slid it down his wide shoulders. Half holding her breath, she tangled her fingers in the wiry mesh of fine silver hair. The sensuous allure of a wet T-shirt couldn't compare with the erotic feel of his firm flesh under her hands.

He fumbled with the buttons of her blouse. His warm fingers skimmed her breasts, making her simmering blood boil. She lowered her arms, slipped out of the clinging silk and let it trail to the floor. He reached behind her and unsnapped her bra. The release had her sucking in her breath and holding it as his hands drew away the confining material. The fire turned to liquid lust as he fondled her peaked nipples.

"I got it wrong," he muttered as he brought his mouth down to one erect bud. He suckled, then released. "I'm the one who's dizzy." He drew the other nipple between his teeth, his tongue flicking its sensitive tip. A high, breathless sigh escaped her slack jaw.

"Maybe you ought to lie down." She threw her head back, her spine arching as electrical shock waves slammed through her.

Suddenly, her head was swirling. Her reflexes had her clinging to his neck even before she realized he'd lifted her into his arms and was carrying her into his bedroom.

"I HAVE TO GO."

Alex felt the sudden panic of abandonment as Rika slipped off the side of the king-size bed. He watched her, naked and alluring, start across the carpet. He couldn't let her go, couldn't bear to have her leave him. No woman had ever made him feel the way she did. Strong. Confident. Content. Was this what they called happiness? If it wasn't, he would settle for it. Paradise couldn't be much better.

He jumped up and snuggled behind her, snaking his hands across her belly, feeling her silken breasts against his forearms, making him doubly aware of his own nakedness.

"Why?" He nuzzled her ear. "It's early yet."

Subtly he pivoted her back toward the bed. The digital clock on the nightstand glowed 4:30. Sunrise wouldn't be for two more hours. "There's still time—"

She leaned her shoulders against his chest. "I want to be home when the folks get up."

He was tempted to remind her she didn't need their permission to stay out after midnight. He nibbled the soft flesh between her neck and shoulder. "Don't you imagine they have a pretty good idea where you are— and with whom?"

"Having an idea and knowing are two different things."

He planted a kiss behind her ear, murmuring, "Do you think they would disapprove?"

She tilted her head, wilted by his hot breath tormenting her sensitized skin.

"They would disapprove of indiscretion." She cradled her arms on his. "I have Emily to consider."

"She's at Micki's house, remember?"

Rika made a pawing movement with her fingers, as if to pull his hands away.

He loosened his hold but didn't release her. "Are

you sorry you came here?'' he whispered in her ear. ''Do you regret spending the night with me?''

She spun around, her bare breasts brushing against his arm before coming in contact with his chest. The sensation sent carnal tremors shooting through his entire body. He groaned with pleasure. She smiled up at him, her lips unbearably tempting, her eyes aware.

''I'm not sorry, Alex.'' Her words were as satiny as the feel of her flesh against his. She skimmed her hands along his thick pectoral muscles, her thumbs teasing his small flat nipples, making them harden. It wasn't the only part of his anatomy responding. ''This night was very special.''

He curled a finger under her chin and lifted. He wanted desperately to kiss her mouth, to taste her acceptance. He locked his eyes on hers. ''But.''

She lowered her gaze. ''I wasn't planning on a man in my life just now.'' She hugged him tighter and pressed her cheek to his chest. ''I'm not ready to get involved.''

Not ready to fall in love. He'd always thought he was immune. But then, he'd never known what the words meant until he'd met Rika. He buried a kiss in her soft brown hair and laid his chin on the top of her head. ''I am.''

She could hear his heart beating, feel his bare skin against hers, feel his arousal. ''Oh, Alex, I wish I could be sure.''

I'm the one who should be afraid, he wanted to tell her. *I've never been in love before. I've never known I could need a woman the way I need you.* Love was as intoxicating as vintage wine. It was scary and glorious and made him thirsty for more.

He eased her back to the bed. ''Let me help you

make up your mind,'' he murmured in her ear, then rolled his tongue along its curves. ''Let me convince you.''

It was six o'clock when Alex drove Rika to her grandparents' home. The moon looked small now, as if it were backing away from the mischief it had caused. The sky overhead was still pitch-black, but the stars would soon be fading. In the east the velvet horizon was paling to dull charcoal.

He kissed her lightly on the lips in the entranceway of the Tierses' residence, then took the key from her hand and quietly rotated the tumblers of the lock. With the door barely cracked open, he kissed her again, this time making sure the sweetness lingered.

''This afternoon at two,'' he reminded her in hushed tones, straining to keep his hands off her. ''At my quarters. Lattimore will have the latest reports analyzed by then, and we can go over the details.''

''Two o'clock.'' She bit her lip as she looked into his eyes and saw her own desire reflected in them. ''I'll be there.'' She raised her hand to the scratchy stubble of beard. *I love you* was on the tip of her tongue, but she managed to rein the fateful words in before they escaped. She cared for him, wanted him, but she couldn't, wouldn't, say she loved him. Not yet. Not until she knew with more than her body that they were right for each other.

He kissed her soft palm. ''I'll be waiting.'' He trailed his hand before him as he backed to his car. He'd left the engine running, calculating this would be less disruptive than restarting it. After quietly opening the door, he slid behind the wheel and blew her a kiss, shifted into gear and rolled discreetly down the driveway.

"DID MAJOR HUSTON take you dancing?" Barbara asked when they sat down to breakfast a little after eight that morning.

"Yes, to the Cowboy Honky-Tonk." Rika took a much-needed sip of coffee and let the caffeine work its way through her system.

"Is he a good dancer?"

Rika nodded absently. "Quite light on his feet, actually."

And swept me off mine right into his bed.

"That's nice, dear."

Out of the corner of her eye, Rika watched her grandmother mask her annoyance at not getting more information.

Nathan Tiers drank half his small glass of orange juice in one gulp and turned from the headlines to the obituaries on page two of the morning paper. "How is your research coming? I understand you're doing a feature on the flying club."

He was checking up on her. She wasn't upset. "I have an appointment today at two o'clock to gather some more details. I don't really have enough so far."

He observed her for only a second, but it was enough to register his understanding that the investigation she and Alex were conducting had not yet yielded significant progress.

How angry at her was he? she wondered. Or maybe the right word was *disappointed*. He'd taken her confession without apparent emotion, asked a few pertinent questions, then suggested she might be in a position to help Alex resolve the problem. There had been no preaching, no accusations of disrespect or ingratitude. It might have been better if he had ranted, she decided. At least then she'd know where she stood. She loved him too much to live with indifference.

Her heart still aching, she tried to concentrate on the sports page in front of her.

"I'm sure when she and Alex have it worked out," Barbara said, her concentration never shifting from the advice-to-the-lovelorn page, "you'll be among the first to know, dear."

CHAPTER THIRTEEN

RIKA DROVE TO THE BASE shortly before two o'clock. Taking her grandfather's Cadillac had been his idea. No one would question the vehicle's presence anywhere on the installation, he pointed out. Maybe he wasn't so indifferent or angry after all. He didn't have to make things easy for her, but he was. She'd given him a big kiss on the cheek when he handed her the keys.

The sentry on duty, seeing the four-star emblem beside the base decal on the windshield, popped a rigid salute and waved her through. She was always uncomfortable with the procedure. She knew the guard was saluting the rank, not the person, yet it seemed impolite not to acknowledge the courtesy. Since she had never been in the military, though, it wasn't correct for her to salute back. The best she could do was smile and wave.

Alex's Ford was the only car parked in front of his quarters. Either Lattimore hadn't yet arrived, was hoofing it on base, or he'd parked at a prudent distance. A swarm of butterflies fluttered in Rika's stomach as she walked up the narrow path she and Alex had strolled the night before. She remembered the warmth of his hand on the small of her back, the light-headedness of anticipation when he'd motioned her ahead of him into the semidark quarters. She knew she was entering a dangerous world. Dangerous and exciting and definitely full of adventure.

She'd had half a day to contemplate his question: was she sorry they'd spent the night together? She'd never imagined the level of pleasures she'd experienced in the bed of Major Alex Huston. She'd never felt more loved. Maybe the two were inextricably related. All she could be sure of at the moment was that his question went far beyond sex and gratification. Somehow he'd managed to touch her soul—and it frightened her.

Her insides quivered as she tapped on the solid wood door, too lightly at first, then too boldly.

Her heart hitched when the door flew open, then chugged into the slow motion of disappointment when she saw Mike Lattimore again in camouflage uniform standing in front of her.

"Hi, Rika. Right on time."

"Hello, Mike." She took two paces inside, waited for him to close the door and allowed him to direct her to the couch. "Where's Alex?"

"I'm right here." He stuck his head through the doorway from the kitchen. "What can I get you to drink?"

She didn't need caffeine. Her pulse was already tripping. "Seven-Up or Sprite, if you have it."

"Your wish is my command." He disappeared once more into the tiny cubicle.

"I understand your grandmother plays a mean game of bridge," Mike commented as he settled into one of the two easy chairs facing her.

Concentrate on the card game, Rika thought to herself, not the slow dancing that followed or the different rhythms they'd explored still later. "The major held his own against formidable odds."

Mike laughed. "He always was a charmer with the ladies."

It was ridiculous for her to feel a twitch of jealousy at the remark. She had no illusions that there hadn't been other women in his life. He was a man of the world who had acted tenderly and responsibly. He'd been very careful about using protection.

The subject of their discussion came through the doorway carrying a small tray with three glasses of iced drinks. "What would you know about charm?"

"I must have had it at one time," Mike retorted with a chuckle. "I won the hand of a lovely lady."

Rika watched Alex. He seemed about ready to make a smart comeback, then caught her eye and apparently reconsidered. He took the other chair facing her.

"Anything of interest on the phone taps?" he asked his team chief.

"Nothing conclusive. Your intelligence on Tilly Silvers having gambling fever clarifies some of the things we've heard her talk about on the phone. Seems she's in debt up to her zircon-jeweled ears." Mike took a piece of paper from his lapel pocket and handed it to Rika. "Here's the name and telephone number of the person she's been talking to downtown. I suspect he's a loan shark. You might want to check him out."

"Thanks."

"Anything else?" Alex asked.

"Brassy's going on leave next week, apparently to visit a friend in San Antonio. But you probably know that from the WAR."

"War?" Rika asked.

"Weekly Activity Report," Lattimore clarified.

Alex nodded. "Rika, I'd like you to tap your source and see what you can find out about Louisa Hartmann."

The name didn't mean anything to her. She wrote it down on the notepad she took out of her handbag. "Louisa. Spell the last name." He did. "Who is she and what exactly are you looking for?"

"Nothing specific. I just have a gut feeling. She's Lacy's secretary. Her continued standoffishness bothers me. Not exactly West Texas friendly. She's defensive about something. I'd like to know what it is."

They spent the better part of the next hour talking about personalities and how they might be involved with the missing drone. Rika tried to be circumspect in the way she watched Alex. When she saw him cross one knee over the other, it was hard not to recall the feel of his legs beside hers, between hers.

At last the meeting ended and the three of them rose from their seats. Rika checked her watch and was surprised to see it was nearly four o'clock. They were almost to the doorway, when Alex patted her on the arm and asked her to stay a minute. "I have something else I need to talk to you about."

"I'm off," Mike said as he opened the door. He shot Rika an amused glance, making her wonder how much he'd guessed about what was going on between her and Alex. "See you later."

The door had hardly closed before Alex swept her into his arms. His mouth consumed hers, his eagerness matched by her response. Her breasts swelled and her nipples grew taut as his hand gently fondled.

"I missed you," he purred in her ear.

She leaned back and grinned at him. "It's only been a few hours."

"Too many hours," he muttered.

He toyed with the top button of her blouse, and would have undressed her right there, had she let him.

"I need to go," she objected, nervously pushing his hands away.

"Tonight," he begged.

"I don't know," she demurred. "Emily will be home, and the folks."

"Emily has to go to bed," he observed. "And your grandparents are not your keepers." When she still hesitated, he said, "Here's an idea. Why don't you and Emily have dinner with your folks at the house? I'll come by around seven and the three of us can go to the miniature golf course I saw down by the river when I was driving around town. Then, after we take her home and put her to bed, you and I can spend the rest of the evening together. Here."

Rika stared at him, unable to keep a smile off her face. He had it all planned. She hadn't missed his allusion to their saying good-night to Emily together.

"Would you like to join us for dinner?"

He trailed a fingertip from the bridge of her nose to the tip. "I've got work to do. For some reason my concentration has been off all day."

There was a knock on the door.

Alex closed his eyes and released Rika. "Mike must have forgotten something." He practically stomped to the door and flung it open.

"Alex!"

He stood there motionless, and Rika wished she could see his face. It took a moment for her to realize why he had gone so still. On the other side of the doorway stood a tall redheaded woman. The bright backdrop of daylight shaded her features, but Rika could see enough to realize she was both statuesque and beautiful.

"Justine! What are you doin—"

"Hi, honey." The visitor threw her arms around his neck and kissed him on the mouth.

Rika watched dumbfounded. This was no sister or cousin, or casual friend.

Alex lifted his hands and gently removed hers. "How did you get on base?"

"In your car, silly. Your windshield sticker did the trick. The guard at the gate waved me right through without asking all kinds of dumb questions like when I'm driving my car. He even saluted. He was sort of cute, too."

"I didn't know you were going to show up today," he muttered. "Why didn't you call?"

"I told you I'd be here this weekend." She patted his cheek again and stepped around him into the room, halting when she saw Alex wasn't alone.

Anger, shame and humiliation exploded within Rika. She felt her face grow hot and her hands ball into fists. Alex had made a fool of her. He'd used her. He was everything she'd been afraid of, everything she'd expected: a selfish, self-centered, manipulative, fighter-pilot playboy. She refused, however, to let mere mortification rob her of her dignity.

"Excuse me, Major. I'm sure you want some privacy, so I'll leave you alone. Thank you for taking the time to see me. I won't be bothering you again. I've got all the information I need."

He spun around. "Rika..." The word was a stunned plea.

For what? she wondered. There was nothing more he could possibly ask from her. He'd gotten what he wanted: her in his bed. As he'd told her just last night, he'd lusted after her the first time he'd seen her.

She bent over the coffee table, picked up her notepad and stuffed it into her purse. For a moment her vision blurred. From anger, she told herself, not from sorrow, not from pain. It was fury, not remorse, that had her chest aching and her stomach clenching in sickening spasms. She straightened and moved toward the door.

"Rika," he repeated softly as she slipped past him. He put out his hand to grab her arm. In the narrow entranceway it was impossible for her to avoid his touch. Almost blind now, she struggled to maintain her composure. Shrugging out of his reach, she extended her hand and clasped his in a cold, businesslike handshake. "Good luck with your career, sir."

She wheeled around, gave the barest nod to the other woman and proceeded in what she hoped was a ladylike fashion toward her grandfather's Cadillac. She could barely hear Alex's voice calling to her, only vaguely perceive his presence by the side of the car when she started the engine. She backed with supreme care into the roadway. She certainly didn't want to scratch the Jaguar parked alongside her.

"JUSTINE, HONEY, I know you came here expecting me to spend some time with you...and I thought I'd be able to—"

He was having trouble concentrating on words. All he could see was Rika's ravaged face. He'd done that to her, twisted her beauty into a mask of pain.

Justine stood in the middle of the room, examining

the two glasses on the end table. She eyed him curiously. "Who was she?"

"She?"

A cynical grin bowed her mouth. "The woman who just left, Alex."

"Oh," he replied, "a reporter."

The grin faded and nearly formed a frown as she pulled in her chin and stared at him. "A reporter? I've never known you to be chummy with journalists before. In fact, I seem to remember a few remarks of yours about newshounds that weren't—"

"This is a special situation."

She ran her tongue across her teeth. "I can see that."

He'd moved over to the wet bar, not because he needed or wanted a drink, but because he had to do something. She slid in front of him and ran a long fingernail along the line of his jaw. He froze.

"Why do I get the impression you're not pleased to see me—"

"It's great seeing you," he lied.

She ignored his statement and let her fingers continue their course down his neck to his collarbone and across the front of his shirt. "And that I just showed up at a very inopportune moment."

When he didn't respond to her words or her touch, she backed off and threw herself onto the couch. Peeking up at him, the gleam under her mascaraed lashes dancing with amusement, she said, "Your female friend was trying very hard to be blasé, Alex, but her heart was pounding so hard I could almost hear it."

"I...uh..." Damn, but he'd become more tongue-tied since he'd arrived in Coyote Springs than he'd

been since he was thirteen and asked Geraldine Cou-
lahan out on his first date.

"She's not just another woman, is she?" Justine's
expression conveyed a strange combination of pity
and mirth. "You love her, don't you?"

There was only one answer he could give. "Yes."

She chuckled and pointed to the chair across the
coffee table from her.

"Sit down, Alex, before you fall down."

"I don't believe it," she went on after a moment's
contemplation. "Alex Huston, confirmed bachelor, in
love." She viewed him with supreme delight. "But
it must be true." She chortled. "I can't think of anything else that could make you look so miserable."

"I..." he started, and dropped onto an easy chair.
"Tell me about her."

It didn't take long to explain the situation—that
Rika was here on vacation from Michigan, that she
had an eight-year-old daughter, that her grandfather
was a retired four-star general and her grandmother a
conniving, manipulative and totally delightful little
old lady.

"I'm happy for you, Alex," Justine finally responded. "Really I am. I just wish you'd let me know
before I'd spent two days driving your precious car
here. I could have brought a friend to keep me company."

He smiled for the first time. "I bet you have them
lined up." Justine was a trooper.

She snorted. "You bet I do. Young men with *dark*
hair." Her glowing grin was marred by a flash of
nostalgia. "Send me a wedding invitation."

"Sure."

She laughed heartily this time. "Don't worry, pal,

I won't show up. It's just that I'm a sucker for those stories that end with 'happily ever after.'"

He reimbursed her for the expenses she'd incurred on her trip, then added a generous bonus.

"Hey, what's this for?" She sounded offended.

"You have to change planes in Dallas," he reminded her, the way he would have a kid sister if he'd had one. "Make it a stopover and buy yourself a trinket or two at Neiman Marcus. On me."

She patted his cheek. "I wonder if your Rika knows what a nice guy she's hooked."

On the short drive from the local airport after dropping Justine off and buying her airline ticket, Alex was hardly aware of his luxury car's polished wood dashboard, its shiny buttons and dials. Only the warm suppleness of soft leather seats registered, in ways that had nothing to do with road transportation.

He didn't give a thought to the possibility of damage to the shiny finish of his car as he kicked up gravel screeching to a stop in the driveway of the Tiers residence.

He shifted from one foot to the other, waiting for Sera to open the door. She greeted him with an easy smile, which quickly faded when she saw the sour expression on his face.

"Is Rika in?" he asked, without even trying to disguise his wretchedness.

Sera nodded and stepped back, allowing him to enter.

Barbara appeared from the living room. "Major, how nice. Rika didn't tell me you were coming to dinner, but now that you're here—" She paused, fixing him with suddenly anxious eyes. "Is something wrong?"

"I've got to see Rika." The words came out in a whoosh.

"She's down at the barn." The old woman's pale-blue eyes studied Alex's face, and he could see her trying to divine the situation. "Has something happened?"

"I just need to talk to her," he explained. "Is it all right if I go out through the kitchen?"

"Yes, of course. But—"

"Thanks." He veered around the two women, made a beeline down the hall and out the back door. Half marching, half running to the metal structure behind the house, he entered its shadows, only vaguely registering its relative coolness. Because he was snow-blind from the bright sunlight, his other senses locked onto Rika moving into the tack room to his right. A few long strides brought him to the doorway.

"Rika, honey." His voice trembled with uncertainty.

She had her back to him. The ache in Alex turned to a slicing pain when he watched her posture stiffen at his calling her name. She said nothing, didn't turn to face him, did nothing voluntary to acknowledge his presence. He'd been expecting heat, not this coldness.

"Rika, please listen."

She reached down, opened a cabinet door, grabbed a rubber currycomb and bristle brush and placed them on the counter.

"You don't understand," he said. "It isn't what you think."

She opened a drawer and removed electric clippers.

"Rika, she brought me my car."

From a second drawer she took out a spray can of Kool Lube and a bottle of blade wash.

"Damn it, Rika, say something."

She whirled around, snagged a metal bucket hanging from a hook on the wall, dumped her grooming supplies into it, took a step toward him, made eye contact and paused. "I have nothing to say to you, Major," she declared in an icy, calm voice. She skirted around him and went to Dark Thunder, who was haltered and cross-tied in the middle of the barn aisle.

Alex spun on his heels and followed her. Fists tight, jaw clamped, he inhaled deeply through his nose, hoping oxygen would dull the hot edge of his rage. Whether at this point it was at Rika, Justine or himself, he wasn't completely sure.

Rika made circular strokes with the currycomb, moving from the horse's shoulder to flank. Alex strode up to the adjacent stall gate and stood there. "Rika, I'm sorry."

Her grooming produced dust, dirt and loose hair, which scattered to the floor. "For what?" Her words were as frigid as teardrops from an icicle. "The lady was only delivering your car, after all."

"Then why are you so angry?"

She continued her ministrations on the docile animal. "I'm not angry."

"Well, you're doing a damn good imitation," he snapped, and instantly regretted it. He was trying to win her over, not put her back up. Except it was already stiff and unyielding. "If you're not angry, what are you?"

She waited a moment to respond, then stabbed him with the pain in her eyes. "I'm stupid, Alex."

She extracted the hoof pick from the bucket, bent over, lifted the horse's right front foot. "I knew from the moment I met you that you couldn't be trusted," she stated as she cleaned. "But I tried to kid myself. Emily adored you. Gram was convinced you were the answer to all her prayers for me. Gramps had only high praise for you." She moved over to the left leg. After cleaning around the shoe, she straightened and faced Alex squarely. "So I cast my instincts aside and made a fool of myself."

"Oh, sweetheart." Her self-recrimination had his gut twisting, his heart aching. He took a step forward, but she turned her back on him. He tried to put his hands on her shoulders.

"Don't." She wiggled out from beneath his touch.

She sounded so wounded, so vulnerable. He wanted to hold her in his arms, hug her, make her believe in him, in herself. Instead he dropped his hands to his sides. "Justine drove my Jag out here for me. That's all," he insisted.

Rika's eyes were narrowed when she confronted him this time. "I saw how she looked at you, Alex, the way she touched you." Her words were a hopeless murmur. "Are you going to insult me by saying her kiss was purely platonic?"

He wanted to laugh, tell her it had all been a joke somebody had put Justine up to, that he hardly knew her. But he couldn't lie to this woman, not if he ever expected her to trust him. Her grandmother was right. It came down to trust.

"On her part, no," he answered.

Rika moved away from the animal, dropped the pick in the bucket and took up the clippers.

"But we're not talking about her," Alex insisted. "We're talking about you and me."

She plugged the long cord of the clippers into a wall socket, flipped the toggle, listened to the appliance's buzz, sprayed the blades with lubricant and shut it off. "You are. I'm not. Because there is no 'you and me,' Alex. There's you and whatever her name is."

"Justine. She's in the past."

Rika made an ugly snorting sound. "Past? Yeah, about two hours past." She moved closer to the bay gelding, flipped the switch and proceeded to trim the long whiskers around the animal's muzzle.

"She means nothing—" he started, but the whine of the clippers drowned out his voice.

He stepped over to Rika, locked his fingers around her wrist and cut the power on the device in her hand. He could feel her pulse pounding. He liked to know he could make her blood heat and race—but not this way.

"She means nothing to me, sweetheart. I swear. She's already gone. I sent her home."

Rika extracted her hand from his. "That's too bad." She put her finger back on the on-off switch. "You're probably going to miss her. Unless you can pick up somebody else while you're here."

This time when she turned on the infernal machine, he walked over to the wall outlet and ripped out the cord.

"Don't!" he snarled, and had the satisfaction of seeing her head pop up in surprise. "Call me whatever you like. You've obviously made up your mind that I fit some stereotype you've created in your head, that because I'm a pilot I'm not good enough for you.

Fine. That's your prerogative. But don't," he barked, and paused, "don't you dare cheapen yourself. What we had last night was not a one-night stand. It wasn't for you—otherwise you wouldn't be so upset. And it wasn't for me, no matter what you may choose to think."

The silence between them was palpable, filled only by the nickering of horses and the shuffling of their hooves on straw.

"Hi, Major."

Alex spun around to find Emily standing by the open doorway. Time for attitude readjustment. He let his face relax into the smile that came easily with children, especially Rika's daughter.

"Hi, Peanut. Neat boots."

She looked down at the shiny, pale-blue Ropers he'd bought her. The girl's face lit up. "Yeah, everybody says they're awesome. Gram wants to know if you can stay for dinner. We're having lamb chops, my favorite, and Gram says there's plenty, even for a man with your appetite."

Rika smirked at him, then shifted her attention to her daughter. "No, sweetheart. The major won't be able to stay. He's very busy and has to get back to work."

"Is he going riding with us by the river tomorrow?"

Rika glared up at him, her expression challenging him to contradict what she was about to say. "He's going to be busy then, too, honey."

An idea suddenly struck him. It was sneaky, underhanded and would probably make Rika mad as hell, but she was obviously determined to be angry at him anyway.

"Your mother's right," Alex agreed, crouching down to be at the girl's level. "Actually, what I have to do tomorrow is go to a very special show, an exhibition. Have you ever watched people fly model airplanes?"

Emily shook her head. "Shawn has a model airplane. He showed it to me once, but I've never seen him fly it. Is he going to be there?"

"I don't know." Alex paused. Opportunity was knocking. Better take advantage of it. "Say, I have an idea. Why don't you and your friends come with me. Shawn can fly his plane, and we can all watch. How does that sound?"

The child started bouncing up and down on the balls of her feet. "Can we, Mom? Huh? Can we?"

He'd definitely gotten to Rika. If looks could kill...

"We're riding tomorrow, remember?"

"Oh, yeah," Alex said fatalistically, and rose to his feet. "Well, it'll just be me then. Besides, Shawn may have other plans, too."

"He'll want to fly his plane. I know he will. Can we go, Mom? Please?"

Alex studied Rika. If he could spend some time with her, he was sure he could make her see she was the only woman for him. He watched a barrage of emotions, mostly anger, shadow her face and linger in her eyes. Glorious green eyes with tiny gold specks. Even when they were seething at him.

"We'll have to check with his mother—"

"Oh, thank you, Mommy. I'll call him right now." Emily darted at full speed from the barn toward the house.

Rika waited a minute before saying anything. "I

don't like being coerced, Alex, and I don't appreciate your using my daughter to get to me.''

"This isn't about us, Rika. You and me. I have a mission to accomplish, a mystery to solve, a bad guy to catch. Tomorrow we'll fly another drone, see where it goes and whom it might lead me to. Apparently now that you've decided to dismiss me from your life, you've given up on your story, too. Actually, I'm glad. I didn't want you in on it to begin with—as you might recall.''

He couldn't deny he was manipulating her. But what else could he do? He had to get her to listen to him. Maybe he wasn't handling this correctly, but he didn't see any alternative.

He lifted his hand to brush a finger down her cheek, but she instantly pulled away. "We wouldn't have to play these games if only you would listen to me—''

"Listen? To what? Excuses? Explanations? Rationalizations?'' She stepped back. "I don't have to listen to you to know the truth, Alex. I've seen it. You want us at the model fly-by tomorrow. Fine. But if you think you can sweet-talk me into your bed again you're wrong.''

"It's not my bed I want you in, Rika.''

She blinked at him, momentarily stunned and perhaps hurt by his sudden rejection. "Then I won't disappoint you.''

"Not *just* in my bed," he murmured close to her ear. "I want you in my life, Rika. Don't you understand? I love—''

"Oh, I understand all right," she snapped, refusing to let him finish. "You'll do or say anything to further your agenda. Well, you'd better adjust your goals, Major, because it won't happen. I'm not going to get in your bed or be a part of your life. You don't love me, and I don't love you."

He'd never known how deeply words could cut. He closed his eyes and opened them again. "Will you be there tomorrow with the kids?"

"We'll be there. But let's get something straight. We're coming tomorrow, not because you manipulated me into it, but because it's important to my story."

"Yes, of course, your story. The one that's going to make you rich and famous."

She awarded him a cruel smile. "It won't make me rich, and I doubt it will make me famous. But it *is* going to give me a great deal of satisfaction."

CHAPTER FOURTEEN

THERE WAS AN AIR of festivity as people unloaded models from the backs of pickup trucks and vans. The flying craft varied in size and design, from simple gliders to barnstorming biplanes, to sleek fighters with sharks' teeth bared. Alex had chosen the role of observer, letting Lacy and his people handle the second drone and all the support equipment that went with it. Riley Cavanaugh, out of uniform, was also present, playing tourist and asking questions.

It was almost two o'clock, and the August heat was intense. Within a few hours the air would be too thick for the little aircraft to be flown. At the moment, the biggest concern was the windsock. A breeze always seemed to be blowing in West Texas, so the people gathered for this event were not only accustomed to it but enjoyed the challenge. There was a limit, however, past which even their practiced skills couldn't cope.

Alex surveyed the crowd. No sign yet of Rika or the kids. Had she changed her mind, decided horseback riding was a safer pastime than being with him? Unlikely. She wanted her story, if only so she could rub his nose in it. Besides, she'd given her word to Emily, and he didn't think she would break a promise to her daughter unless something really serious inter-

250 THE MAJOR COMES TO TEXAS

vened. Could she be ill? Have had an accident? Cold dread soured his belly.

Then he saw the van coming down the middle of the runway. He sucked in a chestful of air and let it out. She was all right. She was here. He was startled when he saw her grandfather get out on the passenger side.

The children poured through the sliding door and ran up to Alex with enthusiastic greetings. The general followed at a vigorous pace. He raised his hand and waved. Alex waved in reply, observing that Rika held back. Because of him? Or was it to take in the scene. He noticed she carried her tote bag. Undoubtedly, a steno pad was tucked inside, waiting to be filled with details for her article about the High Flyers Model Club and a missing stealth drone.

"Haven't been out on this old runway in years," the general said as he shook Alex's hand. "I can tell you, it brings back memories." He glanced at the models scattered about. "As I recall, the planes were a little bigger then, though."

Alex ushered the old gentleman from one group to another. Many of the RCers knew Tiers and greeted him with familiarity but always with deference. He addressed many of them by name.

Over his shoulder, Alex spied Rika trailing behind. She'd taken out a camera and started to snap pictures. Smiling, she questioned the enthusiastic hobbyists about their creations. What were they models of? How long did it take to build them? How were they powered and controlled? Alex decided the best thing he could do under the circumstances was to give her space.

He gathered up the children and took them on a

tour of the planes being prepared for flight, saving the best for last. Off from the others, Riley Cavanaugh, the easygoing farm boy, crouched over the second of three stealth models the lab had built.

Alex had personally and very thoroughly inspected the bird the night before. Today, he'd meticulously examined it again before handing it over to one of Lacy's people. He also made sure a member of his intel team was close by to keep the airman and the aircraft under close surveillance.

Lacy himself was there, as well, but was hardly the PR image of conviviality. He scowled, snapping orders and complaints that were totally inappropriate for what was supposed to be a fun day in the sun.

Neither Nelson nor Brassard was present. This test flight hadn't been scheduled until Saturday afternoon—at Alex's behest—too late to get the information into the WAR. For the two civil servants to come out on a Sunday would have required the base commander's advance approval in writing for overtime. It was a technicality that could be waived in an emergency, which this didn't constitute. Brassard was also signed out on leave. Only a genuine crisis would justify calling him back to work.

Cavanaugh turned out to be a tremendous asset. The freckle-faced airman showed sincere respect and deference for the aged general; at the same time he bonded with the kids like a big brother.

"I really like your Canberra," he told Shawn, who was holding it protectively. "Did you make it yourself? Wow, you did a good job."

The youngster clearly relished the approval, but his real interest was in the sleek black job that resembled a Star Wars space fighter. The other kids oohed and aahed at the sharp lines of the triangular-shaped craft, with its sinister, rapier appearance.

"It looks just like the one the man has down the street from my uncle," Shawn commented as he ran his hands along the pebbly surface of the wing.

Alex raised an eyebrow. "Man down the street?" He tried to be casual as he asked the next question. "Who's that?"

"I don't know his name," Shawn replied as he knelt on the hot concrete and peeked underneath the fuselage. "He's not real friendly." He straightened and brushed off his hands. "But I saw him carrying a model just like this into his house the last time my mom and me went to see Uncle Bill."

Cavanaugh sent the major a meaningful glance.

"When was that?" Alex asked.

Shawn shrugged. "A couple, three weeks ago, maybe."

"Where does your uncle live?"

"306 Hamilton."

Alex recognized the street name and the staff member who lived at 325. In order to confirm what he already suspected, he asked, "Can you describe the man?"

"He's just a guy. Not as big as you. Like that guy over there." Shawn pointed to a middle-aged man a dozen yards away who stood perhaps five-eleven and had a little potbelly.

"Was he fat?"

"Naw, skinny. With real white skin, like he didn't go out in the sun very much."

Cavanaugh, who'd been fiddling with the landing gear, didn't say a word, but his expression indicated he knew who the kid was talking about.

''You said he had a plane just like this. How did you get to see it? Was he working on it on his front lawn?''

Shawn's attention was riveted on the tar-black model. ''He was carrying it from his car into his house.''

Alex thought a minute. If he had it in his car, why hadn't he parked in the garage before taking it out?

''He didn't pull into his garage?''

Alex felt Rika creep closer.

''It's just a little house. He's only got a carport. He seemed like he was in a real hurry to get it inside, but it didn't look like rain or anything.''

''Is the man you saw here today, Shawn?'' Rika asked.

The boy searched the crowd, studying the people gathered in groups around the various models. ''I don't see him.''

Rika hauled Alex aside. ''Do you know who he's talking about?'' Her inflection was low, her voice almost breathless. He didn't want the sound of it to conjure up images of the last time he'd heard that kind of intimacy.

He needed her out of this. Without answering, he strode around her.

''Where are you going?'' she demanded, grabbing his sleeve.

''Stay here with the kids,'' he insisted.

He could visualize the battle raging inside her. He knew who Shawn was referring to, and she wanted desperately to be with him when he confronted the suspect, but she couldn't abandon the children, and she couldn't take them with her.

''Gramps will stay with them.''

"No," he said with hushed sternness. He would do whatever was necessary to keep her safe. "You brought the children, Rika. They're your responsibility, not your grandfather's." His thinly veiled allusion to the swimming-pool incident wasn't lost on her.

"Don't preach to me, Alex." Her chest expanded as she scowled at him, her words ground rough between clenched teeth. "Or give me orders."

He yearned to wrap his arms around her, to quell the anger he saw stampeding through her, to make her trust him. "This is official government business. I don't need a reporter breathing down my neck, getting in the way or second-guessing my decisions."

Eyes locked, neither of them noticed the general moving beside them. "What's going on?"

Rika answered him but kept her eyes pinned on Alex. "He knows who's responsible for the missing drone."

The old man's white brows went up. "Is that true?"

"I'm on my way now to check it out." Alex glared at Rika, then addressed her grandfather. "I don't want her with me, sir. This could be dangerous. It's no place for a woman or the press."

Rika's eyes grew enormous. "You...you... male—"

"Chauvinist pig," Alex finished for her with a grin. "Yeah, that's me. Been perfecting it for years. I'm stepping on freedom of the press, too." He looked over at Cavanaugh. "Watch things," he called over his shoulder. He had already taken the cell phone out of his back pocket and was poking in a number.

"Mike, I'm going over to 325 Hamilton... Yes, him... How long will it take you to form a perimeter around the house? All right. I'll be there in less than ten minutes.'' He pocketed the phone.

Alex opened the door to his Jaguar and was folding himself into the driver's seat, when he saw Rika climb into her van. The general was standing off to the side, a fist upraised at her. Apparently, even he was unable to discourage his headstrong granddaughter from getting in the way.

Again Alex pulled out his cell phone. ''Mike, Rika is on her way to Hamilton. Keep her as far from the house as possible. Sit on her if you have to. Use whatever force is necessary to make sure she doesn't mess this up.'' He snapped the phone closed, turned the key in the ignition and sped across the tarmac.

HAMILTON STREET was less than a half mile from the east gate of the base. Alex kept glancing in the rearview mirror for Rika's van. No sign of her. Maybe the general had dissuaded her after all, or Lattimore had found a way to prevent her from getting off base.

Alex parked at the end of the quiet tree-shaded street and waited a few minutes for his team to take their positions. When he saw the motor home pull over at the end of the block, he knew all the players were in place.

Restarting his engine, he drove conservatively down the street and stopped in front of number 325.

The house, as Shawn had described it, was indeed small, with a single carport formed by the extension of the nearly flat tar-and-gravel roof. The white clapboard walls were peeling, and the scraggly shrubs needed trimming. Alex suspected its owner had chosen the place purely for its proximity to the base. He pressed the bell.

At first he thought the resident wasn't home, though a Subaru sat in the carport. Alex was about to leave, when the door swung open.

The scowl of annoyance on Brassard's face quickly turned to shock. "Major, what are you doing here?"

"Sorry to disturb you." Alex offered a friendly smile. "But something's come up I need to talk to you about."

The man's expression now was one of alarm. "Talk to me? About what? I was just getting packed to go to San Antonio—"

"I know. I'm glad I was able to catch you."

Alex's carefully chosen words had an impact. Brassard blinked nervously several times, apparently unable to decide how to react, what to do.

Alex took advantage of his confusion. "May I come in?" Without waiting for an answer, he slipped past the scientist and entered the modest living room.

Brassard didn't take his hand off the doorknob as he turned toward the interloper. "I really don't have time."

The mild-mannered man was trying to sound forceful, but Alex could hear fear under the uncharacteristic belligerence. "This won't take long."

Leaving the door open but stepping around to block further inroads by his visitor, Brassard demanded, "What do you want?"

Not "What's the problem?" or "Has something happened at the lab?" Alex noted. The man was taking this personally.

He was dressed casually in slacks and open-necked shirt, but his eyes revealed wary suspicion.

"Nice place you have here," Alex said, though it wasn't true. The interior, like the outside, was worn and shabby, but then Alex didn't think the scientist spent a lot of time here. Probably had a state-of-the-art computer system set up in one of the bedrooms, though.

"Really convenient to the base," Alex commented. "How many bedrooms do you have?"

"What do you care? What are you doing here?"

"Looking around." The words, Alex noted, heightened Brassard's apprehension.

"Why? What for?" Anger was beginning to creep into the man's voice.

Alex chuckled. "What are you afraid of? You hiding something?"

"Of course not. It's just that—"

"I know. You're in a hurry, so I won't keep you long. The fact is, I'm concerned about Colonel Lacy. I haven't been getting straight answers from him. I think he might be involved in this missing-drone business."

The scientist's eyes widened, and Alex wasn't sure if the light he saw in them was astonishment or relief. "You're crazy." But the statement harbored more doubt than conviction.

"It would explain a lot—"

"There you are. I was hoping I'd find you home."

They both whirled around to see Rika standing in the open doorway.

"What are *you* doing here?" Brassard snarled, annoyance deteriorating to panic.

"Good question, Mrs. Philips." Alex had all he could do to keep his temper in check.

"Oh, Major. I can't believe I've had such good luck." She sounded breathless, and he wondered if she wasn't taking a page out of her grandmother's book on how to play the ditsy female.

"I'm doing a feature story on the Aerospace Food Lab," Rika continued, "and I wanted to get an interview with Mr. Brassard about his work there. Since you're newly assigned to the lab, maybe you can give me your impressions, also."

She moved to one side and addressed her reluctant host. "I know you have a doctorate in mathematics—" she fumbled in her tote for her notebook "—or is it physics? I have it written down here—"

Brassy automatically faced her. "Actually, it's in electrical engineering, but I can't talk about the lab, Mrs. Philips—"

"Please, call me Rika."

Alex wanted to grab her by the wrist and drag her out the front door—until he realized what she was doing.

"Let's see, oh, your bachelor's is in mathematics from UCLA."

"Mrs. Philips, Rika, I really must ask you to leave—"

Taking a half step back, out of their host's line of sight, Alex slipped into the short, narrow hallway behind him.

"And you got your master's at UCLA, too—" Rika practically gushed.

"I got my master's from USC."

"Oh. Is that right?"

"Yes, but—"

Alex only half listened to the exchange. He was more interested in the two doorways on either side of the narrow passage. The one on his right was to a bathroom that would never have passed a GI inspection. There was a ring around the bathtub and mold on the shower curtain. The door across from it opened into a bedroom with a decidedly lived-in look. Brassy's room. Did anyone live with him? Didn't seem likely.

Alex could hear Rika babbling on. "But your Ph.D. is from MIT, right? I'm impressed."

The third door was wide-open. The computer room—probably where the scientist spent most of his time at home. Alex had been right about the hardware being state-of-the-art. In addition to the wide-screen monitor and imposing tower, there was an impressive array of peripheral components: external drives, scanner, separate fax, and cables going everywhere.

"And that's in physics?" Rika's voice wafted down the hall.

"I told you it's in electrical engineering," Brassy repeated with annoyance.

Across from the master bedroom was the only closed door. Alex had just put his hand on the knob and was turning it, when Brassard appeared at the end of the hall.

"Stay out of there," he ordered, and rushed toward Alex.

Completing his action, Alex pushed the door open.

"You have no right—" Brassy shouted, and tried to block entrance to the room.

It was too late. Several inches taller than the slump-shouldered scientist, Alex had no difficulty seeing into the dimly lit room. There, in the dusky gloom, resting atop a sagging double bed was the missing drone.

"Get out!" Brassard shouted, and pushed against his nemesis.

Alex extended an arm to shove the man aside, when Rika appeared at the end of the hall. Brassy lunged toward her. Her notebook tumbled to the floor as he spun her around with unexpected violence. She let out an astonished yelp, which was instantly muffled by Brassy's arm tightening around her throat.

She froze, her eyes bulging in terror when her captor produced a small pistol from his pocket and jammed it against her temple.

"Don't do this, Brassard," Alex urged. He'd halted his forward movement, unsure whether the man who gave the impression of a physical weakling had the intestinal strength to follow through on his threat.

Even more than the sight of the gun, the naked fear in Rika's eyes had his heart pumping. Her life was in danger. The instinct to protect and defend the woman he loved made him want to strike out, grab Brassy and pummel him, but discipline and training won over. Like a pilot in a nosedive with half his systems dead, he knew this was no time to panic. Cold, calm logic was the only answer.

"Let her go. This is a mistake, a bad move."

Brassy rammed the muzzle of the pistol harder against the side of her head. "She's coming with me," he snarled, his voice rising in panic. "We're getting out of here, and you're staying."

He took a step back and dragged Rika with him. She made a mangled groaning sound as her hands went up to his arm, trying to pull it away—to no avail. Either he was stronger than he appeared or desperation was giving him added strength.

"If you don't follow, maybe I'll let her go later. Follow us and she's a dead woman."

Alex's gut muscles clenched. It took every ounce

of control to keep his hands from balling into fists. Brassy had her pinned snugly against his body. She arched her back and dug in her heels in an effort to make his progress as clumsy as possible.

They were hardly a dozen feet from Alex. If only there were some way to distract him, but Alex was the one in the dead end of the hallway.

"Listen to me." He kept his voice low, reasonable. "Kidnapping and murder will only make matters worse. Let her go. We can still work this out."

"Stay away," Brassard shouted when Alex inched forward.

The click of a hammer being cocked had the impact of a rifle shot. Alex stopped breathing as he watched Rika's face collapse, her body sag. Brassy froze, his posture stiff and awkward.

"Don't move," Lattimore said, the cold metal of his Colt revolver pressed against the back of Brassard's neck. "Point it up to the ceiling."

As soon as the weapon was raised, Lattimore wrenched it from behind. Alex lunged and gathered Rika in his arms, her entire body quivering.

RIKA THREW HERSELF into Alex's embrace. Her heart was pounding and the rest of her body didn't seem to know if it should be hot or cold. She trembled and felt grateful for the rock solidness of Alex's hold on her. But the shelter of his arms lasted only a moment, before he was dragging her out of the house by her arm.

His face set, he positioned her in the middle of the scraggly lawn. "Stay here. Right here, Rika. Don't move. Do you understand?"

The hostility in his voice frightened her almost as

much as the cold steel that had been pressed against her temple.

I...I need you to hold me, she wanted to say, but he was gone before she could speak the words.

He raised his hand in a beckoning signal. As if out of nowhere, people started crowding around, some in uniform, others in civvies. Alex gave a series of orders to back up Lattimore and call the Office of Special Investigation.

"Alex," Rika pleaded. The trembling had subsided, but her voice was still shaky.

He turned to one of his men. "Stay with her. Make sure she doesn't go anywhere."

Anger replaced fear. He was treating her like a recalcitrant schoolgirl. Her grandfather showed up and Alex went directly to him. With an occasional glance her way, they talked in muted tones. She stepped toward them, but the airman or sergeant or whoever he was Alex had put in charge of watching her blocked her way.

"I'm sorry, ma'am, but you'll have to stay here."

"That's my grandfather," she protested.

"Sorry, ma'am."

She attempted another step. He barred her path.

"Gramps," she called out as she tried to see over the man's shoulder. "Damn it, I have a right—"

Alex and her grandfather came over to her.

"Tell this guy to let me go," she demanded of Alex.

"I asked you to stay put," he reminded her curtly.

"You ordered me," she shot back with equal force. "I don't take orders."

"Not from me, obviously. How about from your conscience?"

"What are you talking about?"

His eyes—hard, angry, implacable—met hers. "You almost fouled up this operation, Rika. By your willful disregard for my request, you put me in danger in there. That's okay. I can handle myself. But you also put yourself in harm's way. I guess you have the right to gamble with your life, too, if you want to—"

"Why, thank you very much, Major."

"But you do not have the right to jeopardize your daughter's future." His words had the sharp edge of a knife.

She froze and glared at him. "What the hell are you talking about? What's Emily got to do with this?"

"Everything."

She seethed. "Would you mind explaining it to me?"

Damn it, she wanted him to hold her, to swallow her up in his arms, to lavish her with kisses, not browbeat her. She searched for understanding in his eyes, but all she saw was rage.

"Brassy put a gun to your head. He couldn't have done that if you hadn't been here, if you'd trusted me enough to let me do my job, if you'd listened to reason and stayed away."

Ah, so that's what this was all about. She hadn't shown him enough deference, hadn't played the meek little woman, cowering under his big, strong male dominance.

"He didn't pull the trigger," she reminded him.

"He could have." Alex didn't shout or raise his voice, but his breathing was labored, like that of a man under a terrific strain. She watched his massive chest as it expanded and contracted. "What then,

Rika? Your daughter would have been an orphan, or if you hadn't been killed, she and your grandparents could have spent the rest of their lives watching you vegetate in a coma.''

The image, a possibility she hadn't even considered, brought bile to her throat. Her grandfather stood by, stone-faced. He wasn't defending, wasn't consoling, her. She felt utterly deserted, miserably alone. She focused on Alex.

''Why are you doing this to me?'' *Why are you hurting me this way?*

But he was past hearing her. ''You didn't consider any of them, did you? You thought only about yourself and your precious story. To hell with everybody else.''

By the time she realized her eyes were brimming, it was too late. A tear trickled down her cheek. She started to say something, then stopped, unable to enunciate the words.

Jaw clamped, his lips a thin line, Alex spun on his heel and marched away from her toward the house, then just as quickly halted. He took a long, slow breath, swiveled and addressed General Tiers.

''Where are the children, sir?'' His voice was ragged.

''Airman Cavanaugh is entertaining them out on the flight line. He seems a very responsible young man.''

''He is,'' Alex agreed.

Rika closed her eyes and bit her lip. *He thinks I'm irresponsible, that I don't care about my own daughter, my grandparents—the people I love.* She felt sick inside.

''If things get wrapped up tonight before midnight,

I'll come to your house and report,'' Alex told the general. "If not, I'll see you tomorrow morning. Will 0900 hours be convenient, sir?"

"That'll be fine, Major.''

The old man said nothing as he firmly supported his granddaughter's elbow with his bony fingers and led her away.

CHAPTER FIFTEEN

A FEW MINUTES before nine the following morning, Alex pulled up in front of the Tierses' residence and was shown immediately to the general's office.

He wasn't surprised Rika was sitting in the leather-upholstered chair on the right side of her grandfather's desk, one leg crossed over the other, fingers curled around the handle of a red coffee mug. It took only the briefest of glances, however, for him to ascertain the casual pose was forced. If the shadows under her eyes were any indication, she hadn't gotten any more sleep the previous night than he had.

The general approached Alex with outstretched hand.

"You look like you could use a dose of caffeine, my boy." The old man's tone and expression were friendly, but businesslike. What had he said to his granddaughter yesterday after they left Hamilton Street? That Alex was right and she was wrong? Or that he had been out of line and she would do well to stay away from him?

The general went to the coffeemaker and filled a blue porcelain mug. "Long night?"

"Too short, actually." Alex accepted the steaming beverage gratefully. "We didn't finish up with the feds until after two, and I still had my own reports to write." No use mentioning that when he did finally collapse onto his bed, the few hours of rest he might have gotten never came. His body had been exhausted, his mind swirling. All he could see as he lay on the king-size bed—where he and Rika had lain together—was her tearstained face. She'd been scared at Brassard's house, but instead of comforting her, he'd berated and insulted her.

Reclaiming his position behind the desk, the general motioned Alex into the chair facing Rika. "I've asked Rika to sit in. Unless you have a strong objection."

She was as still as a statue. Waiting. Alex shook his head.

"She has agreed," Tiers continued, "that whatever you tell us this morning will be off the record. Can you fill us in on what transpired?"

She was staring at him with cold reserve, neither confirming nor denying her grandfather's statement. He knew she wouldn't abuse the concession she was being granted. A professional reporter made sure what she was told off the record stayed that way; otherwise she would lose her source.

Hell hath no fury like a woman scorned, he thought, and his words yesterday had scorned her as a mother, as a granddaughter, as a responsible adult. She wouldn't forgive him, and he knew he would probably not forgive himself.

He took a sip from his steaming mug. "First, let me thank Rika for her investigation." She didn't blink or nod or crack a smile, only looked through him as if he weren't there. "I'd like to think we would have caught Brassard eventually—" he spoke to her directly "—but your uncovering his arrest for embezzlement definitely speeded up the process."

She quirked an eyebrow at him, an expression of contempt. "Will I be able to interview him?"

"Afraid not. He's been taken into federal custody and will be relocated sometime today." Alex checked the watch on his wrist. "He probably has been already."

"How did Brassard explain himself?" Tiers asked before swallowing coffee.

"Insisted he'd done nothing wrong, of course."

"But we...*you*—" Rika corrected herself "—caught him with the drone."

Alex allowed a curt chuckle. "Brassy's explanation was that he'd found it in a culvert on his own and was getting ready to take it down to San Antonio to turn it over to Security Command."

"Do you believe him?" she asked.

"No."

"What was his excuse for not handing it over to you?" Tiers inquired.

"He didn't trust me. Said he knew Lacy and I had worked together. He tried to make it sound as if the disappearance of the drone and my coming to investigate it were all part of a conspiracy cooked up by Lacy and me to pirate the technology."

Rika huffed, "Ridiculous."

The old man lowered his mug to the desktop. "He didn't really think that story would fly, did he?"

"If Rika hadn't discovered his arrest before he was hired by the government, it might have."

Alex rested his elbows on the arm of the chair, leaned back and crossed his right ankle over his left knee. "Twenty years ago Brassy was just finishing up his doctorate and was working nights setting up a new computer system for a large shipping company. He was receiving occasional grants, but they didn't come close to covering his living expenses, especially since he was supporting an invalid mother at the time."

"So he needed money," the old man concluded. "Sounds like he should have worked full-time and pursued his education part-time. Selfish of him—putting his personal goals ahead of his duties, then stealing from his employer. How did he do it?"

Alex took a sip of his coffee, very much aware of the woman opposite him, her eyes unflinchingly fixed on him. "The fractional-cent siphon."

Tiers nodded. Rika didn't.

"Are you familiar with the scam?" Alex asked her.

"Perhaps you'd be kind enough to enlighten me." Her voice was flat.

He glanced at the general, whose lips were curled in tolerance. With a nod, he urged Alex on.

"It was an ingenious and novel approach at the time. If, for example, tax on transactions was 7.5 percent and a particular sale was $15.00, the tax due would be $1.0875. Naturally, the payment would be rounded off to $1.09. The leftover quarter of a cent would then be transferred to a separate account. Minor fractions of a penny don't seem like much, but with thousands of such transactions every day, the amount can grow significantly, and auditors, unless they are specifically focused on it, are likely to miss it."

"How did he get caught?" she asked.

"Clever as the scheme was, he wasn't the only one who'd figured it out. When it was uncovered in several other large enterprises, Brassy's company called in a special audit."

"I think I know what's coming." Tiers got up from

behind his desk and walked over to the coffee carafe on the side table. He refilled their cups, then his own and resumed his seat. "But give us the details, anyway."

"While Brassard was out on bail, he was approached by people who offered to get him off the hook—for a price. Remember Brassard was in his midtwenties, a promising scientific career ahead of him, except he was facing a twenty-year felony conviction for embezzlement. So he went along.

"His new lawyer convinced the district attorney that Brassard hadn't written the original software program, that he only adapted it to his employer's use. He argued that his client was totally unaware of the illegal code embedded in it. Since the authorities were unable to find the skimmed money, there was no way to connect the fraud directly to Brassy. At the time, in fact, the creator of the original program was believed to be the actual recipient of the funds through a series of shell transactions ultimately being deposited into a number of Swiss accounts. They'd found some of the money but were never confident they'd found it all."

"How did Brassy get a clearance?" Rika asked.

"The charges were dropped and his influential attorney made sure the records were sealed. When the standard national agency check was run on him, it found nothing—no arrests, no convictions."

"Then came the MADAM program and payback time," the general concluded.

"You're saying he was a sleeper. That for all these years the people who saved his neck let him go on with his life until they had a suitable opportunity to call in their markers," Rika commented dryly.

Alex nodded. "Exactly."

"If the embezzlement charge was twenty years old," she continued, "the statute of limitations must have run out. What were they holding over him to make him still cooperate after so much time?"

"Revelation that he'd lied on his security questionnaire. Not reporting an arrest is a federal offense. It made his job application, still a part of his current official personnel record, fraudulent. Even if the government didn't put him in jail, his career as a scientist would be finished. Having been terminated for cause and unable to hold a security clearance, he'd never get another job involving classified programs or industry-sensitive projects."

"Oh, the tangled webs we weave..." intoned the general.

"There was another element," Alex added. "He was professionally frustrated. The brilliant career he'd dreamed of had languished. He liked his work well enough, but it wasn't getting him the recognition he thought he deserved. I'll give him this," Alex granted, "he's a good scientist. He came up with a few ideas and solutions that went beyond mere competence, maybe even approached genius."

Pensively, the old man rotated the handle of his cup back and forth. "I guess the indicators were there if anyone had bothered to look. A loner, dedicated to his work but getting little credit for it. Was Lacy responsible for that?"

It was a tough question, one Alex wasn't sure he could answer objectively.

"Perhaps indirectly," he conceded diplomatically, "since he knew Lacy had appropriated MADAM from me. That may have contributed to the atmosphere of mistrust.''

Alex leveled an appraising glance at the woman sitting across from him. He wanted to smile at her, wanted to see her smile in return, but it didn't take a rocket scientist to figure out it wasn't going to happen. A forlorn ache of loneliness and lost hope settled in his belly.

''It was your information that really broke the case,'' he told her. ''If you hadn't uncovered Brassy's earlier misdeed, his bluff might have worked. With the records sealed we may never have found the motive.''

''I'm honored to have been of service,'' she said acerbically. She took a hearty swallow of coffee and balanced the nearly empty mug on the arm of the chair.

''So it's over,'' she said, her eyes locked on Alex's. He was all too aware that her words referred as much to their relationship as to the intrigue they'd solved together.

''So it would seem,'' Alex agreed, the quiet intensity of her green eyes confirming his conclusion.

THERE WAS NOTHING to keep Alex in Coyote Springs. He'd filed his reports with the Air Force and the various government agencies involved in apprehending and prosecuting espionage. He'd briefed the general.

He packed his bags with a sense of gloom. How could this unpretentious place in West Texas have unleashed so much turmoil in his life? He'd been assigned here to find a missing drone and protect a government project. He'd done both. Yet...

He'd never intended to fall in love with Rika Philips. Never expected his every conscious thought and midnight dream to revolve around one and only one woman. In a sense, she was right. He'd been a ladies' man. Up until now. But companionship without entanglements and sex for the pure pleasure of it suddenly weren't enough. He wanted more. Much more.

He hung his uniforms on the bar suspended over the back seat of the Jaguar, did a cursory check of the shiny maroon car, climbed in behind the wheel, took a deep breath and started the engine. It was ridiculous to keep checking the vehicles coming on base as he pulled out the gate. She wasn't arriving to say goodbye. He watched, anyway. No sign of her van in the rearview mirror, either, as he turned on the highway going north. He was disappointed but not surprised. He'd lost her—the only woman he'd ever truly loved.

He settled into the plush leather upholstery and tried to concentrate on the bleak road ahead. Investigative reporter Rika Philips, soft brown hair and green eyes, would return to Michigan and write her story. Alex wasn't unaware of the irony of the situation. What she wrote might do more to compromise the MADAM project than Brassard's treachery. Alex didn't blame her for doing her job. If he'd done his better…

WITH THE HELP of her grandfather, Rika wedged the last box securely in the back of the van.

"Emily, I told you to put Scamper's things behind the console. We're not going to have enough room in front for all of them, honey," she added more gently. "You can take one doll and a bone for the pup to chew on, but leave the rest of your toys and games in the back, please.''

Her daughter did as she was told, but with a side-long glance at her mother. Rika couldn't blame the child for feeling apprehensive. The thousand-mile trip from Coyote Springs to Michigan was always difficult for Rika. Her grandparents formed a vital part of her life. Saying goodbye always made her edgy, especially now, as they advanced further in years.

Rika knew it wasn't just the separation from her grandparents, as difficult as it was, that had her snapping and snarling. She'd met a man who'd turned her world inside out, a man who'd exposed feelings and needs she'd tried hard to bury, a man who'd made her feel so womanly and passionately loved that life without him seemed barren. Now he was gone. He'd fulfilled her in a way she could never have imagined. He'd also disappointed her, as she'd known from the beginning he would. Yet late at night, in the lonely darkness of her bedroom, she realized she was more disappointed in herself.

She'd allowed herself to be seduced into his bed by looks and charm and her own rebellious body. She'd gloried in his touch, wallowed in the magic of his strength and power, only to become another of his conquests. In one night he'd changed her life and left her wanting more. It was foolish to blame him for her weakness. She should have resisted. She should have been stronger. Maybe that was why she could never forgive him.

THE MAIL ARRIVED before noon, and Barbara brought her personal correspondence to the lunch table. Today there was a thick legal-sized envelope from Michigan.

Barbara used her dinner knife to slit it open. Rika and
Emily had been back home two weeks, so instead of
recounting Scamper's antics and the problems of
housebreaking the rambunctious pup, the letter rambled on about Emily's first days in school. Scratched
at the bottom of the last page like an afterthought was
a note acknowledging the enclosure of Rika's recent
article in the *Michigan Sun,* a story that was about to
be picked up by the Associated Press.

Barbara unfolded the newsprint and read it carefully before passing it to her husband. "I think she
did a very nice job, dear," was all she said before
picking up a wedge of her grilled-cheese-and-tomato
sandwich.

Nathan's eyebrows slanted to peaks above the
bridge of his nose as he perused the double-wide column.

"Did she say in her letter if she coordinated this
with Major Huston?"

Barbara took a sip of hot tea before answering.
"I'm sure she didn't. I know they exchanged several
letters after she returned to Michigan. Rika says she
made it clear he had no right to censor what she
wrote."

"At least they're talking to each other," Nathan
observed.

"They were," his wife corrected him. "Major
Huston wanted to fly up to Lansing to see her and
Emily, but Rika told him not to, said she needed time
to think things through. He replied that he'd allow her
all the time she needed, but he wouldn't give up."

Her husband chuckled softly. "Good for him."

Barbara frowned. "He hasn't told her about his
promotion or transfer."

Nathan crushed saltines into his steaming bowl of chili, then paused. "Do you think they have a chance?"

"There's always a chance, dear—given the right opportunity." Barbara's gaze drifted off, a satisfied grin slowly curling her lips. "But sometimes opportunity needs a door to knock on."

ALEX WAS FRUSTRATED, physically and emotionally. He'd sent Rika cards, flowers and a two-pound box of chocolates. He'd even offered to fly up to Lansing to help her with her story about what he'd dubbed "The Incident at the Wolf Pack." It had been a mistake. She'd taken it as an attempt to censor her work and pointedly told him not to visit.

She'd finally sent a copy of her article after it had been published in the *Michigan Sun*. It certainly wasn't what he'd expected.

Instead of the sensational exposé of espionage and intrigue at a small Air Force base in West Texas, it was a warm, funny and powerful story about a group of kids who'd saved the day by their vigilance. The article prized not secrecy but integrity, exposed not adult perfidy but youthful innocence. Instead of raising one's ire, Rika's writing warmed one's heart. The lesson of the episode was that our hope lies in the next generation, and that it is our inviolable duty to give them the moral tools to make their lives better.

He certainly couldn't argue with the sentiment and imagined her grandfather was more than a little pleased. Alex had called and thanked her for her discretion, hoping that now, with the issue of her story behind them, she'd be more receptive to his coming to see her and Emily. She wanted more time, she insisted, and he promised to give her all she needed. He felt a tiny glimmer of hope, however. He had a powerful ally.

He picked up Barbara Tiers's letter. She and the general were extending an invitation to Thanksgiving dinner.

"SCAMPER, GET OUT of my lap," Rika admonished, though not very convincingly, as she exited the main highway onto Prairie Dog Lane. The growing pup was a handful, but so eager to please even his bad manners had a way of endearing him.

Emily reached across the console and grabbed her pet, who was trying very hard to cuddle up on Rika's legs.

"It's Thanksgiving Day, and we're almost to Gram and Gramps's house, Scamp," the girl said as she held the writhing bundle of energy behind his front legs and nuzzled her nose against his. As if understanding what his mistress was saying, Scamper wiggled his feathery tail enthusiastically and swiped a slobbery tongue across her mouth.

"Yech."

Rika turned into the driveway of her grandparents' ranchette. The front door flew open even before she pulled under the portico. Her grandmother, wrapped in a pale-blue sweater, had her fingers bunched in front of her chest, her face beaming. Gramps stood behind her, his hands poised comfortably on his wife's narrow shoulders. Nothing American Gothic about this couple, Rika thought with a flood of affection, not with those broad smiles lighting up their faces. Emily was so eager to get out of the vehicle and run to her great-grandparents' outstretched arms she forgot to release her seat belt and nearly strangled herself.

Undeterred, Scamper bounded to the elderly couple and was about to jump up, when Gramps ordered, "Sit." The animal instantly obeyed, tongue lolling, tail wagging.

Rika laughed. "I wish I could get him to do that."

Hugs and kisses met them. It had been less than three months since Rika and Emily's summer vacation, but Rika immediately studied the old folks for signs of illness. She hadn't intended to come to Texas for Thanksgiving, preferring to save the two-day drive for her longer Christmas break, but the letter from her grandmother hinting that her grandfather's health was not what it used to be had been enough to accelerate her plans. Strangely, they both looked perfectly fine. The general definitely didn't have a pallor; in fact, he appeared to have been spending a good deal of time in the autumn sun—on the golf course, no doubt. So what was going on?

It took Rika half an hour to unload the van, unpack her clothes and settle Scamper in the run Gramps had improvised in the backyard. By then, Emily had called Micki Sanchez next door and made plans for them to get together the next day. Rika finally plopped down at the kitchen table with a tall glass of lemonade.

"It smells wonderful in here," she told Sera, who, after an affectionate hug, had continued to move around the steamy room with a casual efficiency that never ceased to make Rika envious. Sera could give Martha Stewart lessons in organization. "When's dinner?"

"Five o'clock."

Rika's watch read just past three. "Good. That'll give me time to relax a few minutes, shower and change into something more comfortable."

Sera uncovered a large crockery bowl and punched down the dough that had been rising in it. "Did you bring your green silk, the one your grandma gave you for Christmas last year?"

Rika glanced up from the table. "Yes..."

"You should wear it," Sera all but commanded.

"It's awfully dressy for dinner at home, isn't it?" She wasn't in the habit of sitting down to Thanksgiving dinner in worn jeans and a tattered shirt, but a washed-silk dress with pearl buttons?

All Sera would say was, "It's a pretty dress."

Barbara came into the kitchen from the garden, carrying a flower basket filled with violet Michaelmas daisies.

"Do you think I should wear my green silk dress at dinner?"

The old woman's face lit up. "Oh, that would be so nice, dear. Maybe I'll put on my blue velvet. You know, the one with the lace collar. Your grandfather loves to see me in blue."

Nathan Tiers strolled into the warm kitchen from the hallway. "Sera, you're smelling up the whole house," he said sternly, then threw the woman a boyish smile. "Delicious smells, mouthwatering smells. I may have to give you a pay raise if you keep this up."

"You must be hungry. Good." Sera continued kneading the bread dough on the floured board at the counter by the wall oven.

"Rika's going to wear her green silk dress for dinner,'' Barbara told her husband, ''and I thought I'd wear my blue velvet.''

''In that case, I guess I'll have to put on my new jacket. Can't have the most beautiful ladies in the world dining with a roughneck.''

''What's going on?'' Rika asked, confused and just a little suspicious. ''Why is everyone getting all gussied up?''

''Whatever do you mean, dear? Wearing the green dress was your idea,'' her grandmother said cheerfully.

''A good one, too,'' the general seconded. ''We don't dress up nearly enough these days. People always running around in dungarees—''

''They call them jeans now, Gramps.''

He ignored her. ''When I was a young man we always dressed properly—''

''Yes, dear.'' Barbara held her flower basket in one hand and with the other gently nudged her husband out of the room.

Rika looked at Sera, but the short round woman merely shrugged, slammed the dough on the board and checked the potatoes simmering on the stove.

Rika opted for a soaking bath instead of a quick shower, after the long drive from Michigan. She let her mind drift as the soft, scented water soothed away some of the tension, but not all. Her grandparents frequently invited single troops from the base, especially those away from home for the first time, to share Thanksgiving dinner. Could that be why they wanted her to dress up? Maybe this time it was a group of junior officers. Or had they snared a more mature officer? Incurable matchmakers.

At least it wouldn't be Alex Huston. In her last

K.N. CASPER281

letter Gram said he'd been transferred from Nellis to some far-flung outpost. She'd hinted that his handling of the MADAM affair had somehow precipitated the move. Well, she wasn't going to think about Alex Huston.

Oh, he'd written, told her how beautiful she was, professed his undying love, insisted his affair with the redhead was over, that there was only one woman for him—the woman with the most ravishing green eyes he'd ever seen. He'd been charming in his letters, almost poetic. He'd also had the audacity to suggest she should clear what she wrote about the Wolf Pack with him. He even offered to fly to Michigan to read it over her shoulder. The recollection of him standing behind her in his bedroom, both of them naked, his hands...

She wrote back, of course—it was the polite thing to do—and sent him a copy of her article. She had never agreed to let him approve her copy, she reminded him. Journalists didn't ask for permission to write their stories. She was confident, however, he would find nothing objectionable in hers.

The tub was cooling. She added more hot water and tried to find the relaxation and comfort this house always brought her. It wasn't working. She couldn't seem to shake off a sense of vertigo, the kind she got on dry land after being on a rocking boat all day.

She put on the handsomely tailored dress her grandmother had given her and the string of pearls that perfectly complemented the scooped neckline. She rarely wore much makeup, but having gone this far, it didn't seem right not to add a touch of mascara to her lashes and apply a few subtle strokes of pale-green eye shadow.

She was coming down the broad staircase, when she saw a flash as the sun glinted off the windshield of a car pulling up the driveway. It was still half an hour before dinnertime according to the grandfather clock in the hall below. Apparently, this guest didn't know arriving early wasn't fashionable.

Then she saw maroon as the car glided to a stop under the portico. Her heart slammed into her rib cage with a thunderous pounding, and suddenly her hands felt clammy. Now she understood the emphasis on the green dress. Why couldn't Gram have left well enough alone?

The doorbell rang. Rika paused midway down the staircase. Her grandmother emerged from the living room, smiled up at her and stepped to the door.

CHAPTER SIXTEEN

SHE WAS EVEN MORE BEAUTIFUL than he remembered, though it seemed impossible, considering his imagination had placed her on clouds of angel dust with a halo around her head. Not that he had forgotten she was a human and very much a woman. Life would have been less complicated if he had. The Justines of his life were past. How empty those relationships had been compared with what he almost had with Rika. They'd been forgotten even before the flamboyant redhead had showed up in Coyote Springs. If only he'd been able to convince the woman on the stairs of his reformation.

It took unnatural concentration to focus on greeting Mrs. Tiers. He kissed her fondly on the cheek, offered the bouquet he'd brought and said polite words of greeting and appreciation for the invitation. If asked what he'd said, he couldn't have answered, because his attention was locked onto the woman staring down on him, her hand clutching the banister. She was still angry. His heart sank.

"Hello, Rika."

"Hello, Major."

"Didn't I tell you, dear?" Barbara puffed a little nervously. "He's a lieutenant colonel now."

Rika raised an eyebrow. "Colonel," she corrected herself.

"Should I address you all evening as Mrs. Philips, or are you going to call me Alex?"

The mask cracked, and she emitted a mild chuckle. "Hello, Alex. Congratulations on your promotion." She descended the last few steps and approached him, her hand extended. He took it, encasing its coolness between his palms. He hadn't forgotten its softness, nor had he been able to eradicate the memory of what the throb of her pulse did to his.

"I've never seen you looking more beautiful," he said, his voice suddenly soft, intimate. "Green suits you. It matches your eyes."

He let her fingers slip away when the general appeared from his study. He thumped Alex on the back before shaking his hand. "Good to see you, my boy. Glad you could make it."

"Where's Emily?" Alex asked.

Just then the girl appeared from the far end of the hallway and ran to him. He scooped her up in his arms and planted a loud kiss on her cheek. "I missed you, kid."

"I knew you'd be here," she declared when he put her down. "Scamper wants to see you, too. He's in the backyard. Sera gave him a bone because he likes to chew on things."

"Is that right?" Alex inquired. "And what does he like to chew?"

Emily lowered her eyes. "Mommy's sewing chair," she mumbled, then raised her head. "But it's all right. Mommy says it wasn't really a good chair anyway."

Alex peeked over at Rika, who was sucking in her cheeks, her expression more one of humor than annoyance.

"It used to have one distinctive feature, though," she commented with a grin. "Four even legs."

"I've got to help Sera put out the appetizers," Emily announced, and darted back to the kitchen.

The adults moved into the living room, where the general served sherry. Rika sat in an easy chair, one leg crossed over the other. Alex noticed she hadn't chosen the couch, where he could have parked himself beside her, where he could have rested his arm behind her and let his fingers creep along her shoulder to her neck, feel the delicate warm flesh beneath the uplifted brown hair.

He opted for the wingback opposite her. If he couldn't touch, at least he could soak in the sight of her.

Sera came in with a tray of appetizers. Barbara passed them around.

"So, you've been transferred from Nellis," Rika said as she lifted a round cracker topped with mild white cheese and chopped black olive—cowboy caviar.

Alex popped a miniature ham roll into his mouth. "Yep. Found a house over in Woodhill Terrace. Moved in last week. Don't really need a swimming pool, and the house is too big for one person—"

Rika gulped, almost spilling her aperitif. "Woodhill Terrace? Here? In Coyote Springs? You're stationed here?"

"I wrote you that he was transferred," Barbara said blandly. Butter wouldn't melt in her mouth.

Rika glared at her grandmother. "You didn't say it was here."

The old woman took no offense at her granddaughter's pique. "Didn't I, dear? I thought I had."

Rika rolled her eyes and grinned at Alex. "I should have known she was holding back when she didn't identify the far-flung outpost you'd been sent to."

When her grandmother made some hemming and hawing sounds in embarrassment, Rika rose from her chair and went over to her. "Gram, you never change." She put an arm around her and kissed the top of her snow-white head. "And I love you for it."

As if on cue, Sera announced dinner, and they moved to the dining room. The general took the head of the table, his wife the opposite end. Instead of sitting Emily beside her mother, Barbara placed her next to Alex, both of them facing Rika.

"What are you doing at the Wolf Pack?" Rika asked Alex between the salad and the main course. They'd already discussed school with Emily, her gymnastics classes and the antics of the growing dog. All the time he'd been watching her. "Don't tell me they're reopening the flight line."

His eyes flashed. "I've taken over the AFL."

A nonflying job? "What happened to Lacy?"

Alex broke open a dinner roll. A tiny curl of steam rose from the center, and its fresh-baked bread smell wafted across the table. "Remember Louisa Hartmann?"

"His secretary." Rika toyed with the stem of her wineglass. "You asked me to check up on her, but I didn't get a chance."

"She and Lacy were having an affair. That's why she was so standoffish and probably why Goodie wasn't minding the store the way he should have. She was afraid I was going to uncover their liaison." He picked up the knife on the edge of his butter plate and slathered a piece of the warm roll. "Ironically, if she'd been more friendly, I wouldn't have given her a second thought.''

"Guilty consciences make people act irrationally," the general contributed. Rika wondered if he was speaking only about Lacy and Hartmann.

"So what's happened to Lacy?" she asked.

"He's still in town, retired now. He's getting divorced.''

She raised the wineglass to her lips and took a delicate sip. "I'm sorry to hear that."

"So am I," Alex said. "His wife and daughters deserve better." He popped the bread into his mouth.

Sera wheeled in the serving cart. The turkey was golden brown, trimmed with sprigs of parsley, and smelled heavenly.

"Who wants a drumstick?" Gramps rose, picked up the carving knife and stroked it against a steel.

"Me," Emily sang out.

They dined for the next hour and a half. The food, of course, was superb. Emily had been excused from the table by the time the adults finished their coffee. Dessert would be served later.

The November sun was skimming the western horizon when Alex escorted Rika onto the patio. She'd relaxed during the long, leisurely meal, but now, as they stood alone facing the gold-and-purple light show of the setting sun, he could feel the tension once more building between them.

"Thank you for the article you wrote," he said. He was close enough to hold her hand, close enough to wrap his arm around her and feel the heat emanating from her body. "I understand it's been nominated for an AP Award. Congratulations."

She seemed unmoved by his praise or his gratitude.

He knew better. The story of the Wolf Pack had been important to her. Professional recognition of it validated its worth.

"Have you given up flying?" she asked.

He knew *his* career would be an issue between them. He'd accused her of putting *her* job ahead of people. Now she was asking about his.

"Flying, no. Being a test pilot, yes," he told her. "I'll still have to keep my aeronautical rating current. Since Coyote doesn't have an active airfield, that means TDYs a couple of days a month to Dyess Air Force Base in Abilene or Holloman in New Mexico to get in my required flight hours. There'll probably be TDYs associated with the work we're doing at the lab, too, as well as long hours testing the drone."

She listened but offered no comment, gave no indication anything he said made a difference to her. He had to break her composure.

He did what he'd wanted to do all evening. He touched her. But it didn't bring the satisfaction he'd hoped for. He rested a finger on her shoulder and with gentle pressure brought her around to face him. Her eyes, wide and almost dreamy, nevertheless avoided his, concentrating instead on his forehead.

"Talk to me, Rika. Tell me what you're thinking, what you're feeling. What I can do to convince you I love you."

"It's over between us, Alex," she muttered, tears in her voice. She turned to her right to face the growing darkness, knowing he would always be in her heart, that the memory of the time they'd spent together would forever be a part of her.

"Why?" he flared, unable to control his frustration.

"Because I'm in the Air Force? Because I'll have to spend time away from you and Emily?"

She combed her slender fingers through her hair. "Long work hours and job commitments have never been an issue," she assured him. "I understand professionalism."

His grip on her shoulder this time was more compelling. He spun her around and bracketed her face with his hands, forcing her to meet his gaze.

"I love you, Rika." The words were soft and tinged with a longing so painful she was forced to close her eyes.

The next sensation she felt was like a galvanic charge to her heartbeat, making it jolt and stutter. His mouth. On hers. It was infuriating to realize it took only the merest provocation by his tongue for her lips to part. His hands slid down from her cheeks to her neck to her shoulders. His fingers brushed the sides of her breasts. Suddenly, his arms were under hers, around her, his hands pressed to her back. He pulled her against his hard torso.

She met his tongue when it searched for hers. The dance they performed brought its own music and beat, its own harmony and heat. Her arms had a will of their own as they rose and circled his neck. As she responded to his passion, his increased. Sensations old and new, desires hot and desperate, needs long repressed exploded in her with a brilliance that had her spinning and soaring. She didn't want him to feel so perfect arched against her body, but he did.

When at last their lips separated, he nuzzled the tender skin below her ear. "I love you, Rika," he murmured. "I'll always love you. Only you."

Her insides quaked; her heart pounded. How long

she'd been aching to hear those words. How much she wanted to believe him. She couldn't deny it; she loved him, too. No amount of will on her part had kept him from occupying all her quiet moments since they'd parted three months earlier. His image, the recollection of his voice and the erotic magic of his touch had consumed her errant thoughts and fantasies. His absence had left her feeling hollow and lonely.

Head bowed, she twisted toward the single ray of light spiking up from the horizon like an upraised sword. For a moment, his grip impulsively tightened, resisting her escape, but then he dropped his arms, releasing her.

"I love you, Rika," he repeated a third time. "I want to marry you, to have you and to hold you for the rest of my life."

She turned her face to him, her lips parted. He saw her deep green eyes darken with fear and what he hoped was yearning.

Cupping her chin in the palm of his hand, he asked, "Can you tell me you don't feel anything for me?"

She closed her eyes. "Of course, I do," she said, opening them. "But it's not enough, Alex."

Hope tumbled to despair, roughening his voice. "What isn't enough?" he demanded. "Your love or mine?"

She pulled away and walked to the far end of the patio, boxing herself in the corner. He came up behind her, placed his hands on her shoulders, felt the tension, the panic. Gently he massaged the taut muscles.

Her mind wanted her body to resist the soothing warmth of his touch, but the flesh was weak. With a muffled moan she leaned into his hands and melted under his firm caress.

She rotated her head as he stroked the rigid column of her neck. "It won't work," she insisted.

She wasn't talking about his massage. He could feel her muscles relaxing, the tension subsiding.

"What won't?"

"Us." Her voice was husky, urgent, sexy. "There are too many obstacles."

He gently squeezed the bunched sinew at the base of her neck. Gathered and released, gathered and released. "What obstacles?"

"You work here. I live in Michigan. You're committed to the Air Force—"

His fingers stopped. "And a fighter pilot. Is that what you were about to say? All fighter pilots are playboys and adulterers. I'm a fighter pilot, therefore I must be a skirt chaser, and if we were to get married, I would be unfaithful." He clamped the outside of her shoulders and whirled her around to face him. "Was your father unfaithful to your mother?"

She shook her head—to his immense relief. If she'd said yes, he didn't know what he would have done—except maybe protest that he wasn't her father.

"Have your grandparents had a good marriage?"

She nodded, her eyes glistening.

"Your grandmother says love is a matter of trust, and you don't trust me? Is that it, Rika?"

"I failed in one marriage, Alex," she replied. "I can't complain. It gave me Emily. But I won't subject myself to the humiliation of being judged inadequate again."

Alex's arms shot around her and gathered her tightly to his chest. "The flaw was his, sweetheart,

not yours. The man was a complete and utter jerk."
He took another tack. "He wasn't a flyboy, but he
was an adulterer. Your father and grandfather were
fighter pilots and they were true to their vows.
Doesn't that tell you something? It's the man, Rika,
not the clothes he wears."

She snuffled, and he arched away just enough to
gaze into her shimmering eyes. "Loving you was the
most beautiful experience of my life, Rika. Being
with you, alone or in the company of others, makes
me feel whole, complete. Having you by my side will
make me the richest man in the world." He held her
face between his hands and kissed her lips gently,
softly. "I promise you, I will never be untrue to you.
I will thank God every day of my life for letting me
love you."

How could any woman resist such a declaration?
Rika wondered. Heaven knew she didn't want to. This
time when their lips met, it was she who plunged first,
enticing, meeting, challenging, demanding.

He led her over to a bench and sat her down, then
knelt at her feet, her hands clasped securely in his.
Looking up, his eyes searching hers in the murky light
of sunset, he said, "Marry me, Rika. I know we have
details to work out, and we will, if only you'll be my
wife."

Her heart was racing. The night air was cool. The
scent of late-blooming roses filled the air. His hands
were warm. The sweet melody of his words echoed
in her mind. The touch and taste of his mouth lingered
on her lips. She'd wanted him for so long, too much
to turn him down.

"I can't," she insisted.

His jaw dropped. "For heaven's sake, why not? I love you. You love me."

"Do you really? You think I'm an irresponsible mother—"

Confusion had him tightening his grip on her hands. "What are you talking about?"

She wanted to pull away, but all she could do was lower her head. "That's what you said at the pool," she murmured. "And at Brassard's place. You thought I was—"

"Rika." The name had a ragged, pleading quality to it. He raised her chin with a curled forefinger, panning his thumb just below her mouth. The sensation had her pulse tripping.

"I overreacted at the pool," he insisted, his voice close, his dulcet touch compelling her to seek his eyes with hers. "I told you why. My mind flew back to a different time, a different place."

He dragged his finger across her lips. "I've seen the kind of mother you are—with Emily and the neighborhood kids, who naturally migrate to you like a swarm of bumblebees to honey. I want to make babies with you, Rika. I want you to be the mother of my children."

The words took the breath out of her. She smiled weakly. "What about at Brassy's house?"

He climbed to his feet, scanned the dark horizon and shifted to capture her eyes. "It was my job to deal with Brassard. I had people available who were trained to handle the situation. It's also my understanding that your job is to report the news, not make it."

She couldn't keep the old defiance from erupting. "You still think I was wrong, don't you?"

The expression on his face gave her the answer before he spoke.

"I think it was reckless of you to barge in without a plan," he admitted, "without prior coordination."

She loved his wanting to protect her, but she valued her freedom more. "I shouldn't take chances, is that it?"

Frustration had him breathing out loudly through his nose. "You shouldn't take *unnecessary* chances, Rika. We could have worked out a plan of action beforehand. You could have trusted me enough to do my job and honor my commitment to you. As it is, you didn't write the sensational story you risked lives to get."

It shouldn't hurt to admit he was right, but it did. His earlier accusation that she had put his life in danger by her impetuous interference still gnawed at her conscience. Suppose Brassy had been more brutal. Suppose he'd actually pulled the trigger. Suppose...

"You're right." The admission was like a dam bursting inside her, freeing her.

His heart stopped. "I am?"

"You needn't act so stunned." It felt good to smile, even with tears in her eyes. "You are right once in a while, aren't you?"

He closed the distance separating them, arms outstretched. She slid easily, naturally, between them, letting their strength surround her.

"I'm right about our love, too," he told her boastfully.

"Hmm." She rested her head against his chest and listened to his heartbeat. "I may have created a monster."

"Marry me, Rika."

The rumble of his voice vibrated through her; the music of his words had her mind floating.

He grazed his lips on hers. "Will you marry me?" he murmured just before he covered her mouth with his. Hard. Aggressively. Yet his tongue probed with a sweetness that turned her knees to jelly. Balance was definitely a problem. She had no choice but to cling to him or crumple at his feet. When at last their lips separated, she blinked up at him and took a long, ragged breath. "I guess I'd better."

The kiss that followed was long and sensual, promising more, much more. They held each other, hearts beating as one.

"We ought to break the news," he finally muttered.

"Gram will be ecstatic. So will Gramps."

"What about Emily?" He sounded apprehensive.

Rika chuckled. "She'll be thrilled, Alex."

"I've never been a daddy before."

"That you know of," she teased, then laughed at the embarrassed scowl the remark produced. She kissed him lightly on the cheek. "I think you'll make a wonderful daddy."

His expression relaxed into a proud smile. "Shall we go inside?" He spanned his arm across the small of her back as they moved toward the kitchen door.

"There'll be a lot of questions," she reminded him.

"And we don't have all the answers," he agreed.

Rika slanted him a comic grin. "Don't worry—" she chuckled "—Gram probably has it all worked out."

"Do you think she knows?" he asked with the same playful tone.

"That we love each other, or that we're going to get married?"

He paused, turned toward her and dragged a finger along her cheek. "Oh, she knows we're in love."

"She probably knew it before either of us did." Rika's mouth curved into a delighted smile. "The old matchmaker."

"Your grandfather isn't too shabby, either."

"They're quite a team, aren't they?"

Alex brushed his lips across hers. "And an inspiration."

Emily bounced up and down at the news of their engagement, begging to be the flower girl at the wedding. Barbara beamed, teary-eyed, and fluttered more happily than Rika had ever seen her before. The general, too, glowed at the news, shaking Alex's hand twice and patting him on the back. Alex wasn't sure if the old man was aware he'd gone from calling him "my boy" to "son." Either way, it sounded remarkably good to his ears.

"Are we going to live here now?" Emily finally got around to asking.

The old woman's eyes went wide with apprehension, as if the idea of their living anywhere else was unthinkable. "Of course you are, dear."

"Babs…" her husband drawled in warning.

She glanced over at him. "Emily, dear, why don't we go help Sera cut the pies for dessert. Didn't you say we have apple and pumpkin and mince? What kind do you want? Or would you like to try all three," the old woman prattled as she escorted her great-granddaughter out of the room.

"When's the big date?" the general asked.

Alex grinned at his bride-to-be. It was one of those

pesky little details they hadn't discussed. "Do you think you can wrap things up in Michigan before the end of the year?"

They quickly reviewed a list of things that had to be accomplished.

Emily wheeled in a serving cart crowded with pies and plates, cups, saucers and a coffeepot. Barbara hovered over her watchfully.

"They've got an opening at the *Coyote Sentinel,*" Rika offered. "It's not as big as the *Sun,* of course, and the pay probably won't be as much, but the paper is on the wire services. Any big story I come up with can still be picked up, and Uncle John is willing to let me contribute freelance pieces to his syndicate."

"Is he now?" Alex asked, gray brows upraised.

"Nathan, dear," Barbara said, taking Emily's hand and leading her gently toward the hall, "why don't you open that bottle of champagne you've been keeping in the back of the refrigerator. Emily and I will get the glasses from the china cabinet."

"Good idea." He joined them at the doorway and, with a gentlemanly sweep of his arms, escorted his wife and great-granddaughter out of the room.

Alex and Rika met each other's gaze from opposite sides of the coffee table.

"So you'd already planned to move back here," Alex stated, his eyes half-closed in a playful smirk.

"I've been considering it for some time. The folks are getting on in years. I thought it would be good to be here for them. Good for Emily, too."

He studied her suspiciously.

She moved around and sidled up close to him. "Major...uh, Colonel Huston, you don't think I was moving back here to be close to you, do you? I didn't even know you were here, remember? All Gram said was that you'd been transferred from Nellis. She didn't mention it was to Coyote AFB.''

"Thank goodness," he said, as he circled his arms around her shoulders and planted a kiss on her forehead. "I was afraid there for a minute I had the whole family conspiring against me."

She pulled back. "Against you? You mean you don't want to do this after all?"

"I didn't say that," he replied defensively, realizing too late the trap he'd set for himself.

"Are you sure? I haven't heard Gramps open the champagne yet. There's still time—"

A loud pop came from the direction of the kitchen.

"Oops, too late." Alex tightened his grip on her. "To have and to hold, from this day forward."

HARLEQUIN®
SUPERROMANCE®

Twins

They're definitely not two of a kind!

THE UNKNOWN SISTER
by
Rebecca Winters

Catherine Casey is an identical twin—and she doesn't know it! When she meets her unknown sister, Shannon White, she discovers they've fallen in love with the same man....

On sale May 2000 wherever Harlequin books are sold.

HARLEQUIN®
Makes any time special ™

HARLEQUIN®
SUPERROMANCE®

*Pregnant and alone—
these stories follow women
from the heartache of
betrayal to finding true love
and starting a family.*

THE FOURTH CHILD by C.J. Carmichael.
When Claire's marriage is in trouble, she tries to
save it—although she's not sure she can forgive her
husband's betrayal.
On sale May 2000.

AND BABY MAKES SIX by Linda Markowiak.
Jenny suddenly finds herself jobless and pregnant by
a man who doesn't want their child.
On sale June 2000.

MOM'S THE WORD by Roz Denny Fox.
After her feckless husband steals her inheritance and
leaves town with another woman, Hayley discovers she's
pregnant.
On sale July 2000.

Available wherever Harlequin books are sold.

HARLEQUIN®
Makes any time special ™